ANTIQUES ROADKILL

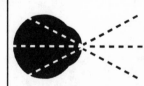

This Large Print Book carries the
Seal of Approval of N.A.V.H.

A TRASH 'N' TREASURES MYSTERY

ANTIQUES ROADKILL

BARBARA ALLAN

THORNDIKE PRESS

An imprint of Thomson Gale, a part of The Thomson Corporation

THOMSON

GALE

Detroit • New York • San Francisco • New Haven, Conn. • Waterville, Maine • London

THOMSON
GALE
™

LIBRARY OF CONGRESS CATALOGING-IN-PUBLICATION DATA

Allan, Barbara.
  Antiques roadkill : a trash 'n' treasures mystery / by Barbara Allan.
    p. cm. — (Thorndike Press large print mystery)
  ISBN-13: 978-0-7862-9140-3 (lg. print : alk. paper)
  ISBN-10: 0-7862-9140-0 (lg. print : alk. paper) 1. Antiques — Fiction. 2.
Large type books. I. Title.
PS3601.L4A84 2007
813'.6—dc22   2006031120

Published in 2007 by arrangement with Kensington Books, an imprint of Kensington Publishing Corp.

Printed in the United States of America on permanent paper
10 9 8 7 6 5 4 3 2 1

For Dorothy Jensen Mull,
who is a treasure

Home is the place where,
when you have to go there,
They have to take you in.
                    Robert Frost

When life itself seems lunatic,
who knows where madness lies?
. . . To surrender dreams, this may be
madness.
To seek treasures where there is only
trash.
                    Cervantes, *Don Quixote*

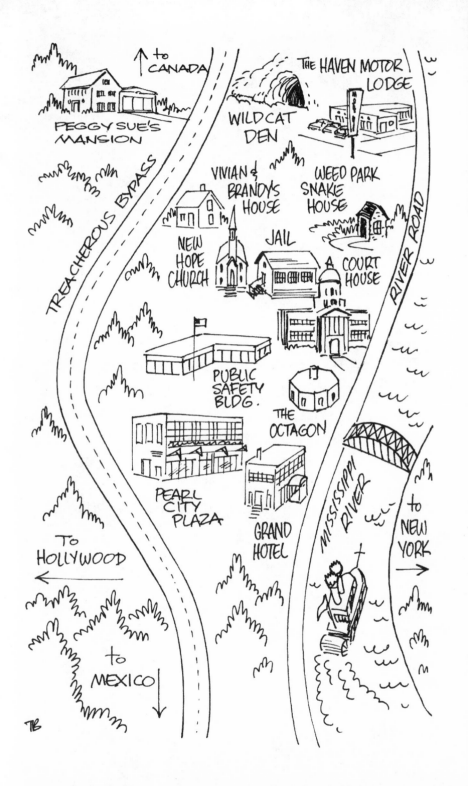

CHAPTER ONE
HOME IS WHERE THE HARM IS

On a perfect June day, late morning sun shining bright, I drove across the steel and concrete bridge over the muddy Mississippi, which actually didn't look muddy at all, wind whipping little whitecaps on the deep azure water beneath a cloudless blue sky.

Like one of those miniature Dickensian villages you'd see in a better gift shop, the downtown of Serenity spread out before me: old, proud, restored Victorian buildings, positioned a cautious distance from the unpredictable flood-prone river, along which a bike path lined with old-fashioned lamp fixtures ribboned its way.

On the car seat beside me, Sushi, my shih tzu, stirred from her travel bed, stretched, and put her furry little face up to the passenger window. But I doubted the dog could see anything.

"We're almost there, sweetie," I said soothingly.

Sushi turned toward me, white eyes staring spookily out of a brown furry face, like a baby Morlock in that great old *Time Machine* movie I caught on TCM one insomniac night (not the terrible remake!). Even before she'd gone sightless from diabetes, Sushi's vision had always been hair-impaired, so when the vet suggested I spend two thousand dollars to restore her vision, I had a good excuse not to . . . also a good reason, which was not having a spare two thousand dollars.

"Almost home," I repeated, more to myself than the dog, and took a swig of bottled Wal-Mart water.

According to Thomas Wolfe, you can't go home again; of course that's not true — many of us can, and do, crawl back to the nest to lick our wounds, regroup, rethink . . . and dream of leaving home again. . . .

My mother, Vivian, much to her surprise, conceived me at the tail end of her child-bearing years, in the mid-1970s, when her only other child was eighteen. Unplanned though I was, I provided Mother timely company, because shortly after I arrived, my father departed.

Now, this is not a sad story of paternal desertion — it's another kind of sad story: my father died from a sudden heart attack, presumably having nothing to do with my arrival.

My dad, Jonathan Borne, had been an army photographer during World War II, really quite a distinguished one among those anonymous heroic shutterbugs; many of the pictures taken at the Battle of the Bulge — which were seen in *Life* and other magazines of the day (and, later, history books and in documentaries) — were his. Dad might have had a big career with one of the news magazines, but like so many Greatest Generation guys, he only wanted to come back home to his sweetheart and start a family and make an honest living — he accomplished the latter by setting up his own photography shop.

Mother named me Brandy, after a corny but kinda cool then-popular song (my older sister, Peggy Sue, didn't fare so well with her own Buddy Holly–inspired moniker). Do you remember that "Brandy" tune? It got to number one, I think. Anyway, it talked about what a "good wife" Brandy would be — well, this Brandy . . . yours truly, Brandy . . . did not grow up to suit those lyrics. Not unless you're into irony.

Point of fact, Brandy Borne was coming home downsized, and not just in the physical sense: my beautiful silver Audi TT Quattro had been traded for this used urine-specimen-yellow Ford Taurus. My forty-something husband had been traded in, too, for . . . well, I'd say for Sushi, only actually I already had her back when I still had Roger, and the affluence that came with him.

Yup. No more retro-packaged Benefit makeup from Stephora, or cute shoes from Aldo's (why have one pair of Jimmy Choos when you could have three of theirs? I'm not stupid), or designer clothes from Neiman Marcus. Now I was strictly drugstore makeup, discounted shoes, and outlet-center apparel. Checking in with my new reality, I changed my subscription from couture-featured *Vogue* to off-the-rack *Lucky.*

In the back of the car, however, hanging from a rod, were some of the clothes I just couldn't bring myself to sell on eBay: a black Stella McCartney satin bomber jacket with tons of zippers; a black Chanel loose-weaved wool jacket with silver chains and frayed edges; and a black (okay, I'd been trying to hide my weight) Versace low-cut spandex dress (the one Angelina Jolie wore to the Oscars . . . except a tad bigger).

I also couldn't give up some vintage pieces: a Betsey Johnson bat-sleeved burgundy corduroy dress with big black patent leather belt, and an orange parachute-material jumpsuit by Norma Kamali that I never had nerve to wear. Since the split with Roger, I'd lost fifteen pounds and no longer fit many of these things; somehow, though, they were the only part of my former life I hadn't been able to cut loose.

According to my mother, the town of Serenity used to be called "the Pearl Button Capital of the World," button factories lining the riverfront like a brick battlement. Then when plastic fasteners became popular (and cheaper), and government restrictions were put on the number of mussels that could be harvested from the river, half the town got a pink slip, including factory owners.

But Vivian Borne had a vision (actually, she's had many, but more about that later); she thought the town could reinvent itself by opening lots of antique shops and cute little bistros, and become a tourist destination. Mother formed the Historic Preservation Committee, and marched on City Hall to stop the demolition of many a downtown building.

I suppose I should interrupt myself again to explain that my mother has always had a touch of the dramatic. She'd been a tall, slender, beautiful blonde in high school (willowy, they used to call it) who had snagged the lead in every play since kindergarten. Her plans to go to Hollywood had changed when she abruptly married her high school sweetheart (my dad, Jonathan — remember him?) on the eve of his marching off to war.

When my father marched home, Mother retreated into community theater and manic depression — in the fifties and sixties, they called this being "nuts" — and some of the therapy Mother got in those days was no picnic, though the plays were pretty good.

Don't get nervous — she's been medicated and beautifully sane for some years now . . . not counting occasional missed appointments, and ill-advised "drug holidays" from doctors who ought to know better.

Anyway, once upon a time poor put-upon Peggy Sue (I was only five) had to post bail when Mother's commitment to preserving downtown Serenity extended to chaining herself to the front door of the old Capitol Theater. The movie house with its great art deco facade didn't survive (it's now a parking lot), and that threw Mother into a deep depression that lasted for months; Sis had to move in for a while and take care of me. And Mother.

I suppose I should appreciate my sister for that, and for keeping an eye on our wonderful eccentric mom when I moved out after high school, leaving all the "fun" to Peg. But I'll be honest with you (you may already have noticed I'm not perfect), I've always resented Peggy Sue, for no reason really, other than her finicky, fault-finding attitude toward me.

Once over the span of the river, I swung onto Elm, one of Serenity's oldest streets, shooting out from the center of town like a spoke in a wheel. Along either side of the tree-canopied avenue, grand old homes built in the late eighteen hundreds, currently looking a little long in the tooth, were occupied by middle-income families, and those foolhardy enough to find romance in a fixer-upper. The local "barons" had long since moved out to the many subdivisions that now bordered the city.

At the end of Elm, I turned into the long driveway of a two-story white stucco house whose green shutters and wraparound porch were solely in need of a coat of paint. Or two.

I got out of the car, stretched from the long trip, then retrieved Sushi from the front seat. I stood under an ancient, familiar forlorn-looking pine, listening to the wind whispering in the tallest branches, while Soosh peed. Many of the lower boughs that I used to climb as a kid (getting sap stuck in my hair) were long gone, sheared off by storms or man.

Leaving my stuff behind in the car, I picked up the dog and headed toward the house.

As usual, the door was unlocked — actually, finding it locked would signal an alarm, indicating Mother might have reverted into one of her "spells," in which case even the sheriff would have had difficulty getting in. But the barricades were down, and I easily stepped into the small front foyer.

Nowhere else smelled like our house. It wasn't unpleasant; it wasn't pleasant. It was just my nostrils welcoming me . . . home.

All the way from the Chicago suburbs, I had been dreading this moment. How would I feel? Defeated? Miserable? Depressed? Would I see the ghost of a little Brandy — skinned-knee, dirty Scooby-Doo T-shirt, long stringy hair — looking back at me accusingly for making such a mess of her future?

But little Brandy wasn't there. And grown-up Brandy felt nothing negative at all . . . in fact, something comforting. And a surprising sense of . . . possibilities. Why, I had practically my whole life ahead of me. A second chance for love, wealth, and happiness. A new dawn was beginning!

Thank you, Prozac.

I went through the mahogany French door separating the entryway from the large front parlor, and put Sushi down on the bare wooden floor. Peggy Sue had tried to prepare me on the phone, but it was still a shock.

Gone were the Queen Anne needlepoint furniture, Hancock straight-backed chairs, Duncan Phyfe table, and Persian rugs . . . family heirlooms, all. Even the colorful collection of small glass shoes (think Cinderella's slipper) that had forever graced the picture windowsill was AWOL. I felt a terrible lump in my throat, and a sense of loss rippled through me in a wave reminiscent of nausea.

"Everything can't be gone," I'd said to Peggy Sue on the phone, knowing how she could exaggerate.

"Not *every* thing . . . but most of the downstairs things."

"Surely Mother didn't let go of the chairs Grandpa caned?" I wanted those.

Her silence was all the answer I needed.

"Can't you get it all back?" I wailed. "Mother was mentally ill — isn't that fraud or something?"

My sister sighed heavily. "I've already talked to our attorney."

"Mr. Ekhardt? Is *he* still alive?"

"He is, and he said the antique dealer bought everything in good faith and had no idea Mother was . . . well . . ."

"Cuckoo for Cocoa Puffs?"

". . . off her medication." Pause. "Why these doctors don't call the family, when a patient misses an appointment, I will never know."

"But those are precious things. It's like the bastard bought our childhood! Stole our memories!"

"Brandy — you *are* taking the Prozac . . . ?"

"Yes, yes . . . they just take awhile to kick in, is all. But even when she's in one of her lunatic phases of the moon, Mother surely wouldn't give away such precious —"

"Brandy," my sister said, voice tight, "I wish you wouldn't refer to Mother's condition in so, so . . . insensitive a manner. You know as well as I that it's a disease."

"I'm sorry," I said quickly, hoping to thwart a probable, inevitable scolding. Peggy Sue had a way of reducing me to six years old. Or five.

"How," she was saying, off on a pedantic

tear, "are we ever to eradicate the stigma attached to this illness, when you keep using words like 'cuckoo' and 'lunatic'?"

Too late.

"Sorry," I mumbled.

"Do you have any idea how lucky we are that Mother responds so well to medication?"

Note that Peggy Sue hadn't said how lucky Mother was.

"I said I was sorry," I said.

Make that four years old.

The strained silence that followed was not unusual in our phone conversations.

Finally Peg asked, a trifle testily, "When are you coming back to Serenity?"

"In a couple weeks. After the divorce is final."

And my medication has kicked in.

"And will Jacob be with you?"

Why did she even ask that? Peggy Sue knew Jake's dad had custody!

"No, Peg — he's better off with his father. For right now, anyway. At the moment, Jake blames me for everything."

Peggy Sue didn't jump to my defense — not that I expected her to. Instead she shifted gears, saying pleasantly, "It'll be such a relief to have you living with Mother."

"Thanks."

"Finally, someone else to drive her to the doctor, so she'll never miss another appointment. . . . You *do* know she had her license suspended?"

"Yes, you wrote. How *are* the cows?" Mother had taken a shortcut through a pasture, on her way to a play at a rural church.

I could almost hear the frown in my sister's voice. "Are you being sarcastic?"

"No." But I wondered if Peggy Sue could almost hear *my* snide little grin.

"If you really want to know, there was only one bovine fatality, though the others were certainly traumatized." She added cheerfully, "Thank God the insurance paid for everything, including the damage to that combine. They're terribly expensive, you know."

"Cows?"

"Combines! Honestly, sometimes I don't know whether you really are that thick, or are just pulling my chain!"

I'll leave it for you to decide.

"Personally, Peg? I'm most relieved that in the accident the only casualties were farm equipment and some shaken-up livestock. That Mother wasn't hurt . . . ?"

After the next strained silence, we had managed to chat a bit longer about nothing

20

in particular, both of us sensing the need to work our way somewhere where the conversation could end on a cordial note of truce.

That was about a month ago.

I watched as Sushi took a few tentative steps from me in the living room, feeling her way along. At least with most of the furnishings gone, the dog wouldn't be bumping into so many things.

I was wondering where Mother was when I heard the muffled sound of the downstairs toilet flush, then running water. In another minute she was gliding through the kitchen doorway, and my smile froze.

Mother was wearing an unbecoming, ill-fitting purple dress — I might have made it in seventh-grade sewing class with my eyes shut — and a huge red straw hat arrayed with plastic fruit, arcs of white hair swinging like scythes on either side of her face, her attractive features bordering on self-parody with an overapplication of makeup and her blue eyes huge behind the big thick-lensed glasses.

My heart sank. Peggy Sue had said she was stabilized!

Mother beamed when she saw me, magnified eyes bright with delight. She had put a few pounds on over the years, but remained a tall, striking figure, despite the ghastly dress. "Brandy, darling! Thank the Lord you've come! And just in time, too."

"Yeeees," I replied. "I think I am."

The big buggy eyes narrowed suspiciously as she advanced toward me for a hug. Then she held me out in front of her like a painting she was considering to buy and said, "Darling child, you look simply stricken — are you all right?"

"I am . . . question is, are you?"

"Of course, dear. Well and truly medicated. Now hurry up, or we'll be tardy . . ."

What was I, back in school?

". . . and this is not the kind of event where a late entrance is considered fashionable."

"Event?"

Mother made a little cluck with her tongue. "Oh, Brandy! At my age, I'm the one with an excuse for being forgetful — you promised you'd go with me!"

"Go . . . where?"

"The Red Hat Social Club luncheon! Remember? The guest speaker is one of the Keno twins!"

Well, I *had* forgotten — or rather banished it to a corner of my mind. The idea of dressing up in a red hat and purple dress was not my idea of a good time, particularly on the heels of a long car trip.

22

I said hopefully, "I thought you meant you just needed a ride. How can I attend? Don't you have to be, you know, uh . . ."

"Old? Why, yes, dear thing, an incredibly ancient fifty! And I know you don't qualify, but didn't I mention it?"

"Mention . . . ?"

"This is mother-daughter day! And I've told simply everyone that you were coming back, and would be with me. Brandy, every chapter in Serenity will be there!"

"Why not take Peggy Sue?" Vaguely I recalled either Peg or Mother mentioning that Sis was a Red Hat, too.

"She and I are in different chapters," Mother said. "She's going to sit with her own group. Now shake a tailfeather!"

I guess I was going. Half sarcastically, I said, "How can I attend? I don't have a red hat!"

"Ah, dear girl, don't you know your mother by now? I think of everything."

She disappeared in a swish of purple fabric and a bobbling of fake fruit.

All too soon she had returned, from the kitchen, saying, "Luckily I found some paint out in the garage . . . I do hope it's dry."

Mother handed me a straw hat that I remembered from some play she'd been in, when I was a kid; she had revamped the nineteen-hundreds-looking affair with bright red paint, which was tacky in more ways than one.

"What," I said, "no fruit?"

Mother put her hands on her hips. "Fruit is strictly optional, as is the purple dress. Now, if you don't want to go, don't. I am perfectly willing to call a cab and go and be humiliated."

My own humiliation in the worst, wackiest "Red Hat" imaginable did not occur to Mother. She had always lent her theatrical production touch to apparel, makeup, and other everyday matters, forgetting that what looks good to an audience past the footlights might seem bizarre in what I laughingly like to refer to as "real life."

Long ago I'd lost every battle over Mother's homemade "solutions" to various fashion crises; now was simply not the time to change my ways.

"I'm coming," I said, dutiful daughter that I am.

Anyway, why not attend a Red Hat meeting, and see what I'd be doing with my free time in about thirty years? Don't laugh (or cry) — that's how Peggy Sue wound up, right?

But I had enough dignity left to say, "Just give me a few minutes, Mother," and went out to the car and retrieved some things.

When I returned, Mother was cuddling Sushi in her arms. I wasn't sure how she would take to Soosh; it had been a number of years since a pet had invaded the house . . . and a high maintenance one at that.

"Look, dear," Mother said, beaming, "the little darling — unlike you — likes my outfit."

"Sushi's blind, Mother . . . she can't see your lovely ensemble."

Mother held the dog out, inspecting her. "I thought something was strange about those eyes. . . ."

Oddly, Mother's eyes and Sushi's looked about the same.

Then Mother shrugged, clutched the dog against her chest, and sighed, "No matter . . . we're all damaged goods around here."

In the upstairs bathroom, I ran a brush through my shoulder-length golden-blond hair (L'Oreal Preference; you can usually find coupons) and applied a little Rimmel makeup (at least it was British, even if it didn't look as good on me as on Kate Moss).

I put Sushi in her bed next to the tub, left a bowl of water (diabetic dogs get *really* thirsty), and shut the door.

"Let's take my car, dear," Mother suggested when I came back downstairs. She had found a big lighter purple purse somewhere, which actually went well with the purple frock. "Automobile engines are like people, you know — if they sit too long doing nothing, they wind up dead before their time."

Even medicated, Mother had no shortage of such words of wisdom. Anyway, it sounded like a plan.

At the end of the drive was a freestanding garage, with an old, heavy door you had to open yourself. If things hadn't changed, the keys to the ancient pea-green Audi would be waiting on its dashboard — and they were. That careless key security had made sneaking out of the house in the middle of the night and taking the car so beautifully easy, way back when.

While I drove downtown, Mother informed me Serenity had six chapters of the Red Hat Social Club, and over twenty thousand in the entire country (I feigned interest), and that each chapter had its own "darling" name like Better Red Than Dead, and Code Red Hat, etc.

When Mother and some of her friends who belonged to a mystery readers' book club — Mother "adored" Agatha Christie — had tried to join various chapters around town, each in turn was told that all the chapters were closed to new members.

Whether she and her fellow eccentrics suspected they had been turned away for any reason other than no-room-at-the-inn, Mother didn't say.

What she did say was: "At any rate, we just started our own chapter, turning our little readers' group into 'the Red-Hatted League.' That's a Sherlock Holmes reference, dear."

"I know, Mother."

At that point Mother launched into a detailed comparison of the relative merits of Basil Rathbone and Jeremy Brett as the great Baker Street detective, making a good case for each.

I parked in a packed lot adjacent to the Grand Queen Hotel, which at eight stories lorded over its loyal subjects, the surrounding riverfront buildings. The view of the Mis-sissippi from the top-floor ballroom (where the luncheon was being held) was breathtaking. For a small town. In the Midwest.

The wealthy publisher of the *Serenity Sentinel* had saved the Queen (named after one of the founders of Serenity, Nathan Joshua Queen, and an ancestor of said publisher) from the chopping block, giving her a face-lift to the tune of three million dollars. People came from all over the nation just to stay in one of the many "theme rooms" — from the serene Grecian-spa bedroom to the way-out moon room, complete with space-capsule bed.

That such funky fantasy suites had nothing to do with the Victorian wedding cake of a building that housed them bothered no one, particularly not the *Sentinel* publisher, who was even richer now than before.

By the time Mother and I reached the ballroom, the luncheon was getting under way; we were among the last to arrive, but we weren't late. Several hundred hats bobbed in a sea of red as the ladies were served what appeared to be chicken salad (not my favorite). Only a few women, however, were wearing purple dresses (good call), and daughter day or not, hardly anyone seemed my age. . . . Maybe they had to work.

While we were standing in the doorway looking for our table, pretty-pretty-pretty Peggy Sue came over, maybe glad to see us, or maybe just feeling obligated. Her red hat was a pillbox, à la Jackie O, but a new number, not something Mother had dredged from the basement or attic for house-paint conversion.

Her skirt and jacket were a lavender Ralph Lauren (and not the Blue Label), though her brunette hair was in the same shoulder-length flipped do as in high school, sprayed to where you could bounce ball bearings off it.

"I was beginning to think you weren't going to make it," she said with a forced little laugh. Even when she was being pleasant, Peggy Sue buried a kernel of criticism in her words. Suddenly her eyes widened to where they were almost the size of Mother's magnified orbs: our homemade hats had just appeared on Peg's radar, alarming unidentified objects.

But Sis did have the good grace not say anything — it wasn't like such "fashion statements" from Mother were unheard of.

Anyway, Peg gave me a cursory embrace, and said, "Great to see you, Brandy. Thanks for being a good sport."

This seemed to be a reference to my red hat.

"Your group is seated over there," Peggy Sue said, pointing in the opposite direction from where she'd come — which was no surprise. Somehow I had the feeling that Peg had been involved in the seating arrangements.

My expression must have conveyed that,

and Peg said, "I do wish we could sit together, but you know how it is."

Actually, I did know.

But Peg was gracious enough to walk us over to the table, even taking me by the arm and asking, "How was your trip?"

"Pretty boring. Interstate, mostly."

Sis gave me a canned smile. "That's nice. Well, I'll see you two later."

And she vanished.

We had been deposited at the table where the other members of Mother's chapter were eagerly awaiting our arrival. The friendly, motley crew consisted of a retired schoolteacher (I had her in fifth grade), a widowed nurse, a homemaker (who might as well be widowed because her husband had Alzheimer's), and a divorcée (she left her husband immediately after their fiftieth wedding anniversary party, and I mean *that night*).

These were Mother's dearest friends (you needn't know their names, just yet), and I didn't mind spending an hour or so with them, and hearing stories (sometimes more than once) about how they did things in the olden days.

I took a pass on the chicken salad and waited for the main course. Then I realized, too late, after they took away the plate, that

that *was* the main course. Next thing I knew I was staring down at a big slice of chocolate cake.

Chocolate on an empty stomach is a no-no for a migraine headache sufferer, which I am (thank God for Imitrex). So I removed myself from temptation and went off to find a bathroom.

Weaving around the tables took me by Peggy Sue, where she sat with a clutch of longtime, so-called friends.

I despised these women, each of whom had at one time or another betrayed my sister. The ringleader of the cattiest clique this side of the Mississippi was Robin (wearing the stodgier side of Anne Klein); she once stole Peggy Sue's fiancé, then threw him over. Lana (looking silly in Lilly Pulitzer — where's a palm tree when you need one?) had had my sister kicked off the Pom-Pon Squad (at the time called Pom-Pom, before anyone realized it meant "whore" in the Philippines) for being "too fat," which had sent Peggy Sue on an anorexic cycle. And my "favorite," Connie (hiding her heft under a voluminous Eileen Fisher dress; it wasn't working), had once spread a vicious rumor that my sister was pregnant, when Peggy Sue studied in France her freshman year of college.

I had heard all of this — and more — as a kid listening at the top of the stairs, or with one ear to closed doors, when Peggy Sue went crying to Mother. Why my sister still cared about what these middle-aged over-Botoxed bitches did or thought or said was a mystery that even the Red-Hatted League's Holmes couldn't have solved. Rathbone *or* Brett.

When I paused at their table, Peggy Sue smiled in her frozen way and said, "Brandy! You remember my friends . . . ?"

I bestowed my sweetest smile on them. "Why, of course. I've heard so many interesting stories about all of you, over these many years."

Several pairs of eyes narrowed — of those smart enough to perceive the dig — while Peggy flashed a glare, as if to say, "Don't make trouble, Little Sister."

Robin turned her Cruella face toward me. "I understand you'll be living here again. Moving back in with Mother? How sweet." Her smile was sly, knowing.

"Yes, and I'll be looking for a job," I replied, then asked innocently, not missing a beat, "Do you think your husband could use a secretary?"

Her hubby, Mel, ran the biggest auto dealership in Serenity. And was the biggest letch.

"Why . . . uh, I . . . don't . . ." She managed an embarrassed smile, then said, "I don't really keep track of such things."

"No problem," I replied, then crinkled my nose, *Bewitched*-style, cute as heck. "I'll call him myself."

I let Robin chew on that and headed for the ladies' room, which proved deserted, everybody but me busy snarfing down that rich cake. I was drying my hands when the door swished open. I half expected Peggy Sue, come to admonish me for being "not very nice" to her supposed friends, but it was even worse.

"Hello, Brandy," the woman said. She held her ground by the door, and was clearly not here to pee.

"Jennifer." I threw the paper towel in the bin.

She was slender and pretty and two years younger than me, with thick auburn hair, a porcelain, doll-like complexion, large green eyes unblinking in her pale face, her thin lips a red lipstick slash; she wore neither a red hat nor a purple dress — just a smart periwinkle suit.

"I'm here with my mother," I said.

"I'm with mine. Spotted you talking to Peggy Sue."

"Ah." That's me, always ready with the

smart comeback.

"I just thought," she began, clutching her black purse like an oversize fig leaf, "as long as you're back in town . . ."

Bad news travels fast.

". . . we'll be running into each other . . ."

Not necessarily. I wouldn't be shopping the better boutiques.

". . . and we might as well get this over with."

She really was quite beautiful; why would her husband have cheated on a ten like her with a seven and three-quarter like me, I'll never understand.

Well, okay — the sex.

And a guy at his high school class reunion, which his wife chose not to attend, who runs into his old steady, might make a sad mistake.

So might the old steady.

I noticed her hand shaking a little as she toyed with a button on the jacket of her suit.

"I just wanted to say," she continued, "that I don't hold a grudge. What happened just . . . happened."

I had no words. None.

"You just came along at a rough patch in our marriage — it could have been any-body."

Gee, thanks.

"And, anyway, Brandy, Brad and I are doing fine now. I have no intention of causing a scene, here, today . . . anywhere, ever."

I nodded.

"That doesn't mean I forgive you, of course, for what you did."

Of course. But *Brad's* forgiven.

She raised her chin; was it trembling, just a little? And I'm happy to say that my marriage is stronger than ever."

Not "our" marriage — "my" marriage.

I really could think of nothing to say, except, "Was it really key to your happiness, calling my husband and telling on me and ruining what *I* had?"

Which of course I said only in my head.

"Well," Jennifer sighed with a half smile, "I'm so glad we had this little chat. Good luck on your new start. Sorry if you thought Brad might be a part of it."

She wheeled and left.

I had to admit, what Jennifer did took guts. I felt about as cheap as my $49.99 cotton dress and Dutch Boy–painted red hat.

As I returned to my table, all eyes were on me, looking for cat scratches, maybe. Thankfully the after-luncheon program was about to begin.

Stepping to the center-front dais was Mrs. Lindel, evidently in charge of the day's historic mother-daughter Red-Hat citywide event; she was a trim, energetic, perpetually cheerful woman in her sixties who, like Mother, had been active in community theater since I was in diapers. Her red hat was by far the most . . . What, you're not interested? Okay, be that way.

The upbeat Mrs. Lindel, however, was looking a little down in the dumps as she spoke into the microphone. "Ladies . . ." She had to repeat this several times before the crowd — eagerly anticipating the featured guest from the popular *Antiques Roadshow* program — quieted. The excitement was palpable, the suspense excruciating — which Keno twin could it be?

"As you know, Mr. Keno is in our little corner of the world for a Des Moines taping of the *Roadshow*," she said. "He was gracious to make time for us in his busy schedule, but unexpected production demands made it necessary for him to cancel at the last minute."

Oh. Neither Keno twin.

"He sends his best and his apologies."

The latter half dozen or so words were barely audible over the moans and groans.

Mother, who always projected well, said, "Well, *shit!*"

Laughter followed — everyone in town

knew my mother (and most knew her favorite swear word), though a mortified Peggy Sue, glancing our way, didn't seem to realize how well received and even cathartic Mother's little outburst had been.

"However . . . however," Mrs. Lindel continued, "we have a wonderful substitute speaker, Clint Carson, who moved here recently from Boulder, Colorado. Many of you already know Mr. Carson, and are familiar with his antique shop in Pearl Button Plaza. So, without any further introduction, let's give him a warm welcome and a big hand!"

And she began clapping wildly to rouse the crowd.

I'd bet Mrs. Lindel had the man waiting in the wings like an understudy ready to go on, should something go wrong with the featured guest. The substitute came out (stage right) to polite applause, and the director returned to her seat.

Clint wasn't bad on the eyes: tall, slender, youthful, yet old enough to have some gray in his brown ponytailed hair. He wore a black Stetson, a tan and brown plaid western shirt, and dark slacks. I couldn't see his feet, but I was betting on tooled leather boots.

"Good afternoon, darlin's," the man

drawled into the mike. "I've never seen so many pretty faces — not to mention *hats* — all in one little ole room. . . ."

I was thinking, *Lame,* but then noticed that the women all around me apparently liked this chicken-fried blarney, some even giggling.

Carson began to talk about his love of antiques, and I looked over at Mother, to see if her disappointment had been placated. Unlike the women surrounding us, who were eating this up, Mother's head was lowered, the wide-brimmed hat mostly covering her face. Her normal outgoing self seemed to be shriveling, as she withdrew into herself, in a way that often signaled a bout with the blues.

And I could see a tear trickling down one cheek.

Now, I knew she loved *Antiques Roadshow* — especially when the Keno twins were on — and surely had been looking forward to today; but her reaction didn't seem right — perhaps her medication made her overemotional . . . or needed adjusting.

I leaned in, peering under her hat. "Hey, we can always go to Des Moines to see the twins. When are they taping — do you know?"

But my normally outgoing Mother said nothing.

And the tears were streaming now.

"What is it, dear?" I whispered, alarmed at her distress. The other ladies at our table had noticed, and concern registered on their faces, too.

"That . . . that . . . *terrible* man . . . is . . . the one . . ." Her whispered words came in little choking breaths. ". . . the one who . . . took advantage of me. . . ."

And I knew what she meant; we hadn't even discussed it at home, I hadn't wanted to upset her, or hurt her feelings, but I knew exactly what she was talking about: folksy Clint Carson had scammed my mother out of our precious furniture!

A ball of fire rose from my stomach to my throat, the worst heartburn I'd ever had.

Carson spoke for fifteen minutes on the subject of unscrupulous dealers who passed off replicas as antiques ("A good way to tell the real antique from the reproduction is to look at the manufacturer's mark . . .").

I sat through it seething, my face getting redder than my hat. But I waited for the Q-and-A portion, at which time I flew to my feet and did not wait to be recognized.

"I have a question, relating to unscrupulous dealers."

Red hats swiveled my way. Dozens of eyes locked on to me, amid murmurings of (no doubt) how rude I as.

The speaker seemed a little thrown himself, and a touch irritated at my presumption, but he gave me a patronizing "Yes?"

"Is it ethical for a dealer," I said firmly, "to take advantage of a seller? I don't mean a seller who hasn't done the research, and is just carelessly getting rid of items that are actually valuable."

Carson was frowning.

"What I mean is, is it ethical for a dealer — let's say . . . oh, you for example — to buy treasured family heirlooms from anyone who is not, well, aware, for one reason or another, of what they are doing?" I thought that came out rather nicely.

He was silent for a moment before responding. "I'm not sure I entirely understand the question, little lady. When you say, 'me,' are you in the hypothetical realm?"

"There's nothing hypothetical about dealers taking advantage of seniors."

The crowd was beginning to realize that this was not a friendly exchange, and I heard some disapproving murmurs. But here and there, surprisingly, were smatterings of applause.

Carson's eyes narrowed and his voice had

a quake that might have been anger, or even fear. "Are you implyin' that I am unethical?"

"No — I'm *saying* it."

He stiffened self-righteously. "You want to be very careful about making such statements. We have laws against slander in this country, you know."

"We have lots of laws in this country, Mr. Carson. And the truth is the best defense against slander."

But now my confidence was flagging; the audience was grumbling, and more seemed against me than for me — I had ruined the Red Hat luncheon!

Time to cut and run.

I turned to Mother, who was looking at me with a big smile and those blue eyes huge behind the lenses, though her face was streaked with tears. "Come on, dear," I said, "we're going."

I took her by the arm, and we exited the ballroom, leaving the stunned group behind. And yet among the rumblings was again more scattered applause. Apparently we weren't the only ones who didn't think well of this Colorado highwayman.

We sat in the Audi in the parking lot, Mother blowing her nose into a big cloth hanky that had seen better days.

41

"Brandy, I'm so proud of you. Not only did you stand up to that man, you showed . . ."

That instability ran in the family? Or maybe galloped?

". . . you showed a great dramatic *flair.* How I wish you'd followed me into theater!"

"Mother — what about the real-life melo-drama? How much did that jerk give you for our things?"

Mother sniffled. "About a thousand dollars . . . I think."

"For *everything?* The pine armoire alone was worth triple that!"

She nodded dejectedly.

"Shit!" I said.

"Brandy," Mother said. "Language."

I started the car and decreed, "I'm going to get that creep Carson — and all of our things back — if I have to run right over him to do it!"

Then I wheeled out of the lot, tires squealing, and headed for the home that unscrupulous dealer had emptied of so many memories.

A TRASH 'N' TREASURES TIP

It's said that one person's trash is another person's treasure, but that's not entirely true. Trash is still trash . . . but there's no law against treasuring it. Just don't expect a lot of resale money.

CHAPTER TWO

A TISKET, A CASKET

In chilly darkness inside the Taurus, Mother and I were slumped in the front, leaning back against the headrests, waiting patiently. Down the block — deserted but for a few empty, parked cars — a streetlight flickered spookily; I could almost see the hockey-masked Jason, knife-blade glinting, running from house to house, seeking teenagers having sex and scolding them as only he could.

Mother had her eyes closed (we'd run out of conversation some time ago) and I took a sip of coffee from the thermos I'd brought from home, even though the strong liquid had long since gone cold. My patience was just morphing into claustrophobia when a light snapped on in the home across the street.

"Mother," I whispered, giving her a gentle nudge. She sat up with a start and batted her eyes behind the magnifying lenses of the big glasses.

44

"Ah!" Mother said. "He's up and around — won't be long now, dear."

But another half an hour had dragged by, the sky blushing with dawn, before the garage door to the split-level house finally began to rise with a slowness that could only be described as ominous. (Which is why I described it that way.)

Out of the car like a shot, I was poised to dash across the street, when Mother trilled a warning: "Remember Aunt *Mabel,* darling!"

Once upon a terrible time, Mabel (actually my great-aunt) had spied a butter churn at an estate sale, crossed the road without looking, and gotten hit by a tour bus of seniors on their way to Branson.

Not being interested in making a trip to the next life, or Branson for that matter, I made sure the coast was clear and was inside that garage before the door was all the way up.

I took everything in all at once — old Christmas decorations (a hard sell in June), glass flower vases (everyone already has too many), some old tools (valuable to some collectors), books (mostly bodice-bursting romances), LP records (no way to play *those* anymore), outdated women's and men's clothing (just donate them, already!) — as I frantically worked my way toward the back of the garage.

Suddenly I was aware of others around me, coming out of the woodwork, like cockroaches swarming toward cake crumbs. But this little bug reached the object of her desire first, which I scooped up and held tightly to my chest, even as hands reached out.

"Did you get it?" Mother was beside me, breathless. "Did you get it?"

I nodded, thinking, *We're not exactly playing it cool, are we?* Tipping your hand like that in pursuit of a precious item, whether at a garage sale or a pricey antique shop, was pretty dumb, I admit. But we'd waited a long time, and the resonance of this little object touched us both.

I waited for the infestation to pass before showing her the portable writing desk. "Desk" brings to mind a piece of furniture, I realize — something substantial, with legs. But this was a simple, small walnut box (about twelve inches square) on which you could write letters while in bed: square glass inkwell, a place for a quill pen, and even a hole for a candle; inside the hinged, green velvet-covered lid was where paper and envelopes were kept.

When I was small, Mother used it as a

place to stash extra cash, and kept it high up in a kitchen cupboard, away from my grubby little hands. Later, the writing desk became a focal point in the music room, displayed on a round oak library table, holding an assortment of old-time sheet music . . . Gershwin, Rodgers and Hart, Cole Porter, and the like. I didn't need to see the tears fogging up Mother's large lenses to know this "desk" was ours.

Or, anyway, used to be.

The day before, we had come home to a message on the answer machine. A certain Marvin Petersen said he was having a garage sale in the morning, and that there was something we "might be interested in," describing the aforementioned wooden box, but he wouldn't hold it for us. I tried calling him back (several times), to see if we could come right out, but got no answer; even a drive-by proved futile — his house remained silent and dark.

Now I looked for the sticker price on the writing desk, finding it on the underside.

Mother read the disappointment in my face. "How much could it be?"

"It could be," I managed, "three hundred dollars . . . and is."

"What?" she asked again, incredulously. Then, "Well, now, that's just ridiculous. I'll

just have to see about that."

I watched Mother zero in on Mr. Petersen like a heat-seeking missile. The old boy had set up shop at a card table near the garage entrance, and her demonic demeanor suddenly softened into something angelic. When she wanted to, Mother could charm the pants off a snake. Assuming the snake was wearing pants, of course.

Best that the diva of the family handle this; garage sale finagling hadn't been covered in *Trump: The Art of the Deal,* required reading for my first college business class.

Idly poking around a knickknack table, Mother waited for this first wave of garage sale shoppers to do their shopping, and buying, and leave. Yesterday's paper had promised good weather, and a couple dozen garage and yard sales around town, so there was much scavenging to be done among the true believers.

In the lull before the next onslaught, I hovered nearby while Mother finally approached Mr. Petersen, seated at his battered card table, putting money away in an old tin cash box, presenting a truly Scrooge-like image.

He was an older gent (but younger than Mother), perhaps in his late sixties, rotund

48

(polite for overweight — okay, fat), partially bald, with bulbous nose and rheumy eyes. He noticed Mother holding the writing box, and put two and two together.

"Well," the man said rather gruffly, "glad you made it, Vivian."

I wondered how long he and Mother had been acquainted, and under what circumstances. Over the years she had often gone out on dates, but after my father, she never had a serious relationship — that I knew about, anyway. Mother bestowed a charming, disarming smile on him, bringing out her still-attractive Swedish features, and spoke in a soft, musical voice usually reserved for the stage, or bill collectors.

"Marvin, thank you so very much for calling," Mother said. "You've always been a dear."

The blush rose all the way over the bald head. "Well, er . . ."

"You know," she said, leaning in conspiratorially, "we tried to contact you last night, but" — she winked at him, and behind those lenses, it was one big wink — "you must have been out on the town."

He coughed, blinked, blushed some more, then grunted grumpily, "More like hiding in the basement."

"Whatever for?"

49

Shrugging, he said, "When I have a garage sale, I turn off the ringer on the phone and draw the blinds, once the ad hits the paper — otherwise, there'd be no peace."

With a sympathetic sigh, Mother nodded and said, "People can be so presumptuous . . . so annoying! Imagine, asking to come the day before so they can have a first look-see." She made a "tsk-tsk" sound, as if discussing some unfortunate breach of not just manners but the law.

"I mean, fair's fair," he was saying. "First come, first served, I always say."

Again she leaned toward him, her voice husky now. "Some folks even park outside the house, hours before the sale begins. I mean, are they people or vultures? Terrible, making a person feel like a prisoner in your own home, simply terrible."

Mother, of course, had been describing us and our actions, but Mr. Petersen didn't seem to know that. But she had melted whatever resistance remained in the old fella — Mr. Petersen beamed; he'd found a kindred spirit.

"Nice to know," he said, "that you understand."

This line of attack exhausted, Mother switched gears. "But however did you know that little box was mine?"

"Ah," he said. "The missus found a small address label stuck inside the back."

"Really? Where *is* Mildred this morning?"

"That's part of the story, Vivian. You see, I bought that piece right after Mildred broke her leg and got laid up in bed for a spell. We don't believe in the Internet, and Milly does love to write her letters."

I was contemplating the notion of not believing in the Internet, as if it were a superstition, while Mother made her move.

Looking down at the box in her hands with a tragic little frown, Mother said pitifully, "Well, again, Marvin, it was awfully sweet of you to call, but you know . . ."

Here it came.

". . . the tag says it's three hundred dollars . . . and on my limited income, well, I guess you know —"

"Pish!" he said.

At first I thought he'd said something else!

But our host at the card table was waving a hand like a graceless magician. "Don't pay any never-mind to that. I just used a figure to keep *other* folks away, till you could have a look."

"Oh, how sweet of you, Marvin."

"For you, it's only . . . how's fifty dollars?"

"Really?" Mother was smiling ear to ear (me too). I'd been inching my way over,

51

wallet in hand containing the shabby remains of my travel money.

Then — if you can believe it (I hardly could) — Mother said, "Oh, but, Marvin, it's worth a least a hundred!"

I gave my mother a short, swift, ever-so-subtle kick in the shin, and her eyes popped behind the magnifying lenses, though she managed not say, "Ouch."

Instead, while I plunked down the fifty before Petersen could adjust his price, she said, "But who am I to question your generosity? You are an angel, Marvin Petersen."

This summoned an image in my mind that I feel a responsibility not to share in any great detail.

As our host wrapped the writing box in yesterday's news, Mother asked, "And how is Mildred?"

"Doing much better. They have her using a walker — you might have seen her at that meeting the other day. Aren't you one of the Red Hat girls?"

"I most certainly am. You just tell Mildred that she has the sweetest husband on the face of the earth."

I managed to keep my breakfast down, while the bald-blushing gentleman handed us the bundle.

In the car, we sat for a few moments; suddenly I was dead tired — Mother's performance had been exhausting to watch. Right now she was lovingly looking over the box, which had a not-so-secret compartment — a false bottom — that I had always romantically thought was intended for love letters. Mother slid it open and withdrew a small yellow piece of paper.

I glanced over her shoulder; it was a receipt from Clint Carson's antique shop for a portable writing box, paid by Marvin Petersen — for three hundred dollars.

"What an old sweetheart," she said.

"Literally?"

Mother's eyes regarded me with magnified innocence. "I have no idea what you're suggesting."

Everybody has their own secret compartments, and I guess Mother deserved hers as much as the next "girl." I started the car and we rode in silence toward Elm, then down our street, when Mother suddenly sat forward.

"Looks like Floyd Olson's having a sale," she said. "Pull over, would you, Brandy?"

She needn't have asked. Mr. Olson, a retired dentist, had been a widower for several years; he and his late wife had traveled the world, bringing back all sorts of unique items. (Mother would make excuses to visit just to see their latest acquisition, to the point Mrs. Olson finally asked, "Vivian, are you after my husband?" To which Mother replied, "Dear thing, the only antique you possess that I'm *not* interested in is your husband.")

Floyd, who had lost considerable weight due no doubt to grief, and the absence of his wife's German cooking, was showcasing his wares out on the front lawn; the buzzards were already picking, a dozen or so people on the prowl.

One buzzard in particular caught my eye. The ponytailed skinny figure in western attire was unmistakable even from behind; he was talking to Mr. Olson.

"You know, Bubbah, if there are other things in the house you'd like to turn into money," Carson was saying in his phony, good-ol'-boy drawl, "maybe I could be of help."

Mr. Olson's eyes were narrowed; he probably had never been called "Bubbah" before, and may well have been trying to figure out whether to be complimented or offended. "Well, now, young man —"

"There's no tragedy worse than the loss of a wife," Carson said, his tone somber now. Then it subtly shifted: "But a man just

54

doesn't need to have the same bric-a-brac and such around the house as a female does."

"I suppose that's true."

Carson smiled and waved a hand. "Oh hell, I know you're busy right now, but I can always come by later. We can sit and jaw and just chew the fat."

Older people often appreciated those who would spend a little time with them. Carson had his game plan all figured out, didn't he?

Mother, drawn to an unframed oil painting of a cabin in the wilderness, had heard this spiel too, and stood frozen in her tracks, Lot's wife staring back at Sodom (or was it Gomorrah?).

Finally she came to life and rushed over, planting herself between the two men, an uninvited referee.

"Floyd," she said firmly, but with her trademark theatricality, "please tell me you're not allowing this vile creature inside your home — you'd be better off with a raccoon or a skunk climbing in. He will cheat you and he will rob you and he will take you to the cleaners!"

That about covered it.

Mr. Olson had assumed a deer-in-the-headlights expression at this intrusion, but Carson remained calm, head *Exorcist-*

swiveling slowly toward Mother, giving her the look a parent might a disobedient child.

"We're having a *private* conversation, ma'am," Carson drawled, "and it in no way that comes to *my* mind concerns *you.* Why don't you just be a good girl, and avail yourself of the opportunity to move along to the various tables, and pick up a bargain or two?"

Mother held her ground. "You know a lot about picking up 'bargains,' don't you, Mr. Carson?" Her eyes were round cold stones behind the glasses; big stones, too. She shook a finger at him, no longer the disobedient child, but the stern parent.

She went on: "Floyd here is a close friend, and when someone intends to take advantage of any one of my friends, well, you can rest assured that it does concern me . . . *especially* when a near and dear friend is about to be duped."

Did I mention Mother had a lot of near and dear friends? Or maybe you received one of the four-hundred-plus Christmas cards she sent out last year.

Dozens of eyes were on us, as I moved to Mother's side, and Carson's expression tightened.

He said to me, "I know you . . . you're the snippy little lady who gave me such a bad time last week." He looked from me to Mother and back, something animal in his gaze now. "You two girls seem to be making a habit of embarrassing me . . . slandering me . . . in public."

Mother said, "People have to be warned."

"They do, sometimes. And right now I'm warning you that if you gals don't back off, and behave yourselves, I'll get *my*self a restraining order that sees to it you do."

We had drawn a small crowd of garage sale shoppers, some clutching items of their desire. So I hated myself for what I did next.

I tried to make peace.

If Carson had any of our antiques, or knew where they were, making a total enemy of him would not exactly help in getting them back.

I tried my best to sound sincere. "Mr. Carson, you do have a valid point. And I apologize for making a scene at the luncheon."

"Brandy!" Mother looked at me as if *I'd* gone off my medication.

"But you of all people should know what family heirlooms can mean to a person. How valuable such things are, in the sentimental sense."

Softly but with an edge, he said, "No one put a gun to your mother's head to make her sell those things."

"I know, I know. And you had no way of knowing that there were . . . other considerations."

"Such as?"

I didn't want to get into that here, and said instead, "Right now Mother only cares that her friend Mr. Olson get top dollar for his antiques, should he decide to sell any."

Mr. Olson roused from his silence to say, "Really this fuss isn't necessary — I'm not interested in selling anything that's not out here on the yard."

"But if you ever *should*," Mother replied, "why don't you call me? I'm kind of a buff, you know, Floyd — and I have all sorts of price guides on what antiques are worth."

"Or let Mr. Carson make an offer," I chimed in, "but then get a second opinion from another dealer or two." I gave Carson a smile that I hoped seemed innocent and sincere. "Just like with a doctor and something serious — right, Mr. Carson? A second opinion?"

What else could Carson say, but, "That's not a bad idea, Mr. Olson. Just let me know how I can be of help."

Mother said, "How generous of you . . . 'Bubbah.' "

Carson sneered a little, then nodded to

Mr. Olson, turned, and went off in a huff. Actually, he lingered at one of the tables, so make that a minute and a huff.

We departed shortly after, ourselves . . . but not before Mother bought that painting for a mere five dollars (I think Mr. Olson would have given it away, just to get rid of us).

Earlier, in anticipation of the return of the writing box, I had dragged up a Formica table with a white-and-red-checkered top from the basement, and put it in the music room. Now, back home, I placed the writing box on its time-honored perch.

The music room also doubled as a library, one entire wall containing a built-in floor-to-ceiling bookcase, books thankfully intact, unplundered by Carson. The room was dominated by a very old ornate walnut upright piano, which had been there as long as I could remember.

Before I was born, Peggy Sue took lessons in high school, trying to get cultured. Then I came along and pounded on those poor black-and-whites (no lessons) (no culture). Sometimes, a really bad smell would permeate the music room, and I'd open up the lid and find a mouse, strangled in the piano wires. Mice loved to hide in there, you see, and it meant an unfortunate end for the poor creatures when little Brandy decided to play "Chopsticks."

Tired after our garage sale trip, Mother trudged upstairs to her bedroom to take a nap. I had something else in mind, but first needed to attend to Sushi.

The little bitch (I mean that in the nicest way) had been dogging my heels since I got home, wanting to be fed, which I hadn't done previously, since we'd left the house so early. Sushi trailed me out to the kitchen (she knew her way by now; only once did I find her stuck in a corner, blindly blinking at a dead end) where I prepared her breakfast.

Diabetic dogs should be fed twice a day, followed by a shot of insulin (same as people). Naturally, animals are not fond of needles (same as people), so I would give Sushi a dog treat after. She always had the same conflicted look in her eyes: *I don't want that bee sting . . . but I do want that biscuit!* Greed got the better of her (same as people).

I went upstairs myself, to change out of my sweats, and put on something a little cooler since it was warming up outside.

Here I was, thirty, with my old bedroom back. Fortunately for me, my prized furniture — a five-piece bird's-eye maple art deco set from the 1930s — Carson hadn't taken. He must not have known about it, or he would have snatched up the awesome set. Or maybe Mother had drawn the line — even off her meds, she had known that this was mine; she'd bought it for me for my sixteenth birthday.

My favorite piece was the dressing table with a huge semicircle mirror and round glass top. An addition since my long-ago departure was a deco-framed black-and-white glossy of Jean Harlow (Mother's favorite old-time movie star) seated at the very same vanity, wearing a white silk, white-fox-trimmed robe, combing her platinum hair. How cool!

In the back of the closet, I discovered (boxed up) some of my childhood toys. Among them was a Cabbage Patch doll that Peggy Sue had stood in line hours for, then got mad at me because I said it was ugly; and the complete set of Pee Wee Herman's Playhouse action figures — except for Clocky; doggie ate Clocky (not Sushi . . . Bluto, a little bulldog, long deceased).

After rifling through the hangers, I picked out a girly pink cotton tulle skirt by Trina Turk that I'd gotten on sale due to a grease spot (no, I didn't put it there; yes, it came out). I paired this with a military-type tee, some bronze-leather Dr. Scholl's slides, and a counterfeit Louis Vuitton hobo bag that a street vendor in Chicago should've been in jail for selling, for copyright infringement (with me in the next cell for aiding and abetting).

And now . . . here are some of Brandy's fashion tips: (1), purchase one, really nice, expensive piece, and buy everything else in the ensemble on the cheap — that one, outstanding item will make you *feel* like the whole outfit cost a million dollars; (2), wear tough with tender, sending mixed signals to keep 'em guessing . . . is she naughty or is she nice? (aren't we both?); (3), put on clothes that you like, then leave and *don't look back* — the more time you have to preen and primp in front of a mirror, the more your confidence will erode and lead to a fashion faux pas; (4), don't wear the same style of clothes or designer (like Peggy Sue) day after day — just like an actor who plays the same role over and over, you'll get typecast. Sometimes I feel like being Sporty Spice . . . other times, Posh Spice. Get it? (They were a fab group, by the way, the Girls, no matter what anybody says.)

Changed and freshened up, I went out to my car.

A beautiful sunny morning awaited me —

in the seventies, low humidity — and soon I was taking in the shops along Main Street, which were bustling already, townspeople and tourists alike, looking for the indispensable item(s) they couldn't live without. I parked in one of the side lots (free) and walked along, looking in the windows.

Which reminds me.

Have you ever been at a mall, waiting for a tardy girlfriend, say, and watching the people walk by? (Perhaps the only thing men and women truly have in common is that in such situations, both are checking out the females.) When was the last time you said, "Wow! There goes a really great outfit"? Almost never! *So where do all the cute clothes in the stores go?* What, are they in closets, with the tags still on them? It's a mystery even Agatha Christie couldn't solve.

At the end of Main Street — that is, where the shops trailed off — was an old four-story building that hadn't been restored to the grandeur of its neighbors. A sign read: CARSON'S ANTIQUES — BUY AND SELL.

I had hoped Clint Carson might still be on the garage sale circuit so I could snoop around his shop, maybe spot something of ours, to size up the prices.

The building (front facing Main Street; side, Pine Street) had a unique corner front entrance with an elaborate facade, and a heavy door with its original etched glass and Victorian hardware. A bell hanging from thin, scrolled metal tinkled as I passed through.

The scarred wooden floor hadn't been refinished (or cleaned) since the building first opened its doors, the old tin ceiling retained, giving the place a rustic (not to say musty) atmosphere. Among all the gentrified antique shops of the downtown's Pearl City Plaza, this one retained a certain junk-shop aura — not necessarily a bad thing, making customers feel bargains were to be found.

As I prowled the place, however, that proved not to be the case: item after dusty item seemed ridiculously overpriced.

I had to wonder how Carson expected to stay in business. Granted, some people could be fooled — not everyone was an expert on antiques — but most shoppers had a rudimentary knowledge of what things were worth, and if not, at least some common sense.

In the middle of the elongated room a raised circular checkout island was overseen by a woman with flaming short red hair. Ginger (well, with that fiery hair, she sure wasn't Mary Ann) was talking on the phone, her voice kind of hushed, so I guessed it was a personal call. She paid no attention to me as I passed.

I couldn't say I was enamored of Carson's taste in antiques, which had a southwestern bordello look (and if that's what you're into, go for it . . . I'll pass); so he must have brought a lot of it with him from Colorado. Peppered in, though, were some midwestern antiques, such as a maple Colonial sideboard, and the occasional fifties modern piece, like a pair of really cool Hayward Wakefield end tables (but at a thousand dollars apiece, gimme a break!).

At the end of the room a vintage pointing-finger sign directed me to the second floor, so I climbed the rickety stairs to another long chamber of more of the same . . . and nothing with the family familiarity that I'd hoped to find.

Disheartened, I returned to the first floor and approached the red-haired clerk. She was about my age and dressed Bohemian but funky: sheer white peasant blouse, black leather fitted vest, multicolored skirt. Her jewelry consisted of tons of silver chains and crosses (of various lengths), which were mixed with colorful 1940s Bakelite bracelets — Heidi meets Joan Jett.

Ginger was busy with some clerical work

(accounts payable it looked like) and barely acknowledged my presence.

Finally she said, "Can I help you?" Pleasant enough.

"I was looking for Victorian furniture . . . Queen Anne in particular."

"Sorry, nothing at the moment," she said with a kind of finality, engrossed in her task.

I wasn't leaving, however. "But . . . you *did* have?"

Her back stiffened. "Once an item is sold, our policy is not to refer —"

"I'm just curious, that's all."

She sighed heavily and put her pen down, giving me a half-lidded look. "We did have some Queen Anne in about a month ago."

"And sold it?"

"Actually, no."

"Then . . . what happened to it?"

She shrugged. "Stored, most likely."

"Stored where?"

Now Ginger was flat-out irritated; she didn't like being stuck on her island dealing with a bunch of boobs.

Her words clipped, she said, "Clint — Mr. Carson — has a farmhouse out on Route 22. There's a barn where the overstock goes."

Hope jumped within me, but then she added, "Sometimes, though, he ships stuff

66

out from there . . . if it's been around too long."

"How long is 'too long'?"

"It varies. Perhaps you should talk to Mr. Carson. He'll be back in tomorrow, around eleven."

So — there might be a chance our furniture would still be within reach. But tomorrow at eleven seemed a lifetime; maybe I'd pay Carson a little visit.

I thanked Ginger and left.

Out on the sidewalk I checked my Chico's watch — almost noon; I was meeting my best friend, Tina (short for Christina), for lunch at a cute little bistro, back in the next (renovated) block. I hadn't seen Teen for a whole year, but we kept in touch by letter (not the Internet where messages bounce back and forth so fast nothing has a chance to happen to you!).

We prefer to send cute, funny greeting cards to each other, and enclose a long tome (hers handwritten; mine WordPerfect) that can be read at leisure over a cup of hot coffee (me) or tea (her). Sometimes we tuck inside magazine cutouts of clothes or shoes we'd like to have, or to be on the lookout for. Other times we pass along bargains we run across, i.e., those pink suede Steve Madden moccasin boots that Madonna wanted so bad; I found them off-season at an unbelievable twenty-eight dollars (75 percent off retail) and bought pairs for me *and* Tina (our wardrobes are practically interchangeable).

By the way — you do know what a real friend is, don't you? It's someone who tries to talk you out of marrying a guy who is older than you (ten years) and not in the same mind-set as you (wanted kids immediately), but when you go ahead and marry the guy anyway, said friend is behind you 100 percent.

That's Tina (and, unfortunately, me).

We met in high school — I was a sophomore, she a junior — and as Tina tells it (because I honestly don't remember), some witchy (with a "b") senior girls were ganging up on Teen in the hallway when I came around the corner. I ran over with clenched fists (and most likely wild eyes) and told them to lay off . . . and they scattered like the marbles in their heads. Later, Tina said she'd never heard such foul language as mine come out of any girl's mouth. Or, for that matter, guy's.

A proud moment.

Anyway, we've been like sisters ever since (I'm going to say it: the one I wish I had).

I arrived at the restaurant first. What I

liked about Pine Creek Grist Mill (besides the food) was that everything — tables, chairs, plates, cups and saucers — were all mismatched antiques; it was like eating at home.

I'd just been seated (the last table available) when Tina came in looking her usual lovely self. She was a slender honey-colored blonde (natural), a few inches taller than me, and wore pale pink capris and a white cotton, fitted, three-quarter-sleeve blouse; the sedated outfit made her David Yurman jewelry (around her slender neck and arms) go *bling, bling, bling!*

I stood for a hug.

"You're too thin to be seen with," she gushed. (I had another ten to go, but it was sweet of her to say).

"And you look younger than *last* year," I said. "Damn it."

The waitress came over; Teen and I were both good and ordered salads with house vinaigrette, after negotiating up front to split a peanut butter cheesecake, Pine Creek's specialty.

And now for the last word you'll ever need to know on dieting, and it's not counting carbs or calories . . . it's something you *visualize:*

There are three men who live in your

stomach — Tom (wiry), Dick (fireplug), and Harry (needs a shave); their job is to keep the furnace (your stomach) stoked with coal (fat from your thighs). All they really do, however, is sit around playing cards, or reading *Penthouse,* or getting into fistfights like drunken sailors on a three-day pass; they get away with such derelict duty, why?

Because you keep doing their work for them!

How? By pouring too much food down your gullet! So the next time Tom, Dick, or Harry sticks you with a pitchfork (hunger pang) douse 'em with a big glass of water, and then eat *smaller portions,* so the boys have to go back to the coal bin.

"How's Kevin?" I asked. Tina's husband (a salesman for a pharmaceutical company) was a peach of a guy, always nice to me, never jealous of our friendship. They'd been trying to have a baby for a couple of years.

"Kev's on the road this week," she said. "Maybe we could go out some night — there's a club on the bluff that just opened up."

"Girls' night out?"

"Absolutely! We're overdue, don't you think?" She leaned forward to add carefully: "You could meet some new people."

Meaning guys. "Teen, I don't know if I'm

ready to get back up on that particular pony."

"Never too early to check out the corral," Tina said, and gave me a sideways smile. "We'll just enjoy the view while we sip some champagne."

She knew my weakness, and it wasn't men, unless the name was Andre. I really wasn't much of a drinker — not with *my* migraines — but sometimes a bit of the bubbly was worth the risk. Actually, these days a big weekend eve for me was champagne, cheese and crackers, and Mad TV. Tina was right: I needed to get out in the world. We set a date for the weekend.

Our salads came and we reminisced about old times — like driving to a Chicago suburb in pea-soup fog (using a semi as a scout) for some shopping, and coming home with only a five-dollar necklace (each) . . . apparently what our lives were worth.

I can only think of one instance when Tina and I got sick of each other, and that was after a marathon shopping trip (nine malls in two days) . . . and then we didn't want to see each other for a *whole week.*

The lunch crowd had cleared by the time we split the bill and left the bistro. We lingered on the sidewalk, promising to call each other about what we were going to wear on our outing (a pointless ritual since we rarely kept our word).

I drove home to discover a large box in the front entryway. Mother was folding laundry in a chair nearby, and she got up.

"It's for you, Brandy," she said, excitement in her voice. "From Roger."

How she had resisted opening it, I'll never know. Where Mother clung to the notion that contact with Roger meant a reconciliation might one day occur, I knew better. My ex had probably found more of my possessions that he couldn't stand to have around. I tried lifting the box, but it was way heavy; a muffled, metallic ringing sound came from within.

Mother, eyebrows raised quizzically above her eyeglass frames, accentuating further her big amplified eyes, produced a pair of scissors from somewhere (she'd had them all along). Inside the box of mystery, I found several canvas bank bags, and within the bags were pennies . . .

. . . my monthly alimony.

Roger must have ordered them direct from the Federal Reserve, and sent them at great expense.

"Poor boy," Mother sighed, and shook her head. "He's still hurting."

I nodded, thinking that pain wasn't what

my ex was feeling: it was rage. And even now, running my hand through the coins, I could hardly blame him.

I could only hope this was a onetime stunt. Pennies were so worthless that retailers would rather round the bill down than have to deal with Mr. Lincoln. Even parking meters won't take the darn things. Then there's the problem people create by "hoarding" pennies (throwing them in a glass jar), which creates a demand, forcing the Treasury Department to print more and more of the little buggers.

Still, I found myself saying to Mother, "Remember the time I found that valuable penny?"

I'd been working a summer job as a bank teller my first year of community college.

"How much was it worth?" For all her drama, Mother likes to cut right to the chase.

"Couple hundred bucks," I said, adding, "And that was way back then." (I'd spent it on clothes, natch.)

Mother's eyes had dollar signs.

In the meantime, Sushi was whimpering at my feet, wanting to go out for a little walk, which I'd been doing about this hour every day lately. Could dogs tell time?

So I went to get the pooper-scooper,

because Sushi always saved up for the glorious fun of making her deposits on fresh territory.

When we got back, Mother was sitting Indian-style, having dumped all the pennies out on the parquet floor. I would have suggested a better way (ever try to pick coins up off a wood floor?) but didn't want to dampen her enthusiasm. She was examining a coin with a magnifying glass, making a beach ball out of her already magnified eye. I squatted and joined in on the hunt.

Hey, valuable coins *do* turn up.

Here's how: sometimes, a kid (let's say a girl named Brandy) discovers her father's old coin collection (from when *he* was a kid) in a trunk in our attic and spends it all on Jelly Bellys, my favorite at the time.

On and off through the afternoon, Mother and I worked at the penny pile (finding several promising possibilities to look up), then broke for supper (Swedish meatballs and rhubarb pie — I gave Tom, Dick, and Harry the night off).

My eyes and neck were burning from the penny search, so I decided to go out and get some air, maybe drive around the old town, and see what was new. I spent several hours just taking in how the place had changed — our high school was now the middle school, fresh facilities for the former taking root where the drive-in movie used to be. A favorite necking and petting spot, Weed Park (no kidding — named after a city founder named Weed) had lost a zoo and gained a new aquatic center.

Enough had changed to make me feel old; however, enough was the same to provide a certain comfort. . . .

Dusk was settling in when I headed back home. As I pulled in the drive I could see that the garage door was open.

Mother's car was gone.

You remember Mother, don't you? The woman without a license? Although, a woman often willing to *take* license. . . .

Inside the house, she was nowhere to be found . . . but a notepad by the answer machine had something written on it: *Carson, 4512 Route 22.*

Had the antique dealer called?

If so, what did he want? Or had Mother decided to pay him a visit on her own?

My mind provided any number of explanations, but none of them made the sick feeling at the pit of my stomach go away.

I had no choice but to go back out.

Route 22 was a scenic road winding along the river's bluff, used mostly by those who lived along it, or sightseers with time on their hands. Other routes were available, and preferable, in no small part because passing was difficult on the hilly, two-lane highway — as attested by the ever-so-often flower-adorned white crosses along the roadside, planted by bereaved family members.

Nonetheless, this was a lovely time of night as I tooled along above the glistening river . . . magic hour, as some called it . . . but in a few more minutes darkness would close in, and with no moon, only my headlights would guide me.

Around a tight curve a deer leaped out of the trees and gave us both a scare. I braked, and instead of swerving, aimed directly for it, thereby missing the animal as it darted across to safety. A few hundred yards farther, however, another deer hadn't been so lucky; the highway was splashed with blood, the twisted carcass thrown by the wayside.

I shivered, and not from the cool night air blowing in my open window; and a sense of sadness enveloped me — the loss of such a beautiful life touched me. But then my emotions were on edge with worry about Mother.

About ten miles outside of town, I slowed, eyes searching the roadside mailboxes with their reflecting house numbers; finally I spotted 4512.

I swung into a gravel drive, which then split into two narrow lanes for incoming and outgoing traffic, separated by an island of trees and brush.

After a distance, I arrived at a nondescript two-story, clapboard farmhouse illuminated by a tall yard light. The house looked dark and quiet. A red Ford pickup was parked in front.

No sign of Mother's car.

While I pondered my next move, I noticed the big red barn just to the left and back of the farmhouse.

Was this the current home of our plundered furniture?

I climbed cautiously out of my car, approached the dark house with my heart in my ears, and knocked tentatively on the front door.

Nothing.

Then I tried again, louder.

Everything remained eerily silent.

Satisfied no one was home, I headed to the barn. I didn't see how taking a look would hurt — reconnaissance, soldiers called it, right?

The rough-wood double doors were locked, and wouldn't budge, even with a good tug or two. I began circling the structure, looking for a window to peer into (or climb inside, if I really got my nerve up).

Around the back of the barn, I tripped in the dark on something, and tumbled . . . my fall cushioned by a pile of garbage. It reeked of farm chemicals; now, so did I. When had I had my last tetanus shot? I wondered. Discouraged, bruised, and rank, I limped back to my car.

Some soldier.

Following the "out" lane, I was going at a pretty good clip when my headlights caught something just ahead. Almost upon it, I again found myself slamming on the brakes.

At first, I thought the prone dark mass blocking the way was just another poor deer. But when I clicked my brights on, I could see clearly that this body was human.

Had been human. . . .

Clint Carson lay on his back, eyes staring hollowly upward, limbs twisted . . . a scarecrow with the stuffing knocked out.

I thought for a moment about getting out of the car and checking to see if he was still alive. But he seemed so clearly dead, as much roadkill as that deer.

Shaking, I drove quickly around him, knocking over some bushes in the process, and sped back toward town. On my cell, I called 911 and told them what I'd seen, but did not give my name.

Just the same, a police car was parked in front of our house, and as I pulled into the driveway, an officer got out.

I was just thinking what a dunce I was — of course their phone system would automatically collect my phone number! — when the policeman approached, asking a question I had not been expecting.

"Is Vivian Borne your mother?"

He was a blandly handsome guy in his thirties, but his brown eyes showed concern.

"Yes . . . what's this about? Has something happened to her?"

"I'm afraid she may be in a lot of trouble."

"For driving without a license?"

He frowned, hesitated, then said, "It's considerably more serious than that. Your mother came into the station claiming she killed someone . . . but that's all the information we could get out of her. She seemed confused . . . disoriented."

My knees buckled and I leaned against my car.

The young officer took my arm. "Are you all right?"

I didn't answer him. For a moment I wondered if I'd *ever* be all right again. . . .

"If you know anything about this," the officer said, firm but kind, "you need to tell us."

"Take me to her," I said.

A Trash 'n' Treasures Tip

Antiques and collectibles should be insured against fire and theft. But if you're short on cash like me, just make sure you unplug the iron and lock the house before leaving.

Chapter Three

JAILHOUSE CROCK

The Safety Building — a two-story redbrick monolith also housing the fire department — was home to the Serenity PD. Behind the seventies-era structure sat a new state-of-the-art county jail, aping the bland red-brick design of its safeguarding neighbor.

To the casual passerby, the jail might seem a law office or a medical clinic, the grounds tastefully landscaped, the premises lacking any barbed wire or electrical fence. The only "tell" as to its true purpose was the row of tiny, too-high barred windows on the second floor, where the prisoners were housed.

Kitty-corner to the jail stood Serenity's grand old courthouse, a breathtakingly beautiful white wedding cake of sandstone and marble. Every couple of years or so, the folks working inside this noble Grecian structure would start grumbling for an ignoble modern facility, because they were hot or crowded or whatever. Mother would hear about a circulating petition for such and scream, "Over my dead body will that courthouse be torn down!" and fly into action, gathering her historical conservation troops and descending on city council meetings like a barbarian horde in support hose.

Rather than deal with the likes of Mother, the council would soon find some money for the purchase of a few more courthouse air conditioners, and recommend that a storage room or two be cleared out for additional offices, and things would settle down for a while. Currently Mother had written her several congressmen (state and national) about protecting the structure with historical status. Nothing had come of it yet, but then you must keep in mind that all of those congressmen likely have a special file for Mother's missives, possibly circular.

You might say the wheels of justice in Serenity worked closely together: a perp could be taken into custody at the police station, then hauled into court, and thrown into jail, all within a block or so . . . almost like one-stop shopping! (Shop-*lifting* location optional.)

Some time past midnight, I pulled my urine-yellow Taurus into the nearly vacant lot of the Safety Building, having dutifully followed Officer Lawson, who had come to the house looking for me.

Businesslike but polite, the officer — tall, brown-haired, brown-eyed, and not at all hard on the orbs — ushered me through the front door of the station, past a small waiting area where a few perfunctory plastic chairs crowded around a scarred coffee table strewn with public-awareness pamphlets. A soda machine hummed an electronic nontune in one corner.

I followed Officer Lawson down a beige-tiled corridor to a large, probably bulletproof window, behind which a ponytailed woman dressed in blues sat surrounded by a bank of screens and computers, like an air-traffic controller at O'Hare Airport.

At the moment, all was quiet on the western front, but the middle-of-the-night atmosphere held the promise of something bad breaking that mood any moment. The female officer took her eyes off a screen and looked at us as if we were a museum exhibit that had just materialized before her.

Lawson nodded; she nodded back, and buzzed us on through a heavy metal door . . . which is to say, a heavy door made of metal, not one decorated with rock-band stickers.

Down another institutional hallway we

trod, footsteps echoing like muted gunshots off the gray walls, which were not at all cheered up by a few hanging pictures, mostly of posed rows of police department personnel past, and shots of the severe, grotesque police station of bygone days, long since torn down (Mother came to her senses on *that* one).

We stopped at a scuffed steel door marked INTERVIEW ROOM — kinder, gentler terminology for Interrogation Room, I supposed.

Next to the door was a small built-in wall safe. This Lawson opened with a key, took his gun out of its holster and placed the weapon inside, then locked it again.

Did he think Mother was really that dangerous? That she might go for his gun? Or did I have a wild look in my eyes that told him I might try for his rod?

He must have read my thoughts, or at least their gist. With a little shrug he said, "Procedure." Then he opened the door to the Interview Room and I went in ahead of my handsome host.

Mother was alone, seated in a metal folding chair next to a metal card table, both fixtures firmly bolted to the floor. The room, sparse, small, seemed claustrophobic, cold. Steel rings for shackling (thankfully not in use at the moment) were attached ominously to one wall like especially ugly earrings.

I was startled and frightened by Mother's appearance — eyes flitting wildly behind the large glasses, lips trembling, hands clutching what remained of a shredded tissue.

I was immediately worried about her mental well-being, but when Mother saw me she stood and pulled herself up to her full height, head high, chin jutting, eyes winning a struggle to focus behind the glasses.

"I am all right, my dear," she announced. The "my dear" designation was reserved for when we had an audience. "The local gendarmes have been very nice to me, even gotten me a tissue or two."

I said, "We should call Mr. Ekhardt, Mother."

She gave her head a toss. "Bosh! He's in bed and I won't bother him at this hour. An older man like him, well, we must have certain considerations."

Mother did have a point.

Mr. Ekhardt had been our family attorney since I was in diapers; now he was old enough for adult diapers. In the late eighties, he semiretired, but kept a handful of clients, including the Bornes (Mother had been best friends with his late wife) and every so often, like an old fire horse responding to a clanging bell, Mr. Ekhardt would take on a criminal case. Even now he made a commanding presence in the courtroom — except, perhaps, when he fell asleep.

Mother once told me about the time in the 1950s when Mr. Ekhardt first made a name for himself as Serenity's go-to trial lawyer when he got a woman off for shooting her sleeping husband in the chest five times "in self-defense" . . . and I mean she went scot-free. This was back when a man could smack a woman around and not get thrown in jail, so it was some kind of victory. Mother said all the men in town were *awfully* nice to their wives for a long time after that!

But if Mother was in the kind of trouble I thought she was in, Mr. Ekhardt should be called, senior-citizen considerations be damned.

I swiveled to Officer Lawson. "Could I speak to my mother alone?"

He nodded. "I'll be right outside."

Soon we were by ourselves in the clammy cubicle.

I sat Mother back down, then took the other bolted chair, probably reserved for the interrogator . . . I mean "interviewer" . . . and I interviewed her. Which is to say, interrogated her.

"Tell me what happened, Mother — *exactly* what happened."

Mother took a deep breath that started out confident but quickly turned quavery, her tough veneer beginning to buckle a bit. "I . . . I . . . came home, and you weren't there . . . and the answer machine was blinking. I checked the message . . . it is *my* machine, after all, how was I to know it was for you?"

"I forgive you. Go on."

"Anyway, it was the girl from that antique shop."

"What girl? What antique shop?"

"She said her name was Tanya and that you'd spoken with her there."

The redhead . . . Ginger, not Mary Ann. . . .

"She's an associate of that terrible Carson person, and said he wanted you to come out to his house. He was willing to talk about letting us have our furniture back."

The redhead had seemed rude and uninterested in me, but maybe she'd conveyed my desire to rebuy our stuff to her boss.

"Well," Mother was saying, "I'd thought maybe you'd already gone out there, and saved the message . . . so I'd know where you were."

"And then what, Mother?"

She nodded. "I got to thinking . . ."

Never a good sign.

". . . and finally I decided to take my car — yes, I know I *shouldn't* have, but I was *frightened* for you. That man Carson can be *awfully* mean."

As the great Inspector Clouseau once said, in regard to a priceless Steinway he'd destroyed, *Not . . . any . . . more.*

"I pulled into that circular drive of his, drove past the farmhouse and barn, but saw no sign of you, Brandy dear . . . so I hit the gas and headed home."

"And also hit Carson?"

"No. Well, yes — he was in the road, prone there, and I didn't see him. I sort of . . . bumped and thumped over him."

Yikes, I thought.

"Brandy, I got out to check — he was, not surprisingly, dead." She straightened. "But. I think he must've been dead already. In fact, I assumed *you* had done it. So . . . so I turned myself in!"

Mother leaned forward, put a hand on mine, as if I were the one who needed comforting; maybe I was.

"Brandy," she said, with considerable

drama (make that melodrama), "you mustn't worry about your old mother. Why, I've lived a good life, a long life."

"Save it for the matinee, Mother. We need to call Mr. Ekhardt."

"And that's exactly why you needn't worry! We will have Mr. Ekhardt in our corner! Don't forget about that!"

Assuming the old gent lived long enough to defend her.

One thing was clear to me: Mother could not survive the ordeal of a trial. Or at least, her mental state couldn't, and I was not about to see her institutionalized again, not after we'd made so much progress.

I stood, sighed, swallowed, opened the door, and asked Officer Lawson to step back in.

Calmly I said, "I don't know what my mother told you, but *I* was the one who ran Carson over."

". . . Really?"

"It was dark and I just didn't see him."

Mother bolted up from the chair. "Brandy! What in heaven's name are you saying? Officer, don't you believe her. She's just trying to protect me!"

I shook my head and pointed at Mother accusingly. "No . . . *she's* trying to protect *me.*"

Lawson raised a traffic-cop palm. "Whoa, whoa, whoa," he said, as if we were a couple of brawling kids. "Settle down, ladies. Do I need to separate you two?"

Mother and I said nothing, not looking at each other.

"If I took your statement tonight, what —"

"*I* did it," Mother and I said.

The officer took a long look at us, giving each of our faces a thorough going-over; he shook his head, sighed, smiled in a rumpled way, then crooked a finger at me, as if I were a grade-school student being summoned to the principal's office.

And he said, "Ms. Borne, a word in the hall, please?"

I stepped out there with him, after he shut Mother back in.

"Can I give you a small word of advice?" He wasn't really asking. "Stop covering for your mother."

"I'm not —"

"Look, it's not gonna take TV show forensics to know which of your cars was involved, and we'll soon know who was behind the wheel, too. Pretty rudimentary police work."

The thought of Mother facing a trial and even a prison sentence sent tears trailing down my cheeks. I didn't have a tissue, but he found one for me. I used it.

His voice softened. "I'm not going to take your statements tonight. Neither one of you is a flight risk, and I know the police chief will want to talk to you, personally. Isn't the chief a friend of yours, Ms. Borne?"

"Y-yes."

"Look," Lawson said, his voice softening. "I'm sure everything will straighten out — it's clear you're covering for each other."

"I can —"

"No, you can't. If either of you were involved, it was likely an accident. Everybody in town knows your mother has a history of mental illness —"

"What are you —"

"Quiet. I'm not going to report that your mother confessed to this, only that she was dazed and confused. And anything you said, well, I hadn't advised you of your rights."

I frowned at him. "Are you *now?*"

"No. But I *am* advising you to contact your attorney, first thing tomorrow. And to stay in town."

"We're not going anywhere."

"You sure aren't. There's a little matter of your mother driving with a suspended license to sort out, at the very least."

I nodded. Sniffed.

"I'll come around to your house in the morning, after I've had a chance to talk with the police chief. We'll know more tomorrow."

Since the PD had impounded both our cars, Officer Lawson had to take us home.

Mother and I sat in exhausted silence in the backseat of the squad car, fenced in behind the wire barricade like a couple of criminals. Maybe one of us *was*. . . .

Lawson pulled in our drive, got out, and opened the car door for us. Mother loped on ahead, disappearing into the darkened house surreptiously, a prisoner making a break for it. Lawson saw me up to the front steps, like a polite suitor; crickets and bullfrogs serenaded us.

I said, "Thanks for taking us home . . . and thanks for being decent to Mother. And . . . and for taking this slow."

"I always take things slow," he said with a shy smile. "By the way, my first name's Brian."

"Brian. Glad to meet you."

"Oh, we've met before."

In the darkness I could see a tiny smile tugging at the corners of his mouth.

"Really?" I squinted at him; I was sure I would have remembered those puppy-brown eyes.

"Yes, about five years ago. Back when I was a state trooper."

State trooper, five years ago . . .

Lawson's small smile got bigger. "I stopped you one summer afternoon . . . along Highway 22?"

My eyes widened. Oh my God, was that *him?*

Okay, here's what happened . . .

. . . I was driving back from Chicago by myself, for Tina's wedding, wearing a St. John's navy and gold cotton knit cardigan and skirt, and a new Victoria's Secret lace bra. All the way home, the bra was pinching and scratching, and I was getting crabbier and crabbier, until — by the time I hit the outskirts of town — I just couldn't stand it one minute longer. Driving with my knees, I proceeded to remove the bra from under my top, rolled down the BMW's window, and flung the offensive item out.

In immediate response, lights flashed behind me.

Pulling my arms back inside my top, continuing to steer with my knees and the occasional elbow, I managed to ease off the road. In the rearview mirror I saw a highway patrol car roll up behind me.

And wrapped around the patrol car's antenna was my white lacy bra, flapping in the breeze like a flag of fancy surrender.

The tall trooper, in those patented high-way patrol wraparound sunglasses, retrieved the undergarment, then handed it back to me with an expression that said, *Well, that's one for the books.*

I had swallowed and placed the bra on my seat. "I guess . . . I littered or something."

"Or something," he said. "Try to stay in that thing, in the future . . . while you're driving, anyway."

". . . Okay."

"Step out of the car, please?"

A few minutes later, after he'd put me through some very demeaning motions, he had smiled, wished me a pleasant day, put a finger to his cap in a small salute, and turned away . . . while I'd created a thousand baby wrinkles in my red-faced crinkly frown that shot impotent daggers at his cocky back.

I number that encounter among my more humiliating moments, so when my new policeman pal Brian brought it all back to me, I was chagrined and dumbfounded and . . . well, not speechless, of course.

"That was *you?*" I asked. "Behind those sunglasses?"

Brian nodded, grinning.

I could feel my cheeks burning — and not

from embarrassment.

Fists on hips, I said, "You didn't have to make me walk a line — right there by the highway, with all those cars going by, honking."

He shrugged. "I thought you might be drunk, way you were weaving all over the road."

"Well, I *wasn't,*" I snapped. "And after *that,* you gave me a *Breathalyzer* test! Was *that* really necessary? You wouldn't have done that to a truck driver!"

Another shrug. "I would have if he threw his bra out his window."

I was gathering steam. "And then . . . *then!* . . . you wrote me out a friggin' *ticket!*"

Brian's smile faded. He went on the defensive. "Hey, you *were* driving recklessly, after all. 'I was driving with my knees' is not the best explanation I ever heard for reckless driving."

I folded my arms across my chest. "So what was wrong with giving me just a warning citation? Or did you have some quota to make?"

"Look, lady, I was just doing my job."
Lady?

I smirked. "Oh, I bet I made some kind of story round the ol' state trooper watercooler. Bet that bra size just got bigger and bigger every time you —"

He turned abruptly and went down the porch steps. A moment later the squad car door slammed in response.

Grumbling, I went inside the house.

Sushi was waiting for me, whimpering a little. I scooped her up and buried my face in her soft fur. "*You* love me, don't you, girl — no matter what."

Maybe I'd been bullheaded. Some things I can never let go. Considering the pickle Mother and I were in, we certainly didn't need to make an enemy out of Officer Brian Lawson. He'd been kind to us tonight, cut us a heck of a break, and I'd gotten all witchy with him. With a "b."

Sighing, I carted Sushi through the kitchen, to put her out back . . . but then saw that she'd already peed by the door. The whimper had been Sushi's confession — every female in this house had confessed tonight.

Anyway, it wasn't her fault; we'd been gone too long for a diabetic drinks-a-lot dog to hold it in.

I put her out, anyway, and wiped up the mess, as if this were the punishment for tonight's crimes.

Of course, cleaning pet pee-pee on bare floors is easy, but what about carpet?

Here's what you do:

Cover the spot with paper towels, and with your shoes on (I know a guy who did this in just his socks!) (don't!) jump up and down on it — you can take your anger at your pet out, this way. Repeat the process until no more moisture appears on the towels. Then pour a pan of lukewarm not-too-sudsy water on the same spot, and do the paper towel routine again. (P.S., keep *lots* of paper towels on hand. Particularly if *your* dog is diabetic, too.)

My legs ached as I trudged upstairs with Sushi. I could hear Mother snoring, and slipped into her bedroom to check on her. She was on top of the covers, still in her clothes. By all rights I should have woken her, confronted her, gotten to the bottom of all this.

But instead I got an extra blanket, drew it over her, then tiptoed back out. Just didn't have the heart, and anyway, I was beyond beat myself.

I collapsed onto my own bed, also not bothering to get undressed, and pulled Sushi close to me, like a living hot water bottle.

Next thing I knew, Mother was shaking me.

"Brandy, Brandy, that policeman's here

again . . . wake up!"

I felt like a tranquilized animal coming around. "What . . . what *time* is it?"

"Almost nine. Get up!"

I groaned. "So early?"

But Mother was gone.

Anyway, once Sushi stirred, that was the end of sleeping, so I might as well get up.

I frowned to myself. *What was that dream I had?* It lingered, just out of reach, an almost memory taunting, a mood that held on, ambiguously.

And while we're on the subject of dreams, remember this: *no one wants to hear your stupid dreams* (except maybe your psychiatrist, who is after all getting paid for the "privilege"). No one else can share your dream experience . . . so don't bore people!

And, anyway, dreams are never as good as you think they are. Case in point: there was this guy I dated in high school who once told me about a dream he'd had. In it, he'd thought up the funniest joke in the world. At the beginning, he told the joke to a class at school. His classmates laughed so hard, they encouraged him to share it. He went on local TV and told the joke, cracking up all within range. He went on a national tour with the joke, on television, finally performing it in stadiums. It was so funny, in fact, that every time he told it, a certain number of people literally died from laughing. He became famous, went on *Letterman,* opened for Chris Rock.

My slumbering boyfriend, sensing a fortune to be made, forced himself awake, stumbled over to his desk, and scribbled down the joke, then went back to bed, secure he would awake a potential entertainment giant.

And in the morning, he eagerly looked at the note, which said: *the banana is yellow.*

And that boyfriend grew up to be Lewis Black. Not.

What annoys me most about dreams is this: with our entire imagination at our disposal, with the ability to make ourselves (in our dreams) gorgeous, rich, talented, young, loved, etc.— why do we dream such vile crap? Like falling to our death, having loved ones burn up in a house fire, being pushed out onstage in a play you've never rehearsed, taking a final exam in a class you've never been to, wandering around in public in the nude, or (the worst) shopping without any credit cards . . . *Come on!* Who is in charge here?

I've been working on a system to combat nightmares. Before I turn in for the night, I give myself a good talking-to. Usually this happens in front of the bathroom mirror, where I waggle my finger, and say things like, "Now no bad dreams tonight . . . only *good* dreams."

The first time I tried this, I snarled, "If you dream something bad, Brandy, I'm going to kick your freakin' ass!" Only I didn't say "freakin'." Bottom line, my psyche didn't like being spoken to like that, and I dreamed I fell down a well.

So, anyway, I dismissed my dream to slumber-limboland and hurriedly got out of bed, after which I brushed my teeth, washed my face, and ran a brush through my hair — there was a rat's nest back there I hadn't been able to comb out for days.

Then I straightened the clothes I'd been wearing since yesterday, dashed toward the stairs, and then . . . nonchalantly descended. Why should I hurry for Officer Brian Lawson, the man who had returned my bra only to humiliate me further?

And there Officer Lawson stood, in the middle of the sparse living room, his demeanor businesslike. Mother sat regally on the couch we'd gotten at Goodwill, hands folded prayerfully (maybe she was praying for a new couch). I sat beside her and slipped an arm around her.

"I don't have a lot to tell you," Lawson

said, "except that a preliminary report from the county coroner could — and I emphasize the word 'could'— clear you both."

Mother and I exchanged hopeful glances.

Lawson continued: "It appears Carson was dead before either of you came along."

With a gasp of relief, Mother turned to me. "Then you *didn't* kill him, Brandy! You *didn't* run him over before *I* ran him over."

"Well . . . *no,* Mother." Did she really think I'd do such a thing?

"Ladies," Officer Lawson was saying, "I'd prefer you waited for your attorney —"

Mother ignored this and blurted, "But, Brandy, in the parking lot of the hotel, you said —"

Before my loving mother could tell the officer how I'd said I wanted to kill the deceased, I gave her shoulder a really *big* squeeze, and she said, "Oww!"

And I whispered, "Mother, that was just an expression. You know I didn't mean it."

Sometimes — *now* for example — Mother could be a tad exasperating. Not very — just enough to make you want to hurl yourself into the Grand Canyon. Or her.

Beaming, Mother patted my hand. "Well, that's nice to hear, dear. I'm glad!"

I rolled my eyes and looked at Lawson.

"Is there anything else you can tell us? How *did* the man die?"

Lawson rocked on his heels, thought for a moment about how much he should say, then shared the following: "We won't know for sure until the tox report comes back, which could take a week or more."

Behind her big lenses, Mother's eyes blinked. "Tox?"

"Toxicology," he said.

Mother sat up straight, as if poked by a cattle prod. "You think he died of a *drug* overdose?"

"Well . . ."

She smiled wickedly. "Or maybe the poor man was *poisoned?*"

"I don't think *anything,* Mrs. Borne," Lawson replied firmly. "And I caution you about repeating any such notions."

Mother put on her most angelic face and touched hand to bosom in genteel display. "Well, of course, Officer. Everyone knows how I *abhor* idle gossip."

I thought it best to get off *that* subject, so I asked, "What about Mother's driving charges?"

His eyebrows went up. "She'll have to appear in court, of course . . . but we'll let you know. In the meantime, may I suggest you both stay out of trouble? And do have a talk with your attorney."

"Certainly," Mother said. Then to me, sotto voce, "Such a nice young man."

I gave her a glazed look, then got up off the couch and trailed Brian out onto the front porch in my bare feet, where just a few hours ago I hadn't behaved very well to him.

His expression was friendly, almost warm. "Listen, about your mother . . . this driving thing. I didn't want to say this in front of her, but . . ."

"But what?"

"Technically, she could be facing jail time."

"Jail time!"

"Wait. Considering her age, and, well, mental history, that's extremely doubtful. Obviously it's not my place to say, but my guess is . . . a suspended sentence."

Relief flooded through me.

"Brian . . . can I call you Brian?"

"I wish you would."

"And I'm Brandy. Brian, uh . . . when can we have our cars back?"

His expression turned businesslike again, and he gave me another "We'll let you know."

At least he didn't slam his cop-car door, this time.

Inside I found Mother in the downstairs bathroom, slapping on lipstick and rouge.

"Where do you think *you're* going?" I asked.

"Nowhere. In particular."

She was sounding like Mr. Toad in *Wind in the Willows*.

"Well, you look like you're going somewhere. In particular."

"Perhaps."

"Muuuhther . . . we've been advised to lie low . . ."

She turned from the mirror and patted me on the head, as if I were still a child, or perhaps a puppy. "I'll be back in a little while, Brandy. . . . You get some sleep, now — you look dreadfully tired."

I groaned.

With no energy to stop her, I went back to bed and pulled the covers over my head.

In my dream, Mother was playing Sherlock Holmes in a play. Just another stupid dream . . .

. . . which, unfortunately, Mother was off making come true.

A Trash 'n' Treasures Tip

If you start to collect something, *don't tell anyone about it!* I know an otherwise perfectly sane woman who has a room filled with ceramic frogs, only about a third of which were her own doing. How would you like to inherit that?

CHAPTER FOUR

TROLLEY FOLLIES

When I awoke, several hours later, I found Mother sitting on the edge of my bed wearing a cat-ate-the-canary smile.

I leaned up on an elbow. "Where have *you* been?"

Her eyes danced with excitement, her smile as mischievous as a North Pole elf who just short-sheeted Santa's bed.

"I have something to report," she said with grand formality.

". . . Report?"

Her eyes flared, and with the magnification of those lenses, it made two small conflagrations. "We now have several suspects in the Clint Carson murder case."

". . . Murder case?"

Mother frowned but there was a smile in it, her eyes narrow now behind the thickness of glass, her hands waving like Al Jolson singing (what else?) "Mammy."

"Oh my, my dear, it's a *murder,* all right."

The frown had held on for a whole four seconds, and the delighted child's smile took its rightful place on her cheerfully demented mug. "Would you like to hear my story?"

"Do I have a choice?"

I did not.

And neither do you: what follows is Mother's story. She has written the following section herself, as she doesn't trust my memory or my ability not to interrupt her tale with sarcasm.

Hold on to your red hat.

After I left my dear darling daughter — poor thing was simply exhausted after our ordeal with Serenity's forces of law and order — I strolled to the corner to wait for the Traveling Trolley to take me downtown.

The old trolley-car — financed by the downtown merchants to encourage folks to do their shopping with them instead of those ubiquitous malls and the dread "super" Wal-Mart — had been converted from electric to gas, and anyone could ride for free, as long as they went downtown, of course.

Mrs. Roxanne Randolf — she had worked at the library, at the Help Desk, until a large world atlas on a high shelf had gotten away from her, the poor woman conked on the head and off a ladder — had fully recovered and was now driving the trolley. Her husband ran a business out of their home (making ceramic lighthouses), and the local gossips insisted he was having an affair with a neighbor young enough to be his daughter, but apparently Mrs. Randolf didn't know about the tryst, and *I* wasn't about to tell her ... although somebody certainly should, because we of the weaker sex should stick together (except for those who are trysting with our men).

But I digress.

Mrs. Randolf dropped me off at Hunter's Hardware, which hadn't changed since I was a dewy-eyed girl back in the forties. The store was long and narrow, typical of the marvelous old buildings of the late eighteen hundreds, and still retained the original hardwood floor and high tin decorative ceiling, not to mention a certain bouquet common to retail stores of days past.

Not typical of a hardware store, however, was the bar located in the back, an ingenious bit of marketing. A husband could actually say to his wife, "Darling, I'm going down to Hunter's for a screwdriver," and still be telling the truth, even when the only do-it-yourselfing he had in mind was imbibing vodka and orange juice.

The downside, of course, was selling ball-peen hammers, actual screwdrivers, and chain saws to patrons who'd had one or two or three or four too many.

I walked in, skirting the racks of wrenches, displays of paint and brushes, and the usual array of tools, to the antique walnut bar in the back. Business was light this time of morning — it wouldn't pick up until the farmers came to town midafternoon to buy seed and grain (albeit already processed into beer) — with only myself and one other patron to keep the bartender company.

Henry (the patron; the bartender was Junior . . . more later) was a poor soul who'd become a fixture in the place, a barfly since I was in petticoats. Once a prominent surgeon, Henry had — under the influence of his own prescription of bourbon — famously removed a patient's gallbladder, an operation that went off smashingly with the small detail that he'd been scheduled to perform an appendectomy.

Once upon a time, I had put Henry in one of my plays (I act *and* direct); believing as I did that art must reflect life, this typecasting seemed not unkind but merely apropos.

Unfortunately, Henry went on the wagon in order to bring his full facilities to the role, and his stone-sober performance as a town drunk was so over-the-top and unconvincing that our local drama critic praised the production but panned Henry. But therein lies a happy ending: stung by criticism, Henry promptly fell off the wagon, and his subsequent performances were perfectly realized, although perhaps too much so on the final performance (he passed out in the middle of the second act).

But I digress.

The proprietor of the store, Junior, was polishing tumblers behind the scarred counter; in spite of his youthful name he was about my age (which is none of your business, and you shouldn't believe everything Brandy tells you). Balding, paunchy, and wearing a short-sleeve white shirt with red, white, and blue suspenders, Junior had a winning if buck-toothed smile.

Back when I was still a legal licensed driver, I would sometimes offer to take Junior's wife places because she had a wooden leg. But it kept falling off, and I didn't want to be responsible. Again I digress. . . .

Junior spotted me and grinned his patented grin. "Well, hello, Vivian. Haven't seen you for a while. Your usual?"

I slid onto one of the torn leather counter

stools, next to Henry. Putting a stool between us would have seemed rude.

"Please, Junior." I waggled a scolding forefinger. "And don't forget the cherries this time."

I could tell immediately that Junior, a terrible busybody, had not heard about his antique dealer neighbor down the block; otherwise he'd have started in on me.

For once I had the jump on him.

"I suppose you've heard," I said, "that Clint Carson is now deceased."

Junior, in the process of assembling my Shirley Temple, spilled a little on his otherwise spotless counter. "No! What the heck happened?"

Even Henry perked up in his permanent daze, and took notice.

Casually, I said, "Struck by a car."

"Really! Who was driving?"

Just as casually, I said, "I was."

Junior's mouth made an O. Henry's rheumy eyes made two Os.

"*But* — he was already dead . . . Somebody murdered him before I ran into the speed bump he'd become." I took a dainty sip of my Shirley Temple and let that sink in. Timing is everything, you know.

Junior was shaking his head, and I would swear I perceived a rattle. "You don't say!"

In fact, I believe I just did.

"Oh, but I do."

"Murdered *how?*"

I leaned forward. Traded conspiratorial looks with my two companions. "Possibly . . . poisoned."

I thought that was being truthful, or at least truthful enough. After all, as Officer Lawson said, the tox report wasn't back yet.

"Pizened," Henry said, nodding reflectively.

"Whaddya know," Junior said, and it wasn't a question. He made a clicking in one cheek. "Well, I can't say I'm surprised. *Nobody* liked that horse's patute. Especially the Downtown Merchants' Association."

Junior was referring to a local retailers' group associated with the chamber of commerce.

I gazed over the rim of my Shirley Temple. "And why is that, pray tell?"

Junior frowned. "Prayin' don't have a damn thing to do with it, Viv. That buzzard refused to have anything to do with the rest of us. We'd hold meetings, you know, to discuss things? Like when to hold the watermelon toss, and what hours we should all stay open Christmas season."

"Coordination between merchants. A reasonable goal."

"*Carson* didn't think so! He said he didn't give two hoots in hell about watermelons, and that he'd set his *own* damn hours! Arrogant SOB, you ask me."

I sucked on a cherry and waited; once Junior got started, he couldn't stop gabbing. Conventional wisdom is that women are the big gossips, but we know better, don't we?

"As a matter of fact," Junior continued confidentially, "a fella came in here just last week, askin' about Carson. A real rough customer."

Delicately removing the stem from the second cherry, I asked, "Who was he?"

Junior shook his head. "Never saw the bozo before. Every second word was the 'f' one, and he had tattoos and lots of hair and a black leather jacket . . . Like I said, he asked where he could find Carson. I gave him directions down the block to the antique store, and he vacated. Didn't even buy anything."

So then he was "rough" but not actually a "customer."

I asked, "What do you supposed he wanted?"

"I was curious, too," Junior admitted, "and followed him out . . . pretended to sweep the front walk. The fellow got in a red convertible with Colorado license plates."

I frowned. "Somebody from Carson's past."

"Funny thing was," Junior continued, "the fella drove off in the opposite direction of Carson's shop . . . didn't even go the way I told him to!"

Interesting.

By this time I'd finished my cocktail, as well as this source of inquiry. "Junior, would you happen to know where I can find the Romeos on Saturday?"

Junior's bushy eyebrows climbed his forehead like a couple of ambitious caterpillars. "Let's see . . . kinda hard to keep track of their schedule, some place different every damn day. They was in here, Thursday."

"Best guess?"

Junior shrugged. "Check the Riverside."

The Romeos — Retired Old Men Eating Out — were sequestered in the back of the Riverside Restaurant, which specialized in the kind of fattening old-fashioned meals the old boys had grown up on, and which none of them should any longer be having. Lunch hour was well under way, with not an empty table to be had in the popular eatery, which was frequented by professionals and farmers alike.

I approached the men — who were a small group today, four seated at a table for six — and asked if I could join them until something opened up; they had been served drinks, and were awaiting their Blue Plate Specials.

Normally, this club of retired widowers does not take kindly to the inclusion of a woman. But I had a feeling that, unlike Junior, they had already heard the scuttlebutt about Carson. As I've said, men are just as hungry for gossip as women, though sometimes more subtle about gathering it.

"Sure thing, Vivian," Vern said. One of Serenity's oldest established chiropractors, he looked like a *Misfits*-era Clark Gable, which is to say his ears stuck out, and he had painfully obvious false teeth. Vern had been forced into retirement when a stack of *National Geographic* magazines caught fire in the back room and burned his office down, and him underinsured. (I couldn't feel sorry for him, having warned him not to be such a pack rat.)

"Sit over here, Viv," said Harold, a retired army captain with Bob Hope's nose but not his sense of humor. He leaned over and pulled out an empty chair next to him. A real taskmaster, Harold had probably driven his wife to her early grave by demanding his meals on time and his socks freshly laundered and set out for him. I once had had a dalliance with the widower, but soon came to my senses. Still, Harold looked pretty darn foxy for a fellow who'd just had a colostomy.

Randall — a former hog farmer who reminded me of a homelier Ernest Borgnine (it's possible) — asked slyly, "And what mischief have you been up to, Vivian?"

Before Randall sold his pig farm, you wanted to stand downwind from him, but he was safe enough now. Of course, he did have glaucoma, and could only see you from straight on, and had to swing around and focus on you somewhat disconcertedly. And he had an unsettling way of smiling at you with a "what'll she bring in at market?" way.

"Yes," chimed in Ivan, Serenity's onetime mayor, a Jimmy Stewart type, only not quite as handsome (but then who ever was?). "What wickedness have you been sowing, you naughty girl?"

Ivan's once boisterous personality had never quite returned after his wife's death, though he always made an effort with me; it was common knowledge his wife'd had Alzheimer's, although for a while Ivan had enjoyed the way he could make her laugh with his same tired handful of jokes. Ivan's health was pretty good, except for a few precancerous moles removed from his face, which he probably got from too much time on the golf course.

I thanked the gentlemen for their hospitality and sat next to Vern. A waitress appeared with their lunches (the Blue Plate Special was meat loaf with mashed potatoes and corn) and I ordered iced tea and a bowl of chicken noodle soup.

Four pairs of attentive eyes stared my way. At their age, that might have represented curiosity or horniness, hard to say. Unfortunately, probably the former . . .

. . . and if rumors were going to fly, they might as well come from the horse's mouth.

"Not *much* mischief," I said, and sipped my iced tea and smiled innocently. "I just ran over Clint Carson, is all."

Two forks clanked against plates, and four mouths yawned open, and a different kind of plate clanked in a mouth or two.

"But it didn't hurt anything," I said.

A narrow-eyed Ivan managed, "Really? Just a fender-bender?"

"Oh, my fender is fine. Carson, however, is dead as a doorknob."

Randal, jaw still slack, said, "Don't you mean doornail?"

"Either way, I mean 'dead'— but he was

already dead, when I happened along."

And, while the Romeos ate, I launched into a dramatization of last night's events, culminating with the morning's visit from Officer Lawson. I omitted only Brandy's admission of guilt in her misguided attempt to cover up for me (while I was nobly covering up for her).

When my performance reached curtain, Vern was the first to speak.

"I never knew Carson, really," he said, eyes tight. "But I seem to remember *one* of us did." Vern glanced around the table, eyes landing on the former mayor. "Ivan . . . didn't *you* have some dealing with Carson?"

The ex-mayor's mouth formed a tight line. "I should say I did."

A few moments passed, tension palpable in the air.

Ivan seemed reluctant to speak, but then at last he said, "This past summer, just before Mary passed away? I came home to find she'd sold nearly *all* our antiques — things that she and I had collected for years, from keepsakes to valuable pieces of furniture we'd carefully selected together . . . each with its own special story."

I thought the old boy might choke up, but he maintained his composure. He had abandoned his Blue Plate Special halfway through the meat loaf.

"Mary was standing at the front door with cash in her hands," Ivan went on, then laughed dryly. "She was so proud of herself! She'd made us some money, after all. Of course, it was a pittance compared to what the stuff was really worth. I went out to Carson's place on the highway, where that barn warehouse of his is, and — in a wholly even-tempered manner, mind you — explained that my wife didn't realize what she'd done, that she'd not been herself lately, was . . . ill. And Carson's response? Well, he just laughed in my face and said, 'So *sue* me, old man — if you think you've got a case!' "

Ivan pushed his plate angrily away. "I could have killed him myself at that moment," he confessed. He looked around the table. "I'll shed no tears for his heartless ass . . . Sorry, Viv."

Randall asked, "Why *didn't* you take him to court?"

Ivan shook his head, then spoke softly. "It may come as a surprise to all of you, but before she passed away . . . Mary was showing certain signs of Alzheimer's."

"No," I said. "Really."

"Anyway, I wanted to protect her. Our attorney said we had a case, a legitimate case, but . . . I just couldn't put her through the pain and embarrassment of a court trial." His head lowered. "I guess maybe it was a blessing she died from pneumonia before that terrible disease *really* took hold."

He swallowed, and got pats on the shoulder on either side from his compadres.

My soup came, and I sipped at it while Harold, the retired army captain, next unburdened himself. He told us that a week after his wife, Norma, died, Clint Carson appeared on his doorstep and had talked Harold into "unburdening himself" of a china cabinet filled with Haviland dishes . . . for only a few hundred dollars.

"I had no idea what that china was worth," he began. "Much less the cabinet . . ."

I didn't have the heart to tell him.

". . . or that Norma had promised them to our daughter. . . ." He paused, shrugged. "I guess I was in shock over her death, sudden as it was . . . and I was thinking about moving into a smaller place, kind of downsizing, not needing so much. . . ."

The other men were nodding.

Harold looked at me, painfully earnest. "You *do* understand, don't you, Viv?"

I almost said, "I bet you didn't 'downsize' by selling your power tools," but restrained myself. And then I felt a surge of affection for the crusty coot, and patted his hand, saying, "Of course."

Now, with the lunch hour past, the restaurant nearly empty, we finally rose from the table. Vern was a gentleman and picked up my check.

Out on the sidewalk, Harold asked if he could drive me home, but I said I had other things to do downtown. I thought it best not to encourage him, and, anyway, I did have one more stop. . . .

Carson's Antiques, on Main Street, was closed, not surprisingly; but lights were on inside the lovely old building, and I knocked on the door, trying to peer through the etched glass, albeit with little success.

Still, I could see movement, and even hear some, so I kept knocking.

Finally a hazy figure moved toward me — even through the etched glass I could make it out — and then a voice behind the door said, snippily, "Can't you see we're closed!"

"I must talk to you!"

"We are *closed!*"

I projected my voice to the last seat in the farthest balcony. *"It's Vivian Borne — would you prefer I talk to the police?"*

Locks were soon unlocked, and the door cracked open. The fiery-haired filly in the peasant blouse and leather skirt might have been pretty if she had not been frowning in such a foul manner.

"What do you mean, police?" she growled.

"I haven't mentioned to them yet," I said pleasantly, "that you called our house and left an answer machine message for us."

Her eyes grew wild, her nostrils flared. "I did no such thing! Are you crazy?"

I have been asked that question before and seldom have I been offended — I understand its colloquial meaning — but I *was* a little put off by her denial.

So, as the young people say, I got right in her face. "You're claiming you didn't leave a call for my daughter, Brandy, last night? Telling her to come out to the late Mr. Carson's house and barn, in the country?"

"No. *Hell* no!" The presumably pretty face grew uglier. "Look, lady, I don't know what the fudge you're trying to prove . . ."

Actually, she didn't say "fudge."

". . . but if you go to the cops, you'll only get *yourself* in trouble!"

And the door slammed in my face!

Mother's expression carried all the indignation it must have held at the moment that door shut on her.

I said, "What then?"

Still seated on the edge of my bed, she

said, "I caught the Traveling Trolley home
. . ."

And now she was off her trolley, and back
again.

". . . because I simply *had* to tell you the
news!"

"What news?"

Mother's eyes grew enormous behind the
exaggeration of the lenses. "That we weren't
the *only* ones who Clint Carson swindled!"

Stop the presses.

"Well, really, Mother . . . I never thought
we were."

Her head reared back, like a horse about
to buck its rider. "But surely you know what
this means?"

"What does it mean, Mother?"

"That we're not the *only* suspects!"

I blinked at her. "Suspects? . . . Oh yeah,
in the 'Clint Carson Murder Case.' "

"Exactly. Didn't we both confess to the
murder already?"

Shaking my head, I insisted, "We didn't
confess to *any* murder — we were taking
responsibility for an *accident.*"

The complication was that we were both
taking that responsibility.

I put a conciliatory hand on her sleeve.
"Let's go have some coffee."

Soon we were sitting at the kitchen table, having Starbucks Caffe Verona, decaf — you don't think I was about to give Mother anything *but* decaf, do you?

"Let's suppose you're right," I said. "And that Clint Carson really *was* murdered."

"Let's suppose that, yes, dear."

I shrugged. "Why should we care?"

She goggled at me.

I patted the air and pressed on: "After all, we didn't kill him. I didn't. You didn't."

"Yes . . . but *somebody* did."

"Right. But who cares?"

"Pardon?"

I spoke slowly and clearly. "Who . . . the fuck . . . cares?"

You'll note I didn't say "fudge."

"Mother, we hated that bastard."

Mother touched her bosom and looked askance at me, her Victorian sensibilities offended by my language and my sensibilities. "That doesn't make murder acceptable! Or that kind of vocabulary."

"Of *course* it doesn't make murder acceptable. But it also doesn't make it your job to do anything about it. What's the idea, anyway, of going out snooping like that?"

Her expression took astonishment to new

heights — or, possibly, lows. "Don't you *know?*"

I thought I did. I knew that Mother had always had a morbid interest in murder — both true crimes and the Christie/*Murder She Wrote* variety that her Red-Hatted League book club found so intriguing — and this Carson mess had tripped some trigger within her that I, frankly, did not feel was conducive to her continued mental health.

But I didn't know how to express that without offending her, and making an instant enemy of her. . . .

"Listen," I said, and reached across and patted her hand. "The police are absolutely capable of looking into this. You met Officer Lawson — he was nice, right? And smart?"

"And handsome," Mother said.

"And handsome. Plus, we both know what a terrific police chief Serenity has."

"Yes. That's certainly true. . . ."

"Why not leave it to them? The professionals?"

Mother leaned forward and grasped one of my hands in hers. Tight. "But don't you *see,* darling? That redheaded wench lied!"

Wench?

"Or if she didn't *lie,*" Mother was saying, and now her eyes were moving quickly behind the lenses, too quickly for my taste, "and she truly *didn't* make that phone call . . . then someone else *did!*"

"Mother . . . please. . . ."

"Someone who wanted to *implicate* us! To *frame* us!"

The kitchen wall phone rang, thank God, and I got it.

It was Tina, calling from her office at the chamber of commerce, where she worked as the tourism liaison.

She had heard about Carson's death, and the rumors about Mother's involvement that were buzzing around, probably in part due to Mother's going clang, clang on the trolley. I quickly brought Teen up to speed.

"How exciting."

"Oh yeah, thrilling."

"Well then, let me ask the *really* important question."

"Which is what?"

"Brandy . . . are we still on for tonight?"

I actually found myself laughing, a little. "Clint Carson being dead won't stop me from going out and having a little fun — I'm not even sure my *own* death would."

"So I can pick you up, then?"

"Sure."

We set the time, said our good-byes, and I hung up.

Mother was staring into her Starbucks de-caf as if it were a crystal ball that held all the answers to the mystery she was cooking up in her fertile imagination.

Which, of course, bothered me.

But not as much as a sense I had — and did not care to acknowledge — that there was something *to* what Mother had said. Someone may well have tried to lure me out to Carson's place to implicate me.

Someone who had no compunction about taking a human life.

Or was I as crazy as Mother?

A Trash 'n' Treasures Tip

Sometimes, treasures can be found set out with trash on garbage collection night. Sifting through a Dumpster, however, I won't stoop to. But Mother will.

CHAPTER FIVE
A FRIEND INDEED, A FRIEND IN WEED

In the midst of Mother's murder suspicions, amateur detective work, and her fear that we'd been framed, I faced my first real crisis . . .

. . . I didn't know *what* to wear!

Clothes were strewn and not just on the floor, but on the bed, hanging from the vanity — the entire contents of my underwear drawer tossed in a jumbled pile. It was as if a bad guy or maybe the cops had "tossed" my room looking for clues.

Only they didn't do it, I did. And I was looking for the right clothes, not clues.

Tina was picking me up in half an hour, and I had to find *just* the ensemble. After all, we were hitting the new nightclub on the bluff, the Octagon House, for our long-overdue "girls' night out," and Tina assured me this was *the* place in Serenity, right now.

This evening I wanted to look chic, but not cheap; hip, but not too trendy — and not for the men. To hell with the men!

Why *do* women dress for each other? Maybe only another woman truly appreciates the effort . . . whereas the chief interest the opposite sex appears to have in women's clothing is pretty much limited to getting them off.

Finally, with fifteen minutes to go, I settled on a hippie-chic Nanette Lepore off-one-shoulder top (which I had eaten Kraft Macaroni and Cheese for a month to be able to buy), some slim-fitting, cropped GAP jeans, and a pair — my *only* pair — of Jimmy Choo turquoise heels, a lucky eBay buy (even so, it cost me a month of Campbell's Tomato Soup lunches) (at least dieting and saving money can go hand in hand).

Now for a purse.

Unlike shoes, a person *can* have too many bags. Besides taking up lots of closet space, purses can all too easily get tangled up. Plus, it's tiresome having to switch contents from one bag to another all the time, just to match your outfit.

And here's another point — I once saw an old black-and-white movie on cable where a man came home, found no sign of his wife, but spotted her purse on the kitchen table; from this he surmised that she had been kidnapped, and on that single piece of evidence the police put out an all-points-bulletin and rescued her from a sex maniac.

Which begs the question: how in this day and age is anybody going to know if you've been kidnapped by a sex maniac with all your purses left lying around?

And one more thing before I get off the subject: how *ever* did bags get elevated to the exalted position of shoes? One strong possibility is that, like shoes, a purse always fits, no matter how fat you get (but unlike shoes, you don't have to shed alligator tears because the shop doesn't have your size).

Here's my bottom-line advice: take all your bags and sell them (eBay, garage sale, secondhand shop — dealer's choice), then buy one expensive *to-die-for* purse for spring/summer, and another for fall/winter . . . and your life will become a lot less stressful.

I selected from the tangle (do as I say, not as I do) a small Nichole Miller evening bag that Tina had given me for my last birthday (it's always nice to show your friend that you appreciate — and use — her thoughtful gifts). Beaded in orange with the yellow word POP! and dangling from the shoulder by a silver chain, this little beauty offered just enough room for some lip gloss, a condom (you never know), a tissue or two (so you didn't have to "drip-dry"), and fifty cents to call your mother (you'll have to decide for yourself what you want to call your mother).

A car horn beeped.

I raced downstairs and dashed into the kitchen to make sure Sushi had enough water — she'd been asleep in her little pink bed, but raised her furry head and turned her spooky white eyes toward my voice.

"If you have to go," I instructed firmly, "go pee-pee on the papers." I'd already put down the nightly edition by the back door.

Mother was rehearsing this evening at the Serenity Center for the Performing Arts (i.e., the Central Middle School stage) in *Everybody Loves Opal* — a lowbrow play catering mostly to midwestern ladies of the blue-haired variety, with a leading role perfectly suited to Vivian Borne's over-the-top talents. She wouldn't be home until late.

I could only marvel at how, in spite of everything that had happened, Mother could still act, but "the show must go on" raced in her blood alongside various out-of-control chemicals. One time, after Mother wrapped her car around a telephone pole, she went onstage in a head tourniquet, arm sling, and with crutches, ad-libbing her entrance — "Watch that last step . . . it's a doooozy!" — and getting an immediate standing ovation for her pluck. (Would it be unkind to mention that she did not receive another ovation, at the end, for her actual performance?)

Sushi seemed to understand my directive about relieving herself on the Fourth Estate. She understood lots of words (not on the paper — the ones I spoke to her), and even some of those I spelled out, in hopes of fooling her . . . like when I would say in an aside to Mother, "I don't have time to take Sushi for a w-a-l-k." Soosh would materialize at my side, and beg relentlessly, until I finally capitulated and went for the leash.

So now, on occasion, I resort to sign language — blind dogs, no matter *how* smart, can't fathom that!

I scurried out the front door, locking it behind me, and in another moment hopped in the front seat of Tina's black Lexus.

"Hi, honey!" I said, and she gave the same right back . . . our usual greeting in a Judy-Holliday-in-*Born Yesterday* voice.

Tina, behind the wheel, looked gorgeous, her blond hair straight with a little flip at the ends. She had on a hot-pink boat-neck top, and black satin cargo pants with a sparkly belt.

"Guess what I found," Tina said with an

impish grin. She shoved a cassette into the dash, and Cyndi Lauper began singing "Girls Just Want to Have Fun."

"Our *traveling* tape," I squealed, and began to sing along as Tina pulled away from the curb. So did Tina. Instant in-car karaoke.

A decade ago, when I was a freshman at the local community college, and Tina was home from Northwestern, we spent a whole summer together, going out every weekend to one club or another . . . often in neighboring cities for a change of scenery (and prospects). Tina made a cassette of all our then-favorite artists, like Madonna . . . and even older ones such as Cyndi Lauper, Blondie, the Motels, and Lene Lovich.

Back then I was the designated driver, because drinking more than one glass of anything alcoholic could bring on an instant migraine, ruining the rest of the night (not to mention next day). I had a "gently used," Leprechaun-green Gremlin that I bought from an elderly couple who'd kept the car hidden in their garage . . . probably because they were too embarrassed to be seen in it.

Tina and I, at the time, had no such shame. The GM Gremlin was the ugliest car every made, bar none. Think of a regular car chopped in half, leaving only the front end and a small hatchback with room enough for a sack of groceries and maybe some running shoes — size 5. The rear sides of the vehicle had a little round window, like on a boat, so Tina dubbed the car "the Green Submarine."

When flying down the highway, if I hit a bump, we'd go airborne for a while, because the GS was so front-heavy. If it was raining, we'd hydroplane all the way because there was absolutely no back traction — I'm amazed we even stayed on the road.

Early on I broke off the flimsy aluminum ignition key in the starter, which was the greatest thing! That meant the GS was always ready to go . . . and I never had to waste time looking for misplaced keys. Nor did I worry about locking the thing — who'd want to steal a green Gremlin? It's not like the car wouldn't be spotted.

Donna Sommer was singing "Hot Stuff" as we wound our way up the drive to the Octagon House, which was situated on a bluff overlooking the Mighty Mississippi.

The Octagon was, in reality, an ancient brick battlement, built back when Serenity was founded in the early eighteen hundreds. The large eight-sided structure had been used by the military for spotting attacks by (in order of appearance) the Blackhawk

Indians, the French, the British, the Confederate army . . . and even Martians in the 1950s, when UFOs were supposedly spotted hovering over town.

Until recently, the building had been a crumbling, seldom-visited tourist attraction, when some local entrepreneurs leased it from the city and turned the edifice into a nightspot. Mother approved, saying it was a win-win situation: the battlement (which was not on any federal preservation lists) got restored, people would come to see it, and the city received extra revenue. (Mother did not include in her lists of pluses the ability for Serenity visitors and residents alike to get drunk on their butts at this historical site.)

The parking lot was packed, but Tina, ever inventive, carved out a space between a Ford pickup and a Toyota, and we soon fell in behind others flocking toward the club.

"Nice wheels, honey," I said to her.

"It's not the Green Submarine," she said with a grin, "but it gets me places."

The Octagon House faced the river, and to get to the entrance you had to utilize a wooden deck that stretched almost to the edge of the bluff. We walked along it, enjoying the attention of the cool night breeze as it ran its fingers through our hair; briefly we paused at the railing to gaze out over the dark churning water.

The Mississippi can be wonderful, but terrible. It's called "Mighty" for a reason: powerful undertows created by swirling currents of swift-moving water. A person should never go boating or skiing on the river without a good life jacket . . . and forget about swimming. Unfortunately, every summer, somebody learns this lesson. Or rather doesn't.

The bridge was like a diamond necklace reaching shore to shore, thanks to an array of lights strung sparklingly along the span; in the distance the melody of a riverboat calliope playing "I'm Looking Over a Four Leaf Clover," floated toward us, in that distinctive muted echoey way, sounding a little forlorn for such an upbeat number.

"You ever go gambling?" I asked her.

Several turn-of-the-century steamboats — with names like *The River Queen* and *Lucky Lady* — trekked up and down the river, offering a scenic ride to take the sting out of relieving citizens of their hard-earned pay.

"Do *you* ever go gambling?" Tina, ever the diplomat, had deftly passed the buck.

"Naw," I admitted, but added, "Just that, with you married, we can't spend all our time bar-crawling."

Her expression was affectionately amused. "Brandy, I'm trying to imagine you putting down a bet on *anything*."

I shrugged; that breeze felt sweet, and the dark river view was strangely soothing. "I dunno — I could *maybe* see taking twenty dollars and playing the nickel machines till it ran out, poker not slots? But I'd really rather buy a pair of designer socks."

She nodded. "Or Chanel nail polish in 'Vamp.' "

"Or another Pandora charm."

Right now we were wearing identical Danish bracelets — demonstrating how Tina and I were always on the same page, right down to the paragraph . . . sentence, even.

When "I'm Looking Over a Four Leaf Clover" morphed into a nearly unrecognizable "Hey, Jude," we made a face at each other and headed into the nightclub to find better ear candy. And maybe some eye candy, too. . . .

The Octagon, we quickly realized, had two separate watering holes: a bottom floor for smokers, and an upper one for those who valued their lungs if not their brain cells. We entered onto the smokers' floor, which seemed to be an older crowd, the decor disappointing: black walls trimmed red, standard small round tables, a few booths, a perfunctory bar in back; nothing that cigarette burns could damage too much (hookah bars have not yet caught on in middle America). Next to a postage-stamp-size dance floor, a band called Geezer was playing — four older guys doing Weezer songs, and not too badly.

I liked the music but not the literal atmosphere. Before the smoke had a chance to permeate our hair and clothes, we hurriedly followed some other females, who seemed to know what they were doing (compared to us, anyway), up a flight of stairs to a red vinyl-padded door meant to keep the fumes out.

Pounding dance music assaulted us as we stepped through, the room crawling with yuppies and guppies, and Xers and Yers. Obviously, this was where the owners spent the bulk of their budget: subdued deco lighting, rich cherry furniture, Parisian dance-hall wall prints. The focal point was an elaborately carved, eight-sided bar in the middle of the room, mirroring the shape of the building. Tract lighting aimed at the large octagonal wineglass holder above the bar — where hundreds of crystal bats hung by their stems — made an incredible chandelier.

As we worked our way through the crowd,

a couple slid off stools at a high-top table, and we grabbed it, beating out others in what seemed like a game of musical chairs.

With the dizzying din of music, it was hard to think, much less talk. A waitress in a white tux shirt and black tux pants came over, and we shouted our order: splits of champagne.

I leaned in to Tina's ear. "See anybody you know?"

She shook her head. "Old married lady — been off the circuit too long."

Our champagne came, and we drank and giggled and drank awhile and giggled some more.

Then I spotted an old childhood friend, Mia Cordona, standing among the crush at the bar. Even though I hadn't seen her for years, that long chestnut hair, those dark sultry eyes, high cheekbones, and full-lipped mouth were unmistakable. Mia's once skinny-as-a-toothpick figure, however, had blossomed voluptuously, putting a strain on her red spandex dress.

Mia had grown up across the street from me. Naturally, I gravitated to the girl closest to my age in the large Hispanic family. The Cordonas ran a Mexican restaurant catering to the ever-growing number of immigrants who'd come north to work in the corn and tomato fields near Serenity. Mia was so much fun, always up for some harmless mischief, which we'd then blame on one of her numerous siblings.

I loved going over to the Cordonas' rambling clapboard house, filled as it was with constant commotion, kids practically hanging from the rafters, one or another constantly in the "time-out" corner. The decor was so different from ours — brightly colored tablecloths, pottery, hand-carved Spanish furniture . . . and always some wonderful south-of-the-border food cooking on the stove.

Sometimes, after I'd already eaten at my house, I'd tie a scarf over my light-colored hair and go over to Mia's, and sit among the mob at their table, unnoticed (or so I thought).

Mia's parents spoke only Spanish (their kids, of course, were bilingual), and on several occasions I ran across the street to get Mr. Cordona to help me with Mother when she was having a particularly bad spell. His gentle manner and lyrical speech had a calming effect on Mother, and the fact that she couldn't understand a word he said helped create enough distraction for me to go and get the doctor.

My favorite memory of Mia is of her at

about age twelve, jumping on her bed like a trampoline, singing "Turn the Beat Around." Sadly, the family moved across town, and because I was older than Mia, we rarely saw each other.

"I'm going over to talk to Mia," I said in Tina's ear.

Her brow furrowed. "You *know* that girl?"

Tina's expression made me ask, "Why?"

"Haven't you heard?"

"Heard what? I'm a stranger in town, remember?"

Tina's expression grew uncomfortable. "When she was on the police force —"

"Mia's a *cop?*"

"*Was* a cop," Tina corrected. "She got kicked off."

"Why?"

Tina shrugged with her eyebrows. "Some confiscated drugs came up missing . . . and she was in charge of the evidence locker. She never got formally charged with anything, but she was fired for malfeasance, and since she didn't fight it or anything . . . well."

I stared across the room at my childhood friend; her devoutly religious, upstanding parents must have been crushed.

Mia seemed to be hanging on the arm of a really cute guy.

I said to Tina, "I'll be back," and slid off my stool.

Pushing through the boisterous throng, getting some flirty self-esteem-boosting glances from guys, I made my way to the bar.

"Mia!" I smiled. "Hi!"

She turned, recognition slow in coming. Her smile seemed halfhearted. Polite. "Oh. Brandy, right? Hello. Didn't know you were back in town."

Not that she seemed to give a damn.

The frantic dance music turned to a slow syrupy song, giving everyone a chance to talk, and for some reason, I didn't accept her near brush-off.

"I'm back living with Mother," I said, hanging in. "Nasty divorce, you know, that kinda thing . . . maybe we could get together some time?"

"I'm pretty busy," Mia said.

I just stood there awkwardly with my hurt feelings hanging out. She hadn't even bothered to say, "Cool, yeah, we'll have to do that," and turn away.

She had really changed.

But the guy she was with was giving me a look that said he, at least, was interested. . . .

Just to be ornery, I gave her my least

sincere smile and said, "Mia — why don't you introduce me to your friend?"

Her "friend" was of average height, nicely put together, with carefully mussed hair, and dark, penetrating eyes.

When Mia didn't answer, I stuck out my hand. "Brandy Borne."

"Todd." His hand was warm, his grip firm, his smile easy. But he didn't offer a last name.

Working my voice over the music, I said, "Mia and I grew up across the street from each other."

Todd's mouth smiled but his forehead frowned as he said, "Funny, I thought I knew all of Mia's friends." He looked chidingly at her. "Sometimes I think you keep things from me."

Mia reached for her drink on the bar and took a sip. I might as well not have been there. The slow number ended and an oldie-but-goodie disco song filled the room.

Raising his voice over the pounding bass, Todd said to me, "Mia's in one of her moods tonight . . . maybe *you'd* like to dance?"

Was he trying to make Mia jealous?

I looked at her; she shrugged indifferently, and faced the bar, her back to us.

I said to Todd, "I didn't come here to sit!"

Was *I* trying to make Mia jealous?

He took my hand and led me through the crowd to the dance floor, where we carved out a spot. He pulled me roughly to him.

Todd was a great dirty dancer, his pelvis grinding against mine . . . and, noticing Mia glancing at us occasionally, I gave as good as I got. Whether I was being bitchy to my old friend who'd snubbed me, or just horny, who can say?

We stayed on for a slow number, and he held me tight, his lips brushing my ear, then my cheek, before landing fully on my mouth, his kiss wet and hot. An electric jolt surged through my body — a feeling I hadn't had in a quite some time.

After the song, I signaled to Todd that I wanted to leave the dance floor, and he walked me off.

"See you later?" he asked.

Maybe I should play hard to get . . .

"Sure. I'm in the book — it's under Vivian Borne."

"Got it. You're a great dancer."

If "dancing" could be defined as allowing him to press himself up against me, I was terrific.

I made my way on rubbery legs to the ladies' room. Part of it was the champagne. But partly it was that guy — something exciting, even dangerous about him. . . .

I was fixing my makeup when I saw Mia's reflection in the mirror behind me.

Her voice was cold. "Stay away."

"From you?"

"From Todd."

Confrontations in bathrooms seemed to be the norm with me these days — particularly with women whose men I'd gotten too friendly with.

I said, "Hey, you were there. He asked me to dance. All I did was say yes."

Mia put her hands on her curvaceous hips. "Next time say no."

"Don't you mean . . . *just* say no?"

She got the drug-reference dig and her upper lip curled.

Before she could speak, however, a toilet flushed. We held a momentary truce as a brunette exited a stall, and hurriedly washed her hands and scurried out of harm's way.

Mia stepped closer and shook a long-nailed finger in my face. "I mean it, Brandy — don't even *speak* to him again . . . got it, girlfriend?"

What, was I on *Jerry Springer* suddenly?

Still, I had to wonder if Mia could still beat the tar out of me, which even when she was skinny she did with ease . . . and I didn't care to find out.

"Okay . . . okay, I hear you. I guess I was just a little . . . hurt."

Eyes flared. "Hurt?"

"We were friends once upon a time."

"*That* fairy tale's over," Mia said, and whirled and was gone.

I leaned against the counter and looked at myself. I was pretty cute, and maybe a little drunk, and definitely a lot embarrassed. Gathering what remained of my dignity, collecting a few shreds of what had been my poise, I exited the ladies' room.

Returning to my table, I could tell Tina was peeved by my extended absence. I took her by the arm and said, "Let's get out of here."

"Good call," she snapped. "Do you know how much fun it is, being married, and sitting by yourself in a singles' bar, getting hit on, and fueling rumors?"

"Not much?"

"Not much."

Neither of us spoke again until we got inside the car; then I asked sheepishly, "Could we go to the Holiday Inn — like we used to?"

Tina bestowed me a small forgiving smile. "All right. . . ."

"Thank you, honey."

"Shut up." But she was smiling.

The Oasis was a typical hotel cocktail lounge, cozy, dark, blandly anonymous. Dead tonight, but for a pair of businessmen in Brooks Brothers, at the bar. And us.

Tina and I slid into a semicircular padded booth off in one corner, to be by ourselves. When a barmaid in a red vest and white shirt and black slacks came over, we both ordered coffee.

When she'd gone, I said, "I don't ever want anything to come between us, Teen. . . . I'd rather cut off my arm than have you mad at me."

"Never mind."

"Let's face it, things are different now. I'm single, you're married. I don't want the dynamics to affect our friendship."

Tina nodded in agreement. "We can stick to shopping and movies . . . Your friend Mia's single, though, right?"

"Friend is not exactly the word."

I told her about my little encounter.

"Weird," she said.

The coffees came. For my penitence, I paid.

Tina took a sip, then set the cup down and gave me a quizzical look.

"What?" I asked.

She crinkled her nose. "You're not going

147

to start *seeing* that guy, are you?"

"What guy?"

"That Todd character."

"Him? No. He doesn't exactly seem to be available."

"Since when did that stop you?"

I gave her a hurt look.

"Sorry," she said. "But I'm glad Mia told you to stay away."

"Why?"

Tina waited a moment. Then, "Let's just say, if you had any pharmaceutical needs, and didn't have a prescription? That Todd could probably fill them."

Too bad. Todd might have been worth pursuing, otherwise; plus, it seemed to confirm the drug rumors about Mia. People sure could change when you left town for a while. . . .

Tina was shaking her head and lost in some private thought.

"What are you thinking, Teen?"

"Just . . . what I don't understand is . . . after what happened to her brother? How Mia could get mixed up with a guy like that."

"Which brother, and what happened to him?"

"I don't know his name, it was just something I saw in the paper, when she got fired and lots of ancient dirt got stirred up . . . but I believe he died from an overdose."

"Oh. Jeez. What of?"

She shrugged with her eyebrows. "Does it really matter?"

No. Dead was dead.

I stared into my coffee cup, hoping the overdosed Cordona brother wasn't Juan. In my mind's eye, I could see him, a few years younger than Mia, gazing at his sister with pure adoration. And, although she never alluded to it, Juan was clearly her favorite. If drugs had taken him from her, she'd have been devastated. But Tina was right — how could she go down that path herself, then?

Sorrow and rage can do funny things to a person.

I switched the subject. "What do you think about what I told you before? On the phone?"

Tina's eyes narrowed. "What?"

"About Mother — about these traumatic events, all this murder talk — I'm afraid it's put her in a bad place."

"Mentally, you mean."

"Yes."

"In a maybe-she-needs-her-meds-upped kinda place, you mean."

"Yes."

"No."

I blinked. "No?"

"No, I think your mother's right — it *is* suspicious. That Carson guy was . . . Remember *Perry Mason*?"

"Sure. We used to watch reruns over the supper hour, Mother and Peggy Sue and me. I loved that show."

Tina nodded, indicating this was yet another shared experience. "Well, remember how there was always somebody so despicable in the first ten minutes, he or she was sure to get killed?"

"Everybody and his duck had a murder motive. Sure."

Tina was nodding some more. "Well, that's Clint Carson. And you attacked him in public the day before he was killed."

"I didn't *attack* him. . . ."

"Verbally you did. You, and your mother, with her well-known . . . problems? You're perfect patsies."

"You *did* watch *Perry Mason*."

"Sure I did. I also watched *Nancy Drew*. I'm not against you snooping a little." She sipped her coffee and shrugged. "You need help, just say the word. Every Holmes needs a Watson."

"I'm *already* Watson," I said with a smirk.

"I'm living with Sherlock Holmes in a red hat."

The barmaid delivered two glasses of white wine . . . compliments of the two businessmen. We guardedly smiled at them, but they didn't come over and hit on us.

Sometimes people do things just to be nice.

Or maybe they were just gay.

I was rudely awakened Sunday morning by Mother singing "Oh, What a Beautiful Morning," off-key, at the foot of my bed. (Musicals were not her forte.) (Not that that ever stopped her.)

Still, I was pleased to discover her in such good spirits . . . but couldn't I, for once, sleep in? I would have belted back "Oh, How I Hate to Get up in the Morning," but I had a frog in my throat, not to mention a haze in my brain, and not a "bright, golden" one, either.

"Brandy, darling, come along," she chirped. "We're going to church."

Then, after I didn't stir, she gave me the singsongy final wake-up call notice I'd heard since I was a child: "Up-ie, up-ie, *up*-ieeee!"

"I'm not *three!*" I whined.

"No, you're a big girl now," she said, and

pulled off the covers.

There was no arguing with Mother when she decided she needed a shot of religion, which (thank God) was irregularly, at best.

When I was growing up, Mother and I didn't belong to any one churchly persuasion, much less individual house of worship; but you might say we belonged to all of them, at one time or another: Presbyterian, Methodist, Episcopalian, Baptist, Lutheran, Catholic, Jehovah's Witness, Mormon . . . we even went to synagogue (Jewish weddings were my favorite). Mother said she believed in God in heaven, but she was looking for just the right earthly fit.

Me, I didn't mind, because at least church never got boring, which was a common complaint from other kids, condemned to weekly bouts of the same old unison chants and dreary hymns. We always signed in as "visitors," Mother putting what she could (or what she considered fair exchange for an hour of "enlightenment and entertainment") in the collection plate. Everyone was always so nice to us, because we were potential converts.

I struggled out of bed and headed for the shower (no time for a leisurely bubble-bath), to wash the product out of my "club" hair.

In record time I was out the front door, wearing a denim DKNY skirt, white lace poncho — already passé — over a pale yellow top, pink Minnetonka moccasins, minimal makeup, and my damp hair left to dry on its own devices (which could be scary).

Mother was waiting for me out on the sidewalk, and I fell in beside her, as we began the ten blocks or so to the church.

After all those years of religion-hopping, we had finally joined the New Hope Church in my eighth grade year of junior high. The church was aptly named, but even more apt would have been the Church of Common Sense and Mild Scoldings. The (also aptly named) pastor, John Tutor, had been a minister at another local church, but when told by the national church-type powers-that-be that he was getting transferred to another state, Tutor balked. When his holy superiors insisted, he left, formed New Hope, and took half the congregation with him.

Upon this base, a roughly equal number joined up, regular churchgoers who had become dissatisfied with their former holy houses for a variety of reasons, which made an interesting mix of tolerant and nonjudgmental folks. For example, when we eventually turn up, nobody wearing a "Christian"

153

smile ever says to us, "Well, we haven't seen *you* at church for a while!"

As Mother and I walked along on this cool, sunny summer morning, I felt myself growing smaller, and slipped my hand in hers, like I used to do. Mother, ever the snoop, had her head turned toward the houses as we passed, studying the tended lawns, flower beds, and yard art, pointing out antique glassware visible on an inside windowsill. If a garage door happened to be open — *whoa, Nellie!* — she'd stop dead in her tracks, eyes growing larger behind the spectacles, searching for castaways that might be destined for the curb come next garbage day.

"Mother . . ."

"Yes, dear?"

"You've got to promise me you'll leave this Clint Carson thing alone."

"I'll do no such thing! We could be the target of a killer!"

I liked her better when she was singing "Oh, What a Beautiful Morning," tone-deaf or not.

I stopped her and faced her and took her by both arms. Lovingly and firmly, I said, "We still have your driving-without-a-license charge to deal with. And we haven't talked to Chief Cassato yet."

"That's true. . . ."

"And you *like* our chief of police."

Mother's eyes perked behind the buggy lenses. "I do! Very much!"

"Then promise . . . I'll make you swear on the Bible at church! . . . promise you'll let me talk to the chief about this, and we'll concentrate on your legal problem, before you take any other steps."

She nodded gravely. "I promise," she said.

Her delivery reminded me a little too much of William Shatner in that old margarine commercial, but I accepted it.

Finally, we arrived at New Hope. Formerly an old fire station, the brick building had been gutted and turned into a church. One thing remained preserved, however: the brass fireman's pole, which bisected the main aisle, though was easy enough to slip around on either side. (After some kid came flying down it and broke both legs, however, the hole in the second floor was sealed.)

A scaled-down replica of the Liberty Bell stood proudly on a concrete pedestal in the church's front lawn. Every so often, a kid (probably the same ornery one who came down the pole) would steal the bell's clapper, and Pastor Tutor would ask the congregation to pray for its safe return. (I got kind of tired of this — at age fourteen — and once yelled from my seat, "Just weld it, already!" I couldn't see bothering God about such a trivial matter.) Of course, the clapper would return . . . until next time.

This morning Pastor Tutor — a small, almost plump bespectacled figure in purple shawl over black robe — gripped the pulpit and said, "When we have problems, we must first look to ourselves before turning to God — the Lord can forgive us, He can grant us grace and give us strength. But only we as individuals can take responsibility for our actions — only we can assume ownership of our problems."

How come this guy's sermon always seemed to be directed at *me,* personally? What did I ever do to him?

We stepped out of the church into a warm breeze. A round-faced boy of about twelve with glasses and Beatle bangs was ferociously ringing the bell until his father stopped him.

Mother hooked up with her four friends from the Red-Hatted League, also New Hope members; they would have a buffet lunch after church (our house today) and spend Sunday afternoon discussing a mystery novel (this time, *The Mirror Crack'd*), while incessantly snacking.

Mother wouldn't have minded if I sneaked a few cold cuts from the Red-Hatted ladies' repast, but I had been invited to Sunday dinner at my sister's house, with Peggy Sue's stated reason that my niece hadn't seen me for a while.

Ashley, an only child, was a senior in high school, and although we got along, I'm sure I was in her thoughts about as much as she was in mine — which is to say, hardly at all. Peggy Sue, I felt sure, just wanted access to me without Mother around, to carp, criticize, admonish, chide, rebuke, reprimand, and generally flay me for the latest mess Mother was in . . . as if I, or anyone, could control her!

Since I was car-less, one of the Red-Hatted League ladies — Mrs. Hetzler, the former teacher — offered to give me a lift to Peggy Sue's. I thanked her and climbed into the front passenger seat of her burgundy Buick.

Mrs. Hetzler had shrunk over the years, her gray-haired head barely clearing the dashboard, white-knuckled hands gripping the top of the steering wheel, like it might fly away. I made sure my seat belt was fastened tight, which was a good thing because we nearly had a few accidents — no more than a dozen.

Or two.

Not because Mrs. Hetzler was driving fast, mind you, but because she was going so damn slow! Like Mr. McGoo, she was oblivious to the disasters she left in her wake, creating an array of angry, frustrated motorists, driven by madness to do whatever they could, including passing ill-advisedly, turning down one-ways, and driving up on the sidewalk, *anything* to get around or at least away from us. Mortified, I slumped in my seat and became her twin.

Finally we reached the new suburb north of town where my sister's house was located, a modern monstrosity in brick, wood, and glass, with the personality of a paper plate (an unused one). Mrs. Hetzler narrowly missed Peggy Sue's street-side mailbox (Hastings) as she bumped up over the curb, and after all the mortifying moments I'd endured on the ride here, I could now only smile at the thought of the tire tracks she'd be leaving behind on my sister's (formerly) perfect lawn.

"Thanks for the ride, Mrs. Hetzler," I said as I quickly opened the car door.

"What time should I come back for you, dear?" the elderly woman wondered. Somebody really should get her a big-city phone book to sit on and strap wood blocks to her feet.

"That won't be necessary . . . I'll be fine! It's a lovely day — I can use the walk."

And I made my escape, heading up the wide, white concrete driveway where a double garage and a half announced: WE HAVE THREE CARS! Good for you.

Attention, home builders: since when did big, ugly garage doors become a part of the front of a house? What was wrong with a nice porch and a couple of bay windows? *Attention, home buyers:* if you can afford a six-figure home, you can certainly afford to pour extra cement around back, where the garage is *supposed* to be! And, men, if the garage was behind the house, you wouldn't be nagged to clean it out so often, would you? Can't see the mess from the street.

Why doesn't somebody put *me* in charge?

My brother-in-law, Bob Hastings, answered the doorbell in one ring. Tall, thin, and gaunt, Bob was in his fifties, but looked older . . . probably from working so hard as an accountant to pay for this place (or just being married to my sister). He had a nice face, though; with an extra twenty pounds, a tan, and a two-week vacation, Bob could make the grade.

He gave me a little smile, and I reciprocated. We'd had a nice rapport from the get-go, I supposed because we were in the same boat — at the mercy of Peggy Sue.

I stepped into a large, gleaming foyer; to the right was an opulent living room that hardly got used; to the left, a dining room, the table spectacularly set with china and silver, massive brocade-covered chairs drawn up.

"Something smells good," I said, and meant it. Peggy Sue was, if nothing else, a crack cook.

"Beef Wellington," Bob told me proudly. I could tell he adored her.

Poor dumb slob.

I turned to him. "And how are you?" Before he could answer, I cocked my head and commented, "If you don't mind my saying, you look a little pale around the gills . . . work running you ragged again?"

He shrugged. "Year-end stuff. You know how it goes."

I shook my head. "I don't understand why June is sometimes considered the year's end. . . ."

We walked back to the kitchen, an enormous room that had an island counter with its own sink and burners, and every amenity that a homegrown Emeril could want —

and then some.

Dutifully, I asked Sis, "Can I do any-thing?"

Peggy Sue, dressed in a blue silk dress and high heels, nary a hair out of place, was taking a roasting pan out of a stainless steel oven with only a few more controls than a jet's cockpit. (Sometime remind me to tell you about *my* experience with Beef Wellington, which ended in a thousand-bucks'-plus worth of smoke damage.)

"No, Brandy," Peggy Sue answered sweetly. "You can just sit up to the table."

To Bob, she crisply ordered, "Call Ashley down."

We both obeyed our respective commands.

Dinner was pleasant enough. I kept the heat off me by asking Ashley a lot of questions about school and stuff, a trick I use when I don't want to talk myself.

Ashley was seventeen — beautiful, smart, popular, with parents that gave her everything. Listening to my niece's bubbly chatter, I wondered if the girl remotely realized how lucky she was.

We'd kind of wrapped up our conversation when Ashley smiled and looked right at me and said, "I'm so glad to see you, Aunt Brandy. You always dress so cute — could we go shopping sometime?"

Peggy Sue was sipping coffee, her eyes frozen.

I said, "Sure, Ash — maybe drive down to the Quad Cities and hit the malls?"

"That would be awesome."

With a brittle laugh, Peggy Sue said, "*Everything's* 'awesome' these days."

Ashley gave her mother a curdled look and I just kind of half smiled, said, "Yeah, uh, sure is," and went back to my food.

After the meal, Ashley disappeared back upstairs, Bob headed out to the garage (whud I tell you?), and I made like the scullery maid, taking charge of the dirty dishes and bracing myself for Peggy Sue's lecture concerning Mother.

But I was in for a shock.

Peggy Sue stood nearby as I fed her dishwater and her expression seemed sincere as she said, "Brandy, I want to thank you for looking after Mother . . . I . . . I know it isn't easy . . . and, well, I want you to know that I do appreciate your effort."

I tried to find a note of sarcasm in there, especially in the last part about my "effort," but couldn't. Peggy Sue, for a change, seemed genuine.

Taken aback, I didn't know what to say.

"I assume there'll be a court appearance,"

Peggy Sue speculated, "for the, uh . . . driving infraction?"

That was an innocuous way of putting it. I said, "Yes . . . but I can handle it, Sis."

She heaved a sigh, smiled a little. "Thank you. Really . . . thank you. I'm awfully busy these days with the house, and Ashley, and everything."

And bridge club and parties and trips to the hairdresser . . . and the last place Peggy Sue would want to be seen is in court with her kooky mother.

Peggy Sue was rinsing pots and pans at the sink as she asked, "Have you heard from Jake lately?"

"I got an e-mail last week . . . which read like his father dictated it."

She shrugged. "Well, that's better than nothing."

"I guess."

Her eyes narrowed. "How about a job? Are you looking?"

"Not yet."

She waggled a finger. "Well, you better get around to that soon. Mother's funds are limited, to say —"

That got my back up. "I'm *not* taking *any* money from her."

"All right, all right. I'm just saying . . . you really should find one."

Peggy Sue was right, I knew. I couldn't put off looking much longer.

I asked, "What would you think about me writing a column for the *Serenity Sentinel?*"

"About what?"

"Antiques. For example, how to spot a bargain . . . how to restore them. . . ."

She arched an amused eyebrow. "Like the time you took the veneer off that valuable table by running a water hose on it?"

"Very funny." I could always count on Sis for support.

Ashley entered the kitchen, dressed casually in Lacoste.

"Honey," Peggy Sue said, "why don't you run Brandy home, so I don't have to?"

My niece wrinkled her pert little nose. "But Mom, I'm going to Sarah's . . ." She looked at me. Her eyes lingered. I could see her reconsidering, but couldn't imagine why. ". . . Well . . . okay, I guess it's not too far out of the way."

Ashley handled her fire-engine-red Mustang as if she really were going to a fire. At first it was refreshing, after Mrs. Hetzler's snail pace; but soon I was getting nostalgic about the world's slowest, shortest driver. . . .

When Ashley pulled up in front of my house, I was relieved to be alive. There had been no small talk — hardly any time for it!

"Thanks for the lift," I said, reaching for the car door.

"Wait," Ashley said. Her expression was pensive. "Can I . . . can I talk to you a minute?"

"Sure." I sat back.

She turned off the engine. *Must be serious.*

My niece began haltingly: "I . . . I know Mom thinks I don't know what's going on — with Grandma, I mean, and that man that got killed — but I've heard people talking."

"Oh-kay. . . ."

She leaned forward conspiratorially. "If I tell you something . . . something that has to do with that Clint Carson guy . . . you promise not to squeal to Mom?"

I blinked. Then I said, "Of course, Ashley . . . you can always count on me."

She moved even closer; the leather seat made a squeak. "You can't tell."

"I won't tell."

"Well . . . one time, me and Troy — that's my boyfriend — partied one night out at the Haven . . ."

The Haven Motor Hotel was a notorious love nest on Highway 22, a cheapie motel for kids and cheaters. (Only heard about it;

never been there.) (Honest.)

". . . and, anyway, there was this terrible fight in the cabin next to ours. Yelling and screaming."

"When was this?"

"Last month."

"Go on."

She drew in a deep breath and let it out. "Well . . . I was curious, you know, to see who it was? And so I peeked through the curtains. *He* was standing outside the cabin."

"He? Clint Carson?"

"*That* guy — yeah."

"You're *sure* it was Clint Carson?"

"Oh yeah. He got around town. He was a real hound. . . . Anyway, at the motel? There are these yard lights —"

"Yard lights. Okay. And?"

Ashley swallowed. "And this woman — whoever she was — she jumped in her car and drove off, really, really pissed off."

I frowned. "What did she look like?"

"I couldn't tell . . . it happened so quick, and she was wearing this hoodie, and had her back to me, mostly."

"Why do you think it was her own car she got in?"

"Well . . . for one thing, older people who

go out there, married people and all? They usually go out in separate cars, and meet there. Sometimes even kids do that, just being careful. Anyway, there was this red truck, which I guessed was his."

"What kind of car did the woman get in?"

"That's why I remember, Aunt Brandy — it was a Montana, I think, like we have."

"And the color?"

"Brown . . . also like ours."

"Are you sure? Could be important."

"Definitely." She laughed. "I remember because I had this ridiculous thought. . . ."

"What?"

She shook her head. "It's so silly I don't even wanna say."

"*What,* Ash?"

Another swallow. "I didn't get a good look at the woman, but the way she moved . . . see, I only saw her from behind."

"Ashley — what are you getting at?"

"It might have been my mother." She laughed again, but it sounded almost like crying. "Isn't that silly? Isn't that hilarious? I'm sure I just thought that, 'cause of the car, y'know?"

I just looked at her.

". . . You better go, Aunt Brandy."

I got out of the car and the little red Mustang squealed off.

And suddenly I didn't think Mother was crazy to want to look into Clint Carson's murder.

A Trash 'n' Treasures Tip

Buying an antique that's cheap because it "just needs a little fixing" is like getting a pair of slacks on sale that just need a little hemming. Before the dust settles, you've spent more on restoration than on the item.

Chapter Six

NO PAIN, NO VANE

The day dawned hazy, with a threat in the air of heat and humidity that was really a promise.

In the midwest we have a saying: if you don't like the weather, just wait a minute. The center of the country is a meteorological microcosm of the rest: we have on occasion the kind of perfect, low-humidity days thought only to be found in southern California; but we also get the kind of insufferable summer temperatures of central Florida . . . with the added bonus of the bone-chilling cold of northern Minnesota.

In the heart of the heartland, you learn to appreciate the good days, settle for the bad, and never, ever get complacent.

Complacent I wasn't; but in a grumpy mood I was, because I dreamed that I'd spent *hours* in a really cute boutique where I couldn't find anything in my size (and I had credit cards this time!).

For those keeping score, that's Dreamworld 876,761,800, Brandy zero.

I was also crabby because there was no shampoo in the house, which led to me trying to wash my hair with bar soap. Man oh man, does *that* not work!

But soon I climbed out of my funk. Officer Lawson had returned my car, which showed no signs of having made contact with the corpse; Mother's wheels had, however, shown such contact, and the vehicle was still being held, pending the outcome of the inquiry into Carson's death. (Or, as Mother put it, the murder of that horrible person who took advantage of her and who she would tell a thing or two if he weren't the horrible person recently murdered.)

What Ashley told me about the mystery woman with Clint Carson at the Haven Motel was troubling, but I really didn't take the notion of my sister being the murdered man's shack-up partner — let alone murderer — very seriously. Peggy Sue didn't fit either profile.

On the other hand, this was not information I intended to share with Mother. I had problems enough already.

In celebration of my newfound automotive freedom — I never thought I'd be thrilled to see *that* yellow bucket of bolts again! — I planned an outing for Sushi and me. I had a hidden agenda, which for now I'll hide from you, because if I didn't, it would just be an agenda.

After packing a picnic lunch — leftover meat loaf sandwiches, stale potato chips, frozen Girl Scout cookies (chocolate mint), and tap water in washed Evian bottles — I scooped up the pooch, who had been dancing at my feet, sensing (and smelling) that something was up.

Dressed for the occasion in a light blue tank top, dark denim shorts, and a pair of Peggy Sue's old Chris Evert Converse white tennis shoes (an attic treasure), I asked Sushi, "Ready for an adventure?"

She gave a quick, positive yap in response.

I placed Sushi — a pink bow holding back the hair that usually covered her eyes — in a pet tote bag, like the one Paris Hilton carries her Chihuahua in. I saw a picture of that in *People* magazine — pink leopard print with pink fur trim and sparkly faux jewels . . . I wonder if Paris, like me, made it herself.

Frankly, my version was a little pathetic, but Sushi didn't mind because (a) she was a dog, and (b) she was a blind dog.

Shortly, we were cruising along the River

Road, windows rolled down because the air conditioner was busted, my poochie in the passenger seat, head high, little pink tongue lolling . . . both of us enjoying the fresh air mussing our manes (although my tongue was in my mouth) (make that my cheek).

Traffic was light as I zoomed along without any music blaring, preferring the blessed silence. The dazzling sun — haze now dissipated — had magically transformed the rambling river into an unwound bolt of gold lame, flung to the horizon.

My reverie, however, was interrupted as I glided by the entrance to Clint Carson's place, where yellow police tape drawn across the drive (and tied between two scrub trees) warned of no entry . . . as if that could keep anybody out.

I wondered what evidence the police had found, or more importantly, what they *hadn't* found that *I* might, given half a chance.

But I resisted the urge to stop, passing on by.

In another fifteen minutes or so, a sign pointed the way to Wild Cat Den; I almost missed the familiar marker, having been away so long. So I wound up turning a little too sharply onto the secondary road, and if Sushi-in-a-bag hadn't been strapped in, she would have tipped over.

"Sorry, girl!"

She gave me a don't-do-that-again frown, punctuated by her ghostly eyes.

The popular tourist destination, Wild Cat Den, had been so named because of the abundance of bobcats and cougars that once roamed the thick forest, living in the dens of the limestone cliffs carved by glaciers centuries ago. These mountain lions no longer hung out in the park, driven away by the ever-increasing presence of man; sightings are reported from time to time . . . although no one has actually caught one of the wild animals, not even on film.

I tooled down the road, going by a rustic bungalow nestled among tall pines, where a female park ranger lived (a nice enough person unless she caught you with booze on the grounds, which is prohibited) (not that I'd know), and then passed the Pine Creek Grist Mill, a rambling gray wooden three-story structure built precariously on the edge of a swollen stream. A century ago, the mill's big paddle wheel churned with the help of a man-made waterfall, which in turn cranked the mill's inner workings, grinding grain into meal.

Once a blight of disrepair and broken windows, the old mill had been restored to its former glory by the tireless effort of some citizens, including . . . you guessed it . . . Mother. Today, the old mill conducts weekend tours (and if you go, be nice — leave a five-spot in the donation box, and tell 'em Brandy sent you).

Before long I came to a long steel gate, yawning open to proclaim the park open. At 9:00 PM, that gate swings shut until the next 7:00 AM, and if you linger to camp out under the stars, I wouldn't sweat the wildcats, but I would keep an eye out for that truck-driver-size park ranger lady (and *don't* tell her Brandy sent you).

I came to a fork in the road, which designated that big decision all Wild Cat Den visitors had to make: *You take the high road, and I'll take the low road. . . .*

The park was laid out on two levels — seasoned hikers might start at the bottom, choosing one of the many paths (of varying levels of difficulty) and work their way to the top. Those who prefer taking it easier would begin at the summit, letting a gentlemanly gravity help them down. But there's always a moment, at the end, either way you go, when you realize your car is parked on the opposite level. That's when you could use a friend to bring the darn thing around!

A little hiking goes a long way . . . or is that short way?

You probably already know well enough to figure I'm a low-road kind of girl. This gravel strand soon dead-ended in a flat, pounded-out dirt picnic area surrounded by lush green grass, towering shade trees, and a sun-glinting, babbling brook.

Sushi, feeling the car slow to a stop, barked wildly, her spooky eyes crazy with possibilities. *Hurry up, you dumb human! There's virgin territory to pee on!*

Hooking the wicker basket on one arm, Sushi-in-a-bag on the other, I got out of the car and drew in a lungful of the kind of wholesome fresh air that makes life worth living, and allergies a real threat to it.

Already, a fair amount of tourists were on the scene: hikers in shorts and T-shirts, toting water bottles, making use of the footpaths before the afternoon heat set in; families who'd laid claim to tables and benches, some already cooking on charcoal grills, the delicious aroma wafting our way and putting Sushi into a doggie dilemma (*pee or food, pee or food — priorities!*); and a few couples were stretched out on blankets, gazing mooningly at each other under the sun.

Still plenty of room for Sushi and me, but

actually — I had another spot in mind. . . .

Boldly choosing one of the more difficult upward routes (stone steps instead of dirt path) to the top, we began the climb.

Before long I was huffing and puffing, the ol' thigh muscles stinging. I did my share of walking back in Chicago, particularly on the Magnificent Mile, but not at this steep angle; muscles I didn't know I had were saying howdy do.

So I stopped to catch my breath at a rest station next to a wood-staked plaque that read STEAMBOAT ROCK. The huge looming boulder indeed resembled the prow of a big ship. At the moment a couple of boys were on top of it, arms spread wide, yelling, "I'm king of the world," though Leo DeCaprio they weren't. An echo encouraged repetition, which got old real fast, so Soosh and I moved on.

After a while the stepping-stones turned into a damn near perpendicular path made all the more treacherous, and slippery, by strewn pine needles; the once light-filtering trees were becoming more and more dense — dusk might as well have fallen. Suddenly both my Nature Girl and Nancy Drew instincts seemed ill-advised, the forest growing eerily silent . . . no chirping birds, or pecking woodpeckers, or chattering squirrels . . .

Where have all the critters gone? I wondered, almost channeling Peter, Paul, and Mary. More to the point: what did those *critters* know that I didn't?

A sudden quick movement in the brush startled me, but before I could react, a huge beast leaped into my path, snarling savagely, its rabid fangs drippingly bared, claws sharp as my Ginsu knife (before it fell into the garbage disposal), the creature eyeing me for its dinner — and Sushi for dessert.

Not really.

Just seeing if you're paying attention — didn't I tell you there are no mountain lions living in Wild Cat Den anymore?

The next attraction on the state park's program was Fat Man's Squeeze, a fissure in the mountain wall that offered a shortcut to the top for the slender . . .

. . . the rest of us had to keep on climbing.

Why didn't I at least try? After all, I'd lost weight after the divorce, hadn't I? Well, I'll tell you. Once, a weight-challenged youngster got stuck in there for two days until the park ranger greased him up with a bucket of lard by pouring it down the crack over his head.

That's what I heard in grade school, anyway.

Sushi squirmed inside her faux Paris Hilton bag; she'd had enough of climbing, and let me know in so many barks. Hadn't I taken her away from the smell of fresh grass and charcoaling hamburgers? How much optimism could one blind dog summon?

"Just a little farther," I promised, picking up my pace. "And then we'll have our lunch."

Sushi was one of those rare dogs who could smile, actually smile — and "lunch" was a word she not only recognized, but beamed at.

And then we were there: the Devil's Punch Bowl.

Unlike most of the other natural attractions at the park, a sign no longer announced this one's time-honored nickname. The Park and Recreation Department wished this particular phenomenon had never occurred, and some effort had been made to change the ancient moniker . . . the lamest being the Angel's Punch Bowl. But no self-respecting kid is ever going to trade the devil for a mere angel. . . .

About one hundred feet in diameter and six deep, the Devil's Punch Bowl might have been created by a small meteorite eons ago;

back when the ranger gave walking tours (grade school), that had been the story, though the park's Web site, in a grudging description, now described the more likely explanation: a pooling of an underground spring, having nowhere to run off, had formed the bowllike shape over time.

The "Devil" designation came from a disturbing, reddish goop that oozed from the ground in the bottom of the bowl and — when it rained — made a pink, toxic-looking slushie.

The Devil's Punch Bowl attracted everyone from benign Wicca practitioners to scary Satan worshipers, and others who just found it a cool place to hang out.

This would, apparently, include the two young men who just popped out of the punch bowl . . .

. . . and planted themselves in front of me.

One was tall and druggy thin, with stringy black greasy hair, and dark, dead eyes that were scarier than Sushi's; he wore a dirty black T-shirt with a heavy metal band logo so badly faded as to be unrecognizable, his ensemble completed by torn, worn cutoffs and self-inflicted tattoos, badly drawn.

The other kid was stocky, and the proud bearer of an acute case of acne, courtesy of a merciless puberty past, and multiple piercings, mutilations of his own making. He was better dressed than his friend, though, in cargo shorts and a short-sleeved shirt with dragons, unbuttoned and open over a hairy, protuding belly.

I was kidding when I told you about the mountain lion jumping in my path; this, I'm afraid, really happened. . . .

Not that I was too concerned; in broad daylight, with hikers around?

Only none were around right now.

"Yo, Red Riding Hood — what's in the basket?" the thin one said, his voice as thin as himself; he was smirking at his cleverness.

"Lunch," I said, having no desire to banter.

The plump one with his belly hanging out sneered and said, "You're right on time with the goodies, bitch!"

Eyeing the silver spear through his lower lip, I said, "Does that hurt?"

"*Hell* no!" He seemed truly offended.

"Your mouth looks a little red . . . swollen — is that a recent addition to your collection? Could be infected, you know."

The plump guy didn't know what to say; "bitch" was the best move he could bust, apparently.

"Give it up!" The skinny kid with the bad

skin art stepped forward and wrenched the picnic basket from my hands.

And at that, with a vicious growl, Sushi jumped out of her bag, landed on all fours, and — forgetting she can't see but heeding her other well-honed senses — leaped right at the skinny one and sank her little sharp teeth into his bare narrow ankle.

Now, don't think for a minute that Soosh was trying to protect me. She'd just been smelling that meat loaf for a twenty-minute car ride, its promise trumping the grass and burgers below only to be subjected by me to a half-hour hike, and, by God and Rin Tin Tin's testicles, if anyone or anything tried to come between her and lunch, there would be bloody hell to pay!

They really were dealing with the wrong bitch. . . .

"Get that thing offa me!" the thin kid hollered, shaking his leg as if in a native dance of an unknown tribe. But Sushi stuck to him — she had hold of him, and this was the closest to actually tasting meat she'd come today.

The plump pierced guy was no help whatsoever to his friend, frozen there, stammering, "Look . . . look at its *eyes,* man . . . it's . . . it's like — puh-*sessed!*"

Sushi's eyeballs *were* awfully scary, I had

181

to admit, especially with her hair tied back. I called to her, and she obediently if half-heartedly detached herself from that bony ankle.

The kid jumped up and down on one foot, holding the wounded ankle in his hands, doing a sort of Funky Chicken this time, while swearing at me and Soosh in a cascade of profanity as filthy as it was unimaginative.

I said, "Come on, you aren't hurt, you big sissy — it's hardly even bleeding. You may wanna consider a tetanus shot, though."

More profanity blurted from the hopping, hopping-mad beanpole. I'd have been amused, but finally the fat one unfroze himself and his lip curled back as he took a step toward me.

I was wondering if I should hold the spooky-eyed pooch up, like a cross before an oncoming vampire, when a family of three thankfully chose this moment to swing by the fabled Punch Bowl — father, mother, and a boy around ten.

Dad, a strapping guy in his early thirties, noted the tension, the overturned lunch basket, and looked at the two guys sternly, and me sympathetically, then said, "Any trouble here, miss?"

I said, "I don't think so." I smiled and

arched an eyebrow at them. "Boys?"

They responded by pouting and stalking off, down the path, the plumper in the lead, the skinny skin-art guy hobbling after.

The little family lingered awhile, making sure my two hungry "friends" didn't return. The mother offered to help me with the spilled basket, but I declined, and the little family moved on, the kid turning back to look in fascination at the crazy-eyed little dog who'd so spooked the big bad wolves.

Sushi had found her way over to the spilled basket and was sniffing around, making sure lunch was still there. I bent to gather everything — the food, in various plastic bags, had survived — when someone began to clap, the sound reverberating off the rock walls.

I looked up toward the source of the applause.

Sitting on the ledge overlooking the Devil's Punch Bowl, khaki-clad legs dangling, was the real reason for my trip — Joe Lange.

"You handled yourself well," he said in his overly enunciated baritone. ". . . For a civilian."

Annoyed, I straightened, basket in hand. "And where were *you* when I needed you?"

Joe didn't answer, just tossed a rope over the ledge of the rock and began to climb down. I was impressed until he lost his grip and fell about ten feet to the ground with a *whump!* Seemingly unhurt, he sprang up in the cloud of dust he'd raised, and I suppressed a smile.

I'd known Joe since biology class in junior high. Basically, he was a would-be man's man who was really an eternal boy, and a nerd who saw himself as much smarter than he actually was. I'm not saying that he didn't have brains, but he had sporadic black holes among the gray matter that he'd fall into.

While Joe wasn't hard on a female's eyes, tall and loose-limbed with nice features, those features were a wee bit off: one eye higher than the other, mouth a little too wide, nose leaning to one side. And as long as I'd known him, he seemed perpetually forty years old, as if he'd come out of the womb that way (ouch!).

Joe had a penchant for pretzels and hard liquor — almost always to ill effect — believed in Nostradamus, and was a certified (and certifiable) gun nut. He was a Trekker — not Trekkie! — and strictly orthodox (classic Trek, only). Come to think of it, he was kind of like Mr. Spock — an incompetent Mr. Spock.

That said, he was essentially harmless, a

loyal friend, and interesting if bizarre company, guaranteed to be funny . . . although the latter was not always intentional.

Back when we both attended community college, Joe had joined the National Guard; he loved being a weekend warrior . . . but then along came Desert Storm, and his unit got called up, something I think he never expected.

The war must have been rough on Joe, because he got sent home before his tour was finished, for reasons never explained (to me, anyway), and he hasn't really seemed right since.

Joe said, "I thought your ETA was oh-ten-hundred."

"What?"

He sighed. "Estimated time of arrival? Ten o'clock?"

"Oh." I'd forgotten to adjust to military-speak. "Revelry was late this morning."

"That's *reveille*."

"Whatever."

Joe eyed the basket. "I see you brought provisions."

"Yes, provisions. But if there's dirt among the protein and vitamins, it's your own damn fault."

He waved me off dismissively. "I'd have

stepped in if it got ugly."

"*Got* ugly? Didn't you get a good look at those two? It *started* ugly."

He gestured for me to follow him. I scooped Sushi up and we left the beaten path, climbed up some rocks, and sat under a leaning, half-dead tree that threatened to topple at the slightest breeze.

I spread out a festive red tablecloth and began to dole out the food, serving up the yapping, drooling Sushi first.

"Not bad rations," Joe said after a moment, his mouth full.

"Thanks."

Sushi had already gobbled up her portion — one corner of my sandwich — and began stalking ours. Joe made a friend for life, giving her tiny bites now and then, mindful of her sharp teeth.

Sidebar: my other dog, the late Bluto, was the greediest animal I ever knew. Once, while Mother was away, he got up on a chair and ate my entire pancake and sausage breakfast when I went to answer the phone . . . and he'd *already had* his own dog food! That made me mad. And I wondered just how much Bluto would eat . . . if given the opportunity. So I took a fifteen-pound turkey out of the fridge, cooked it, placed it on the kitchen floor, and left the house to

186

go play with some friends. Well, when Mother came home late that afternoon, she found Bluto passed out over the stripped-clean turkey carcass. I was in *so much trouble* because (1) the vet had to pump the dog's stomach, and (2) that turkey was supposed to be for our Thanksgiving dinner!

Bluto never hankered after turkey much, after that.

As we moved on to the thawed Girl Scout cookies, Joe asked, "So what's this covert meeting about?"

I said, "Well . . . I could use some information."

His eyes narrowed; with the one eye too high, it gave him a vaguely demented look. "Reconnaissance?"

"Call it . . . research."

The eyes tensed. "Explain."

I shifted to get a better look at him, trying to convey a certain seriousness without setting him off. "Way I see it, Joe, when you hang at the park, you always try to kinda fly in under the radar . . ."

"Affirmative."

". . . and are in a position to hear and see things."

He nodded curtly.

"And I suppose you know about Clint Carson's death."

"I've heard the scuttlebutt, affirmative."

Encouraged, I pressed him. "Ever see him out here with any of the drug crowd? Crackheads, dopers, whoever?"

He thought for a moment. "Negative," he said. But then he leaned forward and quietly said, "Not that a lot of trafficking hasn't gone on, in and out of this place."

"Local?"

This time he gave me three whole nods. "And as far away as Colorado."

Remembering the Colorado license plate Mother had heard about from her bartender friend at the hardware store, I chewed thoughtfully on a cookie.

Joe said, "Look — if it's drug dealing you're 'researching . . .' "

"Yes?"

"I did witness something odd out here one night."

I waited for the shoe to drop.

"You know that cop that got kicked off the force?"

Mia.

What a clunk *that* shoe made. . . .

Swallowing, I bobbed my head. "We were friends as little kids."

"Well, the grown-up version was up top with another cop. They sat in an unmarked car for a long time, having a real confab.

Then she got out and drove off in her own vehicle."

Shaking my head, I asked, "What did you make of *that?*"

Joe shrugged. "I thought something was going down — and I don't mean sexually."

"Did you know who the other policeman was?"

"Negative. He never got out of the car. All I saw was the blue uniform."

"So . . . it could have even been another woman?"

"No. That wasn't my impression. I can differentiate the sexes with some ease."

"Good to hear. . . . You wouldn't happen to know Brian Lawson?"

"Yes. A good man."

"Could . . . could it have been *him,* meeting with Mia?"

"Affirmative."

My eyes popped. "You mean it *was* Lawson?"

"No. Affirmative it *could* have been Lawson."

"Oh."

Sushi was getting restless, and I was afraid she might take a tumble off the rock, so I began to pack up the trash.

As I did, I asked him, "How come you

hang around out at the Den so much, Joe?"

"Surely you jest?"

I squinted at him sideways. "Uh, no. . . ."

He squinted back. "Because of the terrorists, of course."

My eyebrows headed north. "Here? In Wild Cat Den?"

He looked at me as if I had lost my mind. "Of course! Don't you see?"

"Uh, no. . . ."

Very quietly, leaning close, he said, "It's the perfect place. No one would ever expect them to strike here."

I said, "Uh, gee. Never thought of it like that."

Joe smiled, filled his scrawny chest with air. "That's why you're lucky you've got *me*, watching your back."

Then he gave me a loose salute for good-bye and headed back toward the Punch Bowl.

I had started the downward trek with Sushi and basket when he called out after me, "Hey, Brandy! Heads-up! I spotted a cougar this morning!"

Oh dear. If Joe was seeing cougars now, how could I believe anything else he'd seen?

I called back with my thanks, and headed on down.

Then I was alone on the trail, every

sensible human being in the Wild Cat Den vicinity having had the sense to get out of the heat and humidity.

I had passed Fat Man's Squeeze and was approaching Steamboat Rock, when an unmistakable scream came from close by, making me all but jump out of my skin.

Not a human scream, an animal one — a wildcat!

And I'm not kidding, this time.

I tossed the basket, clutched Sushi to my pounding chest, and raced down the path as fast as I could. Nearing the bottom, I stumbled over a tree root snaked across the path, skinning both knees, but managed to hang on to Soosh.

Finally I burst into the clearing and looked over my shoulder expecting to see a mountain lion leaping out. . . .

But there was nothing.

I had the sudden quick image of Joe sitting up on a rock, pushing a button on a boom box to play a prerecorded wildcat screech, grinning crazily to himself. Wouldn't put it past him . . . a great terrorist deterrent, wildcats. . . .

A few lingering tourists, packing up their belongings, stared at the frazzled young woman with disarrayed hair, frightened expression, and skinned knees, clutching a dog with even wilder eyes, as she walked on wobbly legs toward her car.

No way was I going to go back for that basket!

"Don't go up there," I told them, and booked.

After we were locked safely in the Taurus, I said to Sushi, "And how did you like our little outing?" My heart was beating like a disco bass line.

Even Soosh looked a little traumatized.

Driving back on the River Road, I noticed that the police tape across the entrance to Carson's place had been removed.

What the heck? I thought, and pulled in, cruising down the one-way lane, and came to a stop in front of the farmhouse.

I got out and stood near the car, appraising the place. Funny how everything seemed different in the daylight — the tan clapboard with its gingerbread accents looked homey and inviting . . . not like the Amityville-like house of the night I'd come out here. The barn, too, with its funky old rooster weather vane, appeared nothing more than a facility for farm equipment storage, rather than a good place to bury bodies.

I swiveled at the sound of another car coming down the lane, tires snapping tiny twigs. A silver sedan pulled into view, and I wondered who else was anxious to look around the murdered man's digs.

The car came to a stop behind mine, and the woman behind the wheel eyed me as suspiciously as I did her.

Could she be the mysterious lady Ashley saw with Carson at the Haven Motel? Assuming the motel woman wasn't my sister Peggy Sue, of course. . . .

She climbed out. Middle-aged, dressed in a brown linen suit, sporting short helmet-hair, she asked in a coolly professional manner, "Can I help you?"

It was as if I'd just entered a dress shop and the manager had deemed me too dowdy to trade there.

"Just having a look around," I said pleasantly.

Her demeanor suddenly became more friendly. "Oh! Then you're interested in the place?"

I wasn't sure what she meant, so I said, "Maybe."

She stuck out a slender, manicured hand. "I'm Sue Roth," she said. "My company is handling this property."

Now I knew what she meant. At least she didn't consider me too dowdy to be a customer.

"Would you like me to show you around?" she asked.

Recalling some recent advice given me by a fortune cookie — *Confucius say: Better to be lucky than smart* — I smiled and said, "Very much — could we start with the barn?"

"The barn?" The Realtor was looking at me curiously, even skeptically. "Most women want to see the kitchen right off."

"That'll be my second stop! But that barn looks perfect for my hobby."

"Hobby?"

"Refinishing furniture."

She brightened again. "Oh! Are *you* an antique dealer, too?" Instantly her face fell. "Oh . . . sorry. That was tactless."

Shrugging, I said, "Doesn't bother me that someone died here."

Sue let some air out, in obvious relief; then she rolled her eyes. "Good . . . good. Because some buyers, well, find that a little off-putting, about a property — especially if there was . . . foul play."

Which explained why slick Sue hadn't turned her nose up at a sweaty girl with skinned knees, a beat-up jalopy, and a shih-tzu with white eyeballs. A prospect was a prospect. . . .

I retrieved Sushi from the car, then followed the crisply professional Realtor to the barn, where she used a jangling key chain to unlock the padlock on the double doors, and together we swung them creakingly open.

I don't know what I expected to see . . . my beloved furniture stacked in a corner, just waiting for me, maybe?

But, of course, the barn was empty. Zip, zilch, zally, zero . . . no furniture, and for that matter, nary a backhoe, salt lick, or bail of hay — only floating dust motes.

I turned to Sue. "What happened to everything in here?"

Her eyes narrowed. "Oh — you mean all that furniture that was stacked to the ceiling?"

I nodded.

"Why, the police took it, naturally."

"Why would the police 'naturally' do that?"

Sue shrugged, not terribly interested — how did this help her make a sale?

"All I know," she said, mildly annoyed, "is that everything in the barn, and everything in the house? Was confiscated. *Why,* I don't know. Maybe you should go talk to the police, if it's the furniture you're after. Do you care to have a look at that kitchen, or not?"

A Trash 'n' Treasures Tip

To revarnish or not to revarnish, that is the question. You might be stripping away value along with the old coat. Consult an expert before proceeding . . . after which, you can say good-bye to your thirty-five-dollar manicure.

Chapter Seven

TOOLS RUSH IN

If nothing else, traffic court serves as a reminder that the average midwesterner is still in abject fear of the law's long arm. The anxiety in the air was palpable — you could almost hear the knees knocking.

I sat with Mother and Mr. Ekhardt in a secondary courtroom of the Serenity Courthouse; the much larger trial room — reserved for murders and mayhem, where Mr. Ekhardt had won many a high-profile case — was located on the top floor. In my opinion, traffic court should have been moved up to those spacious digs, considering how all of us were stuffed into these pews like ancient frat boys cramming phone booths — granted, horizontal ones, but we'd have set a campus record, if this had been a campus.

Every walk of life was represented this morning: young, old, rich, poor, white, black, Asian, Hispanic . . . all equal in the eyes of the law (that's the story), all equal in their sweat-inducing fear (no question), waiting for the gavel of fate (nobody here was thinking "justice") to fall.

I was wearing a sleeveless retro floral-print dress by Too Cool and Brandy-affordable lime rubber Juicy Couture thongs. Mr. Ekhardt looked the elder statesman in his navy pin-striped suit, crisp white shirt, and red-patterned tie with elegant pearl stickpin.

But the getup Mother had chosen to don was as mysterious as what goes on in the books her mystery reading group tackles. She might have been an old frontier school-marm in the shapeless, austere gray skirt and jacket, high-necked blouse, and cameo-brooch, her thick, wavy, silver hair pulled back in a severe bun. Maybe she wanted to appear forthright and upstanding before the judge.

Hey, it worked for Lizzie Borden.

This much I knew about Mother, how-ever: she had a reason for everything . . . even if it wasn't always clear, or logical, or even sane. But there would always be a *reason.* . . .

I had the feeling Mother felt very much at home here. This was, after all, a theater of sorts, the players talking among themselves, sotto voce, defendants going over their alibis, family members expressing concern, lawyers explaining procedure . . . the side door next to the judge's bench opened and an official-looking woman in a brown uniform entered.

She may have been attractive once, but years of unpleasantness — from her job, initially, from herself, later on — had taken a toll, etching permanent scowl lines on her spade-shaped face.

The official woman planted herself next to the American flag and barked, *"Quiet!"*

Pin-drop silence followed as she slowly scanned the room like the Alien trying to sense potential lunch in a dark spaceship. That she was chewing gum in a cow/cud manner took the edge off for me, but it was pretty chilling nonetheless.

Finally she said, in a wholly unnecessarily nasty way, "This is a courtroom and deserves *respect!*"

Then from the pack an anonymous voice (it sounded a lot like mine) said, "Then why are you chewing *gum?*"

"Who said that?" the court clerk snapped.

Everyone looked around, including me. Frowning, my expression seemed to say, "Yeah — yeah, who said that? How rude!"

"One more outburst," the woman threatened, "and I'm going to clear the court-room."

And then what? We'd have to come back another day? As if a reprieve wouldn't be welcomed, even for twenty-four hours.

Besides, did she really have the authority to do that? I sure didn't think so.

But the voice that sounded strangely like my own seemed to have nothing to say now — in fact, everyone fell into submission, reinforcing the gum-chewing bailiff's self-deluded power. (With a certain satisfaction, though, I noticed the witch ditching her gum in a wastebasket when she thought nobody was looking.)

After what seemed like forever, a male judge in a flowing black robe came through the side door — our little theater at last had a star (besides Mother). His hair was thin on top, long strands unsuccessful in covering a bald spot, the black bags under his eyes packed for a badly needed vacation.

The judge took his dignified if weary position behind the raised desk and called court to order with a bang of the gavel that, even though we saw it coming, made us all jump.

We sat through several hearings, waiting for Mother's turn.

A father and mother, dressed like they had money, came before the bench with their teenage son, a round-faced boy with long hair that had been slicked back for the occasion; the kid seemed incredibly uncomfortable in a suit and tie. Their well-dressed attorney lawyer pled not guilty to the charge that the boy drove sixty miles an hour on a downtown street, the lawyer's confidence at odds with the kid who was staring at the floor, as if waiting for the blade to fall. They were dismissed pending a trial date.

A young black man in a black T-shirt and jeans, with no lawyer, admitted to various parking violations and took his lumps: two hundred dollars and court costs.

A middle-aged woman with overbleached hair got fined for parking in a handicapped place without displaying the necessary tag. She claimed a recent injury had inspired her to use the spot. Even though she sort of limped on her way out, it looked faked, and she won no sympathy and a couple of "boos."

The courtroom was an oven baking the defendants and their retinue, the old-time ceiling fans ineffective in circulating what paltry air a single rattling window air conditioner was able to pump out. Maybe the town *did* need a new courthouse . . . and maybe the gum-chewing witch had reason to be crabby.

Slender, white-haired, handsome Mr. Ekhardt had fallen asleep, head bowed, snoring ever so softly. But when Mother's name was called, he suddenly snorted awake, eyes clear, with some of the old fire that had gotten more than one husband killer off scot-free (ironically, one of those husbands had been named "Scott").

Earlier, at his office, Mr. Ekhardt had told us just how Mother's hearing was to go, a director laying out the script for his star actress, detailing her disappointingly small and unchallenging role:

Judge (to Mother): *And how do you plead to the charge of operating a motor vehicle with a suspended license?*

Mr. Ekhardt (speaking for Mother, who was instructed to say nothing): *Your honor, my client pleads not guilty.*

Judge: Then trial will be set for . . . (consults calendar, names date).

Gavel.

Curtain.

No applause.

Mr. Ekhardt had explained that there would be no trial (the same as with the sixty-mile-per-hour boy above), for behind closed doors he would cut a deal with the district attorney that would be more lenient than had Mother pled guilty.

Why?

Because no court wants to waste the taxpayers' money on a minor traffic case.

But, naturally, Mother double-crossed us.

"Your Honor," she said, chin up, head high, a noble frontierswoman facing a hanging judge, "I . . . am . . . *guilty.*"

Her voice could have reached the last row of the last balcony in any Broadway theater; in this cubicle, it rang and echoed and made everyone (but Mother) shut their eyes. In my case, I considered not opening them again.

She was rattling on, in her best Katharine Hepburn–esque manner: "How can I say that I am not? Why, that would be dishonest . . . and honesty means everything to me."

Half of little Brandy wanted to run away, but the other half was glued to her seat, captivated — the woman could deliver a line.

Mr. Ekhardt, for his part, sighed and stood by dutifully, long since resigned to Mother's theatrics. Truth be told, he probably expected this, and had only been going through the motions when he explained a script that he'd known would go out the window.

"Your Honor," continued Mother, gesturing with Shakespearean flare, "may I ask you a personal question?"

The question was apparently rhetorical, for when the judge's mouth dropped open — possibly in surprise, but perhaps to reply — she rushed on, "Do you have any children? For if you do, you'd know that you would do *anything* to protect them . . . even — and I will say this proudly and un-ashamed, before this court and my country and my God . . ."

"My God," Mr. Ekhardt muttered.

". . . a good mother will, if she must, to protect her child — *break the law!*" She whirled to the audience, as if they were the jury. She smiled in a beseeching manner that made me wonder if she were suddenly Peter Pan, asking the audience to believe in fairies so that Tinker Bell could live.

"When I thought that my daughter —" Mother suddenly went off-book and pointed. "That's her sitting there . . . such a lovely young woman, and unattached at the moment, by the way. . . ."

I cringed and did my best to disappear down into the pew.

She shook her head, as if reassembling mechanical parts into the correct order, and picked up again.

"When I thought my daughter was in mortal danger — that she might even be *harmed* — I . . . went . . . to . . . my . . . automobile! Did I have a license to drive? No. But I had the license to look after my child's welfare, which is the right of every parent, every father . . . every *mother. . . .*"

The judge's hand was on his gavel but either he was so astounded by this performance that he'd been frozen mute, or perhaps had decided to let the defendant save him the trouble by hanging herself.

She was really going now: "And so I got in my car, even though my license had been suspended — unfairly, I might add . . . what were those cows *doing* there, anyway, at that time of night, in an unlighted field? Where was their supervision? Where was sufficient *lighting. . .* but I digress."

She sought out the faces of individual women in the gallery on each of her following "lines."

"As a mother, what *could* I do? What *should* I do? Indeed, what *must* I do!" She looked from female face to female face and a low, resonant voice intoned: "I . . . rushed . . . to . . . my . . . child's . . . *rescue!*"

Mother paused for much-needed breath. "Of course, my daughter, as it turned out, wasn't where I thought she'd gone, where I thought danger was waiting, when I went to

save her, not knowing she was not there.
. . ."

The audience was getting lost. So was I. So, for that matter, was Mother.

Finally she raised a finger like Mammy Yokum making a point and said, "But . . . she *could have been!*"

"Aaaahl riiiight," the judge said in a gravelly voice, and banged his gavel, putting an end to the melodrama.

"License no longer suspended," the judge said.

Mother beamed.

"License *revoked* for a full year," he stated. "Three-hundred-fifty-dollar fine and court costs."

Mother bowed grandly and, with ludicrous charm, said, "Thank you, Your Honor."

His expression was stern, his tone the same: "I'm not finished, madam — *plus* sixty hours of community service."

Mother smiled like a little girl and waved that off. "Oh! I can do *that* standing on my head!"

"That," the judge said, an eyebrow raised, "is strictly optional, Mrs. Borne."

Outside the courtroom, in the small marble rotunda that echoed nonetheless, Mother, smiling primly, looked from me to

Mr. Ekhardt and said, "Well! I think that went *very* well . . . don't you?"

Mr. Ekhardt's smile was curdled and he somehow managed to say, "It could have been worse," patted her arm, as I smiled weakly. No use crying over spilled milk — but three hundred and fifty–plus dollars is a lot of cow juice, whether their pasture was well lighted or not.

"You understand," the ancient, elegant attorney said, "that today dealt only with driving without a license. There is still the matter of the corpse you ran over, and the murder investigation. . . ."

I said, "Neither one of us had anything to do with that, Mr. Ekhardt."

"I know, I know. But both of you behaved, well, in an eccentric manner the night of the incident."

Shaking my head, I said, "But Officer Lawson said he wouldn't put any of that in his report. . . ."

The attorney nodded. "And we're lucky he decided to be a nice guy about it. But the word is around at police HQ that you two were eager to confess and cover up for each other. If your mother weren't well known locally for her eccentric behavior —"

"Wayne," Mother said sternly. "Don't talk about me as if I weren't here."

"Viv, I apologize. But I'm keeping an eye on that murder investigation. Just to play it safe."

So was I. But I thought it better not to share my Missy Marple activities with the attorney.

Our little party exited the courthouse, but parted company on the front steps. Mother and Mr. Ekhardt were going back to his office, where she wanted to amend her will. She did this quite frequently. Her Last Will and Testament had more codicils than a vintage tugboat has barnacles. One would think Mother had a fortune to consider, which of course she didn't; but it was important to her (as Mother so often stated) that she had her house in order, even though that house didn't have much in it at the moment.

With Mr. Ekhardt's misgivings about the Clint Carson murder ringing in my ears, I walked a few blocks over to the police station — time, I thought, to sit down with Chief Tony Cassato.

Perhaps three years ago, Tony had come from the East to head up the department, and even now was a man of mystery to most Serenity-ites, which caused a myriad of stories to circulate as to why a person of his caliber and experience might end up in these particular boonies.

One rumor was that he had taken on the New York mob, and in retaliation they killed his family (this sounded suspiciously like an invention of Mother's, however). Another story had him in charge of a Lower Manhattan precinct on 9/11, where he witnessed firsthand the collapse of the Twin Towers with some of his own men inside (which sounded a little too much like a TV movie). A more sinister tale making the rounds was that the chief had been caught by his own NYPD vice squad, and forced to resign in disgrace (this was probably spread by a small core of local cops jealous of an outsider getting the top slot).

Whatever Tony Cassato's reason was for coming here, we were lucky to have him.

Shortly after he took over, gangs from Chicago tried to infiltrate the town's youth, and the chief rounded them up and busted them and stayed on their butts and soon they were scurrying back for the big city. Then he initiated programs to educate students and parents on how to prevent that kind of thing from happening again.

This was not to say that Tony Cassato didn't have a few enemies, besides the criminals he put away, and those jealous longtime local cops. Some citizens, and the city council in particular, often got annoyed with his brash, sometimes rude, shoot-from-the-hip manner. My mother reported hearing one old-timer refer to the chief as "that dad-blasted city slicker," but on the other hand, she'd been watching *Green Acres* on TV Land that morning, so consider the source.

My view? In spite of his "perceived" shortcomings, the town was a lot safer with Tony Cassato.

Inside the station, I spoke to the dispatch officer, a woman again, through a hole in the bulletproof glass, asking if I could see the chief. She took my name and advised me to make myself comfortable — always a challenge, considering those hard plastic chairs in the waiting area next to that humming soda machine.

During the next fifteen minutes or so, I read pamphlets on the evils of drugs, learned how not to catch VD, and brushed up on my rights as a citizen; I was in the process of picking dead leaves off the corner rubber-tree plant when the door to the inner sanctum finally opened, and Tony Cassato strode out.

He was in his midforties, stocky, with a barrel chest, gray temples, a bulbous nose, square jaw, and bullet-hard eyes. While at first glance the chief didn't seem terribly attractive, he had a confident charisma that radiated like heat shimmer over asphalt.

His eastern accent was subdued but definite, and to these midwestern ears, charming. "What can I do for you, Brandy?"

Softly, I said, "It's personal, if you don't mind. Could we go to your office?"

"Sure," he said, managing to make that one word both brusque and friendly, a uniquely New York accomplishment.

Now, you may be wondering why the head of Serenity's law enforcement department would be willing to take time out from his busy day to see little old me. You might assume it was because he was keeping an eye on the Clint Carson case, and you might be partially right.

Partially.

Once, when I was home visiting, and still married, Mother had a really bad episode, and I had to summon the police.

The officers who came out — while competent and knowledgeable in a case of spousal abuse or even a rampaging crackhead or for that matter a full-blown hostage crisis — were clueless when it came to dealing with a mentally ill subject like Mother. After the crisis passed, I approached the chief and suggested he put together a team that had training in crisis management, specifically tailored for the mentally disabled.

These poor souls, I pointed out, should not be treated like regular criminals. He saw my point, and cited a precedent back in New York, and not only created a mobile unit that could travel to the site of such a disturbance, but held periodic seminars for his men using a qualified teacher from NAMI (the National Alliance for the Mentally Ill). He and I had spent hours together working on this — sometimes in Serenity, sometimes over the phone when I was back in Chicago — and we had become friends . . . a kind of professional friendship, but a friendship nonetheless, colored by mutual respect.

I followed Tony down the beige-tiled corridor to the last corner room. He sat behind his desk, while I took a padded visitor's chair.

The chief's office was nothing fancy, strictly functional; no one could fault him for squandering the taxpayers' hard-earned money on expensive furnishings. Several nice prints spotted the walls (of the duck hunting variety) and a few framed awards and accolades were on display, but this could have been any executive's office, really. Missing, however, were any family photos.

"How's your mother?" he asked, settling back in his chair, the leather squeaking.

I told him about her impromptu court performance, her outlandish theatrics, and the sentencing.

A small smile tugged at the corner of his mouth. "Maybe the community service will keep her out of trouble."

"Don't count on it," I said.

"Her meds are right?"

"They're right — it's just . . . certain things get her juices going."

"Ah."

"You, uh, know, of course . . . about her — *our* — involvement with the Clint Carson matter?"

"Matter or murder?"

"You're the detective."

He smiled vaguely, then waved it off. "I wouldn't worry about it."

I'd been hoping for more — figuring he might share details about how Carson really died before Mother ran him over — but Tony, ever the professional, was properly tight-lipped.

"So, Brandy," he said, over tented fingers, "what's this visit about?"

"Well," I began, tentatively, "I thought I

should mention that when I went out to Carson's house, yesterday —"

He cut me off by raising a reproachful eyebrow.

I sat forward and couldn't keep the defensiveness out of my voice. "The crime-scene tape was down! I didn't trespass or anything."

"Go on."

"Anyway, all of his property was gone — not just his personal stuff, but the antiques warehoused in his barn. I ran into the Realtor out there — Sue Roth?"

His nod indicated he knew who I meant.

"Ms. Roth said you took *everything* . . . Is that true?"

"Yup. It's in storage right now."

I frowned. "Until the estate is settled, or . . . ?"

The chief leaned forward, elbows on the desk. "Ever hear of the Crime Control Act?"

"Not really."

His tone turned crisply businesslike. "It gives the government the right to seize any and all property at the site of a criminal act."

I blinked. "What criminal act was Carson involved in?"

Tony just stared at me.

With a shrug, I said, "Am I out of line asking?"

He thought for a few seconds, then shook his head, once. "No . . . Carson was operating a meth lab in that barn."

"Holy shii . . . Well, Tony, I appreciate you sharing that with me."

He twitched something that wasn't quite a smile. "You might as well know. It'll be in the papers, statewide, 'fore long."

I wasn't surprised Carson was dealing drugs — everything had been pointing that way — but I figured it was something more upscale, cocaine supplied through his contacts in Colorado, maybe. Meth labs were more common than cornfields in this part of the world.

And then I remembered the horrible chemical stench of my first nighttime visit to Carson's place.

Boy, was I dumb.

You don't have to *agree* with me!

"So," I said, "what happens now?"

"Ongoing investigation — involving us, the sheriff's department, BCI — feds, too."

"No, I mean — to his possessions."

"Oh. Well, they'll be sold at auction."

I sat way forward. *"When?"*

His eyes narrowed. "We'll get a directive from the Treasury Department . . . I don't *know* when . . . It's early days yet."

This was a new world to me. Somehow I had the presence of mind to ask, "Where does the money from the auction go?"

The chief smiled a little. "That's the beauty part — back into law enforcement."

I sighed. "Makes sense."

Tony, sensing my bummer vibe, asked, "What's your interest in Carson's personal effects, anyway? Not thinking about going into the meth business, are you?"

"Not hardly." I made an embarrassed face. "Some of the furniture in the barn belonged to us."

His eyebrows tensed. "You don't mean stolen?"

I shifted in the chair. "Not technically, maybe — for what Carson paid Mother? Just as good as."

Tony made a clicking in his cheek. "Your mother?"

I nodded glumly. "Yeah — Carson took advantage of her last episode and bought everything on the cheap."

I opened my purse, withdrew a piece of paper, and placed it on the desk.

"This is the list of the precious things that snake took," I said. "We'd be forever grateful if you'd give us a heads-up about that auction — maybe we could manage to buy back a few memories."

He nodded, but said nothing.

I decided to take a shot. "Do you have any leads? On the Carson murder?"

Surprisingly, he answered straightaway: "Well, we have had a couple of confessions already."

"Really?" Then I noticed the twinkle in those bullet-hard eyes and understood. "Oh . . . Officer Lawson told you about that."

"Yes. And I stand behind his decision to leave all of that off the record. But, Brandy, you stopping out at Carson's place, to check on those antiques you lost . . . ?"

"Yes?"

"Was that the *only* reason you went out there?"

"What else would there be?"

He studied me for a moment. "I heard a rumor your mother was snooping around downtown, asking questions about the case. I'd appreciate it if you'd advise her of how *ill*-advised that is."

"Oh. Well. Sure."

"And that advice would apply equally to you."

I grinned. How convincing it was, I couldn't say. "You don't think I'm out playing Nancy Drew or anything, do you?"

He grinned. And it wasn't convincing at

all. "I hope not."

The chief was escorting me back down the hallway when I suddenly heard myself blurt, "If Mia took those drugs from lockup, Tony, she *must* have had help from someone else in your department."

"What gives you *that* idea?" he snapped.

The corridor had gotten decidedly chillier.

Still, I forged ahead, recounting the clandestine meeting between Mia and another officer at Wild Cat Den, but without mentioning Joe.

He put a hand on my arm. "Where did you hear that?"

"I just heard it, that's all. You know what a gossip mill this town is."

"Brandy . . ."

"Yes?"

His grasp tightened. "Leave it alone."

"Mia used to be my friend, that's all. Makes me sad that —"

"It's over and done with. Remember what I said. Stay *out* of it . . . and that goes for your mother, too."

"You're hurting my arm."

He released his grip.

I straightened myself. "Are you saying Mia's situation and the Carson case are related?"

"Good-bye, Brandy."

He opened the door to the lobby and followed me out.

I wondered why my words had struck such a raw nerve with our cool police chief. If Mia wasn't the only dirty police officer, wouldn't Tony want to root out the other bad apples? And was Clint Carson's drug-related murder tied to my old friend's disgraced removal from the force?

And was Mia's clandestine cop-shop rendezvous at the Den with Officer Lawson?

I exited the station, mind spinning with questions, but with an overriding feeling of discomfort, as if eyes — *Tony's eyes?* — were following me to my car.

I was half conscious of Sushi nudging my face . . . No, *scratching* my face, and it hurt.

She'd been out to do her business just before I'd gone to bed, and I had put down water for her, so what the heck did she *want*, anyway? No more dogs! No more *blind* dogs, anyway. . . .

I tried to shove the pooch away but my arms were like lead.

More scratching, along with whimpering.

This really *was* my last dog! I forced my eyes open, and became acutely, overwhelming aware of a sickeningly unpleasant odor . . .

. . . *Gas!*

I struggled to my feet, and the room whirled; but I managed to steady myself, and stumbled out into the hall.

Mother's bedroom was closer to the stairwell, her door — I could see, thanks to the night-light from the bathroom — was open; I moved toward it virtually in slow motion, barely able to lift my feet, as if walking in a swamp.

I saw Mother's form under her covers, and I lurched forward, falling to my knees by the bed, as if about to pray, but instead grabbing her, shaking her, yelling to her, "Mother! *Mother!* Wake up!"

She was limp as a rag doll.

I turned to the nearby window — closed for airconditioning — threw it open, and knocked out the screen, slamming my fist into the wire like a punch-drunk boxer. Then, summoning strength from somewhere, I dragged Mother out of her bed and carted her bodily over to the window, and propped her head up on the sill.

A warm breeze blew in, fluttering the white lace curtains, and I gulped deeply.

I never knew air could be so damn delicious.

Mother gulped, too, and snorted, taking in air finally, and then moaned, as if having a bad dream.

"Mother! There's *gas* in the house — we have *got* to get out!"

Her voice was weak, and for once in her life, all theatrics were drained out of her. "Oh dear, oh dear . . . Oh, my head, aching *head*. . . ."

Sushi had found her way next to us, and I picked the pooch up and held her out the window as if about to drop her, but the point was to give her some fresh air, too.

"Take a deep breath, Mother," I instructed. "And then we'll go."

Mother grabbed some air, and then I helped her to her feet . . .

. . . but she was so damn wobbly that it took both my arms to keep her from falling!

I had to put Sushi down.

"Follow us, girl!" I commanded. "Mother, keep your breath held till we get out!"

She managed to nod, her mouth sealed.

As we descended the stairs, I could hear Sushi's nails clicking on the wooden steps behind us. I didn't dare breathe — the gas smell was everywhere.

Just as we got to the front door, Mother ran out of wind and gulped, taking in toxic fumes, then immediately collapsing in my arms.

But I dragged her out on the porch and unceremoniously down the steps — *klump! klump! klump!* — no doubt creating a few bruises, which was better than the alternative. Then I hauled her across the lawn and propped her up against one of the pine trees.

I was about to give her artificial respiration when she came around. "I'm all right, Brandy . . . I *am* all right."

That was when I noticed Sushi wasn't beside us.

I stood and frantically called the dog's name. Distressed, sick physically *and* emotionally, I looked toward the house.

Mother said weakly, "Brandy, no! Don't go back. It's probably too late. . . ."

"Since when did I ever listen to you?" I said with what was probably a grotesque smile.

And I dashed across the lawn and up the front steps.

At first I didn't see her, because I almost stepped on her: Sushi had made it to the foyer, where she lay, a little brown puddle. I scooped her up and dashed back outside, petting her all the way.

I was sprinting down the steps, wondering if it was possible to perform artificial respiration on a dog, when the world exploded behind us, the blast propelling me through the air, like I'd been shot out of a cannon.

I think I saw the red-hot fireball, consuming the house, before I passed out.

Or perhaps it was just another terrible dream. . . .

A Trash 'n' Treasures Tip

Garage-sale owners will often come down on the price of an item if you let them know the trashy treasure will be loved and cherished. Then they don't feel so guilty about selling Uncle Edgar's spittoon.

Chapter Eight
A CHURN FOR THE WORSE

I was *not* having an out-of-body experience, nor was I floating through a tunnel toward a bright light where dead relatives waited with open arms. Maybe that's because I was on my way to the "other place." Or maybe my idea of heaven wasn't dead relatives. . . .

I was, however, dimly aware of pain and discomfort, and a command to "cough," over and over, which hurt like hell. I couldn't understand why I was being made to do this, so my brain came up with a scenario. I was apparently caught in a simple computer program loop:

START,
COUGH,
GO BACK TO THE BEGINNING,
START,
COUGH,
GO BACK TO THE BEGINNING,
START,

COUGH,
GO BACK TO THE BEGINNING. . . .

And the realization that I would go on coughing and hurting for all eternity was like being buried alive. I'd have panicked if I weren't busy starting, coughing, and going back to the beginning.

If this wasn't bad enough, someone kept sticking the back of my hand with something sharp, which really irritated me. I managed to grab on to a hank of hair, before receiving a particularly sharp jab, then drifted off somewhere.

The first I was fully aware of Mother, sitting next to my hospital bed, she was smoothing my brow with her fingers, talking soothingly in Danish . . . a nursery rhyme she used to say to a sick little Brandy:

"Klappe, klappe, kage, I morgen skal vi bage, en til mor, en til far, og en til lille Brandy."

("Clap, Clap, cake, tomorrow we shall bake, one for Mommy, one for Daddy, and one for little Brandy.")

Slipping in and out of my drug-induced haze, I finally clung to wakefulness long enough to have a semblance of a conversation with Mother. I'd already taken stock of myself — little Brandy seemed to have all of her fingers and toes — and all I could think of past that was Sushi. Was she all right? Had my rescue effort been successful? But as I asked these questions, I knew in my heart my beloved pet was dead; still, I needed to hear it and start the grieving process.

Mother said, "Sushi's *fine,* dear. You somehow held on to the little dog, protecting her from that terrible explosion. And once out in the fresh air, she came around, scampering like a puppy."

I refused to believe that, and began to cry, which really made my chest hurt. "You're luh-lying," I said, sniffling. "You just don't want to tell me the truth."

Mother's expression was loving and, for once, nothing at all theatrical was in her manner. Her voice was gentle, soothing, as she said, "No, dear, I'm not lying, she's fine, just fine. . . ."

"Yes, you *are!* You think I can't —"

She squeezed my hand and said, "I *promise* you, Sushi's fit as a fiddle. I'll sneak her in here, next time I come."

I continued to sob. "It won't really be her . . . it'll be a stuffed animal and you think I won't notice 'cause I'm so messed up. . . ."

"Dear —"

"Or a look-alike Sushi, wearing white

contact lenses . . . That'd be like you! Just *like* you!"

A hatchet-faced nurse, in white slacks and a hideous teddy-bear-arrayed smock, appeared and, all business, told Mother that visiting hours were over and said that I needed rest.

Mother kissed me good-bye as the nurse fooled with my drip, checked her watch, pushed a button to release more pain medication, and I went to sleep again.

Klappe, klappe, kage. . . .

At least the tape loop had broken.

When I became conscious next, Peggy Sue was hovering over me, as if addressing a corpse in a coffin at visitation.

"I'm sorry, Brandy. I . . . I only did what I thought was right. What was best. Please forgive me."

My eyes popped open. "For what?"

My dry croaking voice seemed to startle her — it was like that moment in a slasher movie where the fiend who's taken enough punishment to be dead six times suddenly opens his peepers.

Touching her bosom, Peggy Sue said, "Nothing . . . I . . . I'm just so *glad* you're *alive*."

"For once we agree."

Sis swallowed and said, "When I think

227

what could have happened to you and Mother. . . ." She hugged herself and shuddered, as if from a cold breeze.

And breezes don't come any colder than death, do they?

After a moment she said softly, "Brandy, I know we don't get along, sometimes . . . so many years between us, but I hope you know . . . that you *do* know . . . that I love you very much."

Actually, I hadn't known that. I was moved to see my cold fish sis actually respond with such feeling to my dire circumstances, but also a little pissed. Did it take me nearly getting blown to smithereens to finally pry those words from my sister?

Well . . . maybe it *was* worth it. . . .

Then I heard myself saying, "I love you, too, Sis."

I meant it, I guess. Or maybe it was just the drugs talking. Maybe I was the narcoticized equivalent of a sloppy drunk getting sentimental.

My sister squeezed my hand, smiled a lovely smile — she really was pretty. "Can I get you anything, Bran'?"

She hadn't used that nickname in years.

"Well . . . there're some ice chips in that cup . . . that's all I can have."

Peggy Sue handed me the plastic cup. I

put some chips to my parched, cracked lips. Ice never tasted so good.

I asked, "What about the house?"

Peggy Sue shook her head. "Sorry."

"Sorry? That bad?"

"Worse. Gone."

"Everything?"

"Everything but the foundation."

I was almost afraid to ask the next question. No — scratch the "almost."

"Peg — the house *was* insured, wasn't it?"

Peggy Sue nodded, and relief flooded through me like another soothing drug.

"Yes," she said. "Thank *God* the premiums had been paid!" Her face brightened. "As a matter of fact, Mom's meeting with an insurance adjuster this morning. They're making plans to build a new house."

I must not have looked too happy because Sis said, "What's the matter? Don't you *want* a new house?"

"No," I said, pouting like an eight-year-old. "I want the *old* one. I *like* the old one."

She waved a scoffing hand. "Oh, the old drafty one with a leaky roof, you mean? With the peeling plaster, and rattling pipes?"

I countered with, "*And* beautiful woodwork, and unique parquet floors, and original light fixtures, and marble fireplace . . ."

Peggy Sue winced. "I wouldn't go singing the praises of that fireplace, very loud, if I were you."

Surprised, I sat up straighter in the only partly cranked-up hospital bed. "Was *that* the cause of the gas leak?"

My guess would've been the old sediment-filled water heater, or perhaps a ruptured underground gas line caused by Mother planting bushes without locating the main line first.

Peggy Sue chided, "Why in the world were you using that gas fireplace in the middle of a heat wave, and with the air-conditioning on?"

"What? Don't be silly, Sis. We *weren't*."

She arched an eyebrow. "Well, it didn't turn itself on. Mother's fired that up in summer before. She doesn't exactly stand on ceremony when she gets a notion."

"It wasn't even cool enough to shut off the air conditioners and open the window, let alone use the fireplace."

Peggy Sue half smirked. "Maybe that blind mutt of yours did it . . . accidentally, of course."

Whether she meant that to be funny or not, I can't say — I know she didn't care for my having brought a dog into that house. Either way, I laughed, even though it hurt.

"That's right," I said, "blame a blind, ten-pound dog for our misfortune."

"She does have the run of the place . . . *did* have. Could she have bumped into that old-fashioned dial — maybe gnawed on it like a bone and —"

"Are you *serious?*"

She stiffened. "I'm just exploring the possibilities."

"Way things are going for the Borne girls, I wouldn't be surprised if Sushi *did* turn on the gas — to put us all out of our misery."

Peggy Sue, who was humor-impaired, seemed miffed and said, "Well, you don't have to be sarcastic about it. Don't you think it's important to know how it happened?"

"Sure — but let's start some place more logical than my blind dog mistaking a metal dial for a bone."

That was Sis and me — destined to mix like oil and water, even a loving conversation degenerating into the dumbest argument possible.

Peggy Sue gave her well-shellacked brown locks a toss, not that they were going anywhere. "At any rate, you and Mother will get a brand-new house, out of this misadventure — not to mention two hundred thousand for the contents."

I nearly choked on my ice chips. "*What* contents?" I asked. "The valuable stuff was sold to Clint Carson for peanuts!"

Peggy Sue shrugged, and her thin smile had something almost wicked in it. "I wouldn't mention that to the insurance company, if I were you. I've already advised Mother not to . . . Anyway, who can put a price on memories?"

Sometimes my sanctimonious sister could be rather unethical, to say the least. But this was Mother's call; my impulse at the moment, at least in my current half-drugged state, was to stay out of it.

Before our conversation had a chance to deteriorate even further, Mother swept in, cheeks flushed, carrying the large red tote bag with purple boa feathers that she usually lugged along to her Red Hat meetings.

My first instinct was that Mother was smuggling in some of her wonderful Danish cuisine — rhubarb pie sprang to mind — when she reached into the bag and produced . . .

. . . *Sushi!*

And I don't mean raw fish.

I cried out with joy, which hurt, but who cared?

Sushi, for her part, was so happy to "see" me that she squirmed out of Mother's hands, barking, and scampering up the thin bedcovers to my face — which she licked ferociously — and, in her excitement, peeing on my pillow. Just a little.

Mother, vindicated, said, "See! I *was* telling the truth! Dead dogs don't pee!"

Sis smirked. "Is *that* the name of the mystery your Red-Hatted League's reading this week?"

Well, maybe not *entirely* humor-impaired. . . .

Perhaps now would be an apropos time to mention that I was in a semiprivate room, which of course means not private at all — I shared this space with another female patient. Except for almost getting blown up, I had lucked out, landing the bed next to the picturesque windows overlooking Serenity General's beautifully landscaped grounds; my roommate was stuck with the bed close to the noisy hallway.

My roommate — whom I hadn't actually seen because of the privacy curtain between us — called for the nurse, and when the nurse came, ratted on us, tattling that we had a dog in the room.

Within moments, Mother and Peggy Sue and Sushi were told in no uncertain terms by the nurse — the teddy-bears-picnic-smock-sporting harridan — to leave . . . immediately.

"Having an animal in this sterile environment is a serious breach," the nurse informed us.

As my visitors were escorted out of the room, I heard Mother say, "Don't you know there have been studies about the positive effects animals can have on the infirm? Perhaps this environment is *too* 'sterile'!"

I only caught part of the nurse's response . . . something about one more word and calling security.

After a glare at the curtain separating me from my invisible (but pain-in-the-butt) roomie, I turned my slightly yellow-stained pillow over, pushed the pain medication button myself this time, and happily sailed off to sleep, with nary a tape loop nor a Danish lullaby.

Next morning, Officer Lawson dropped by.

I was in no mood to talk to anybody, much less a cop, much less a *handsome* young cop, having had a terribly restless night — seemed every time I'd fallen off to sleep a nurse came in to check my temperature, or blood pressure.

Nor did I care to be seen by anyone other

than family, who would be required to excuse my disheveled appearance and bad breath.

But a man's gotta do what a man's gotta do, and Officer Lawson was a police officer doing his duty, so I did my best to be civil.

As Lawson jotted notes on a little pad, I recounted the evening of the explosion as I remembered it — Mother and I went off to bed about the same time; no, I didn't smell any gas at the time.

"First I noticed it was when Sushi — my dog?"

"Yes, your dog."

"When my dog woke me up."

"What time?"

"I have no idea — early morning hours. I was tired, and would've been groggy even *without* the gas."

He nodded, the puppy-dog brown eyes sympathetic (and by "puppy-dog" eyes, I don't mean he had cataracts). "Ms. Borne, did you hear anything out of the ordinary during the night?"

"What happened to 'Brandy'?"

He smiled a little. "That's what I'm here to try to find out."

I smiled back; he was pretty cute — probably as cute as I wasn't right now.

I asked, "What did you mean by, did I

hear anything 'out of the ordinary'?"

"Like someone in the house. An intruder."

"A burglar, you mean? Fat lot they'd find at *our* place!"

He shook his head. "It's a nice house, and a burglar wouldn't necessarily know about the lack of furnishings, till he or she got inside."

I shrugged. "Maybe — but I didn't hear anything. Like I said, I was way tired, sleeping pretty deeply."

He nodded. "Do you usually lock your doors at night?"

"Well . . . sometimes Mother can be lax about that," I admitted.

"Some older people are," he said, with a smile and a head shake. "They grew up in a different world than we did."

"Mother's *still* in a different world . . . If someone *had* broken in, wouldn't it be hard to prove? I mean, what with the house blown to smithereens?"

"It would." Lawson scribbled on his pad.

"What *is* a smithereen, anyway?"

He smiled again. "I've never actually seen one. But I'm glad you weren't blown into 'em."

"You and me both . . . By the way, who called 911? I'd like to thank whoever it was. Talk about a good neighbor."

Lawson stopped writing. "You mind if I sit?"

"No. Please."

He pulled up a chair, settled in. "Actually, Brandy, I was the first one on the scene."

"Really? You weren't responding to a call?"

"No — I'd been patrolling a few blocks away when I heard the explosion. I was the one who called it in."

"You always seem to be around when we're in trouble."

His expression turned shy. "Small town," he mumbled.

"You know my first name — what's yours? Or is it really 'Officer'?"

He grinned. "I told you before, Brandy —"

"Sorry. I'm a little . . . 'almost blowed up.' "

"Good excuse."

"Anyway, thanks for being there, Brian."

Lawson swallowed and became business-like again, flipping his notebook back open. "Has anything unusual happened recently to you or your mother?"

I half smiled. "Brian, it's starting to feel like every *day* is unusual for us."

The officer studied me, then said, "For somebody in a hospital bed, you're sure dancing around, aren't you?"

"I don't know what you're getting at," I said, but of course I did.

"What's been going on with you and your mother, since that night out at Carson's?"

"Not that much."

But I wasn't feeling well enough to lie worth a damn.

The flirty friendliness was out of the air. Brian was gone and Officer Lawson was back, frowning at me. "I understand you don't feel well, Ms. Borne, but I'd appreciate a little more cooperation."

My smile was weaker than I was. "Sorry."

"I'm waiting," he said, pen tip to pad.

I began tentatively: "Mother and I *have* been doing a little . . ." I searched for a word not as silly (and for that matter, self-condemning) as *snooping*. ". . . *inquiring* into the death of Clint Carson."

I could tell he didn't like the sound of that. An edge — and some amped-up volume — was in his voice as he said, "After the chief advised you *not* to?"

My roommate moaned.

I put a finger admonishingly to my lips. I whispered, "Please — people are trying to recuperate, around here."

Lawson lowered his volume but the edge remained. "All right, Kinsey Millhone — who have you and Jessica Fletcher been bothering?"

I put as much innocence in my tone as I could muster. "We haven't been 'bothering' anyone. You know how this town likes to gossip."

He just arched an eyebrow at me — an attractive if intimidating gesture.

"Mother talked with two other people — men — who were also swindled by Carson. I don't remember their names, they're some older gents she numbers among her friends — you'll have to ask Mother . . . I believe one was a former mayor."

"That takes care of what your mother's been up to. What about you? Who have you been talking to?"

I shrugged. "Besides you and Chief Cassato? Only one person, really. Old high school pal."

"Who?"

"Uh, Joe Lange. You probably don't know him."

Did I detect a reaction in those brown eyes? Or was the pain medication distorting my perception?

"I probably *do* know him," Lawson said. "That oddball who likes to hang around out at the state park."

"That's harsh — he's just a guy who enjoys the great out-of-doors. No law

239

against it. Anyway, Joe's in a position to see lots of things."

His eyes narrowed. "Such as?"

Such as you and Mia having a little get-together, maybe? I thought.

But I said, "Excess activity around Carson's place. It's not Wild Cat Den, but it's in the same general vicinity."

Lawson grimaced and flipped the notepad shut. "All right, Ms. Borne — I guess that's all for now."

He was on his feet again when I asked, "The explosion? It *was* an accident, wasn't it?"

His expression told me nothing; his words weren't much more informative: "We won't know for sure until the gas company and fire department give us their reports — and maybe not even then."

I sat up some more. "You don't think . . . Do you think Mother and I stirred something up?"

He shrugged.

"Brian — are we in any danger, Mother and I?"

A long sigh. "I don't think *anything* at the moment . . . but it could be possible that one of you's come too close to the killer for comfort."

"The killer's comfort?"

"Anybody's comfort. Where's your mother right now?"

I swallowed. "Staying with my sister. She lives out in the Mark Twain addition with her husband and daughter."

He drew in air, filling his admirable chest, and nodded again. "I'll have a patrol car make a few extra more runs through there — especially at night."

"Officer Lawson . . . Brian . . . you're scaring me."

"Good," he said. "Meddling in police work is a dumb idea."

I must've looked white around the gills, because Lawson said reassuringly, "You'll be all right in here. I'll stop by the nurses' station and fill them in."

"Thank you," I responded weakly.

"See you . . . Brandy."

A while later, Dr. Englund came by on his rounds. He'd been working in the ER when I was brought in, and now he was stuck with me.

The doctor was in his early forties, slender, with black wavy hair, dark penetrating eyes, and a thin long nose.

"And how are we today?" He had a nice smile that included lots of very white teeth.

"You're the doctor," I said.

Dr. Englund consulted the chart in his

hands. "Well, Miss Borne, you have three broken ribs, a punctured spleen — which we've operated on — and a mild concussion. I'm going to order another CT scan, to make sure there's no fluid buildup on the brain . . . so you're going to be with us for another day or two."

I raised my black and blue hand with the IV. "When can I get this thing out?" I asked. "Gives me the creeps."

"It gives you what you *need,*" he said. "For today, anyway . . . and in the meantime, I want you to do some leg exercises, every hour — just bend your feet back and forth slowly, to prevent blood clots."

Didn't *that* sound scary?

"Okay," I said timidly.

"And we're going to get you up and walking this afternoon."

"You have to be kidding! I can barely sit up."

"Sooner the better. You want that IV out, right?"

"Right — but how can I go for a stroll hooked up to it?"

The doctor shared the nice, toothy smile with me again. "You'll take it along," he said. "That's your new best friend."

"I guess I can use a friend about now."

"I hear you. Hang in there, Miss Borne."

Dr. Englund moved on to my neighbor, their voices muffled behind the drawn curtain. But soon the woman's high, whining pitch came through loud and clear.

"I was supposed to have a *private* room!"

"I'm sorry. If one becomes available we can move you, Mrs. Taylor, but as it is right now . . ."

I only caught snippets of the woman's indignant but lowered-voice rebuttal, including "like Grand Central Station," and "can't get a moment's rest," and "is this a hospital or a kennel, are you a doctor or a vet?" and "like something out of *The Beverly Hillbillies.*"

I called out to Dr. Englund.

He poked his head around the curtain. "Yes?"

"We could trade bed stations," I whispered. I really didn't care where my bed was. "That is, if it won't confuse matters, or make things any more difficult for you or her. . . ."

The doctor thanked me for being so magnanimous (I was just trying to minimize the whine, tell the truth) and said he would take it under consideration. Then he disappeared behind the curtain again, returning to his consultation with my unhappy roommate.

In the afternoon, as promised, another nurse clad in one of those unfortunate teddy-bear smocks came around and made me get out of bed. The pain medication had worn off, and it was too early to get more, so I was in a lot of discomfort.

At first, I was too dizzy to even stand; the nurse, steadying me, told me to keep my eyes open and focused. Then slowly the three of us (me, nurse, and my new friend) (you remember IV Poley) made our way to the door, down the hall a smidgen, then turned around. The ties on my thin hospital gown did little to keep me from feeling that my personality was hanging out.

As I returned to my bed, I got a good look at my roomie, who was also hooked up to her own friendly IV: middle-aged, shoulder-length curly light brown hair, puffy eyes, blotchy face. Well, no patient looks good in the hospital. But surely the dirty look she shot me wasn't necessary.

The nurse helped me back into bed and was gone before I could ask for another blanket. *God,* but the room was *cold!* I was staring at the blank television high on the wall, wondering if I dared watch *Reno 911* and risk the wrath of my neighbor, when another visitor took me completely by surprise.

Jennifer Kaufmann stood at the foot of my bed with a vase of yellow roses in her hands.

You may remember Jennifer from our rest-room confrontation at the Red Hat mother/daughter day. And I could not process her presence here: why would the wife whose cheating husband had cheated with yours truly be bringing me flowers? I would have doubted she'd do that for my funeral, much less hospital stay.

Then I noticed the pink and white candy-striped apron over her lilac silk blouse and slacks. She was one of the volunteer workers from downstairs in the gift shop, and I was nothing special, just her latest stop.

"I, uh, heard what happened," Jennifer said, her voice soft. "How awful for you and your mother."

I tried to look beyond the compassionate smile and the sympathetic eyes, for the slightest hint of malice.

None.

Damnit.

This was truly rotten of her — the last thing I wanted to do was *like* her.

I said, "Those are for me?"

Jennifer blinked, then said, "Oh yes," as if she'd forgotten about them. She handed me the little envelope that had accompanied the roses and asked, "Would you like me to set these with the others?"

"Oh, ah, yes, please."

Jennifer made room on the window ledge, which was already loaded with arrangements: Mother had given me a pot of red geraniums; Peggy Sue a mixture of white mums and pink roses; Ashley, yellow daisies; and Tina, some of her own prize-winning irises for me to plant later. If I couldn't find a job, I could always open a slightly-used-flower shop.

I said, "Thanks for bringing these."

"That's all right. It's my job."

"I know. But when you saw it was me . . . you could have asked somebody else to bring them. And you didn't. And that was decent of you."

She swallowed — I actually heard the gulp. "We'd be kidding ourselves if we thought we'd ever be friends, Brandy. But it's a small town, and we have some mutual acquaintances, so . . . the past is the past. Let's just leave it at that, and move on."

And she moved on.

I waited until she'd gone before opening the small white envelope and pulling out the card, which read: *Dear Mom, hope you get feeling better. Love, Jake.*

The message wasn't in my son's cramped

handwriting, of course — the flowers having been called in, probably by his dad (whose presence by way of flowers was noticeably absent) — but it still meant the world to me. I clutched the little note to my chest and allowed myself a few tears.

Midafternoon, Tina breezed in, carrying a black gym bag loaded with lotions, makeup, and other assorted goodies.

First, she gave me a sponge bath, mindful of the stapled slit on my stomach, about which she commented, "You were never much for bikinis, anyway."

Next she slathered on this great-smelling Victoria Secret's body lotion, followed by a foot massage.

We didn't talk much, throughout all this attention, and that's one of my favorite things about my friendship with Tina: we're comfortable enough with each other *not* to make conversation for its own sake.

But she did say, "What happened, honey — did it have anything to do with this silly Sherlock Holmes stuff?"

"I don't know, Teen. I really don't."

"Well . . . I know I kind of encouraged you to do that."

"Not really."

"No, yeah, but I did. And that was probably stupid. I hope you'll forgive me."

"I will if you'll wash this greasy hair of mine."

She did, which we accomplished by me hanging my head over a plastic tray, with her blowing it dry, and styling my naturally wavy locks with a straight-iron. When Tina was finished, I couldn't believe how sleek and modern my hair looked. Wow!

Suddenly, I felt 100 percent better — I could've done cartwheels down the hall . . . only IV Poley probably would have objected.

"Brandy, one other thing . . . and maybe I shouldn't even mention this, but . . ."

"Well, you *have* to now!"

Uneasily, Tina said, "Kevin and I were at the Octagon last night, and I saw your old friend there again — that Mia?"

"I had the feeling she kind of hung out there."

"Well, I saw her talking to somebody at the bar, and it might . . . never mind."

"Teen!"

"Well, she was talking to that redheaded clerk from Carson's shop. I don't remember her name."

"Tanya."

She shrugged. "They weren't doing anything suspicious, but . . . they were talking. I hope mentioning that was the right thing to do."

If Mia knew Tanya, then Mia probably knew Carson — and maybe in a pharmaceutical way.

Finally, my sweet, dear friend did my makeup using Benefit pink face power in "Dandelion," Shiseido eyeliner in "Bronze Goddess," Bobbie Brown mascara in "Coal Black," and Chanel lip gloss in "Cry Baby."

As if I weren't spoiled enough already, out of her seemingly bottomless bag, Tina produced a pale blue cotton-knit DKNY robe and matching nightgown, plus a pair of warm blue UGG slippers.

What did I ever do to deserve a friend like Tina?

As my wonderful spa and salon treatment came to an end, the latest teddy-bear nurse arrived with a wheelchair to take me down for my CT scan (the results of which I hoped would confirm that I still *had* a brain).

Ever have one of those? (A CT scan, I mean — not a brain.) (Well, obviously you have a brain.) (No offense.) You have to lie still, entombed in a big cylindrical X-ray machine, for what seems like a thousand years, give or take. If you're the least bit claustrophobic, you're in trouble.

Of course, none of the technicians appeared to know anything about my results

— or if they did, they weren't talking.

Be that way.

I returned to my "suite," only to discover that Dr. Englund had indeed taken me up on my "magnanimous" offer, my bed having been switched with my roommate's. *Yes!* Less whining, fewer steps to the facilities. Anyway, I sincerely hoped that this new arrangement would turn her disposition sunnier; it's no fun being around a grouch.

Supper was clear broth, orange Jell-O, apple juice, and vanilla ice cream. Nothing to write Duncan Hines about, but I ate every morsel.

After the trays were cleared, my roommate spoke to me for the first time, her voice timid and a tad embarrassed, from behind the curtain.

"Thank you for trading places," she said.

I reached out and pulled back the barrier. "No prob — and I'm sorry about this being Grand Central Station." I wasn't being facetious.

She smiled a little and her wan face looked almost pretty. "I apologize for being such a . . ."

Bitch? I thought.

But said, "No problem, really."

"I guess I should have been more understanding. . . . I'm Linda Taylor."

"Brandy Borne. What are you in for?"

I was making it sound like jail, but then there *were* similarities, including not being able to pick your roommate.

She said, "Hysterectomy."

"Oh." Something I hoped never to go through.

She laughed dryly. "My doctor acted like it would be no big deal. . . . That's a *man* for you."

"Dr. Englund?"

"No, he's fine! It was my gynecologist who ripped everything out, then went on vacation."

No wonder the woman has been temperamental.

She was saying, "It's not like I wanted more children — I have two — but now, it's just . . ." Her hand with the IV went protectively to her abdomen. ". . . it's like the door's completely closed."

She seemed near tears.

To ease her through the moment, I asked, "Where are they, your kids?"

"They live with their father."

"We're not so different. My son lives with *his* father."

"You been divorced long, Brandy?"

"Not very."

"I'm an old hand at it, I'm afraid. My kids

wanted to come visit — Robby's thirteen, Matt's nine — but I really didn't want them, you know . . . *seeing* me this way."

"Sure."

Linda seemed to study me for a while before saying, "I shouldn't bother you with my problems."

"It's okay."

"I mean, you seem to have your own share."

"That just might be an understatement."

". . . sorry. I never *meant* to eavesdrop."

I laughed a little. "How could you *not,* when my family's around?"

We talked for another hour, bonding as you do with someone who shares a like experience. When Linda began to yawn, I said good night and closed the curtain.

I gave myself another dosage of pain medication and pulled the covers up around my neck.

"Brandy?" Linda's voice seemed far away.

"Uh-huh?"

"What do you want to do about your flowers?"

"There's no room over here . . . you enjoy them."

"Thanks . . . they are nice."

I yawned. "Sleep tight."

"Thanks . . . thanks. . . ."

Sometime later, the night nurse tiptoed in and took my blood pressure.

Shortly after which, the world turned wild, the mundane hospital tedium going haywire — doctors and nurses pouring in, frantically pushing equipment.

Panic spiked through me. *Was something wrong? Something wrong with* me?

But the parade passed my bed, converging on Linda's side of the room.

Soon it was clear . . .

. . . my roommate was in serious trouble.

I clasped my hands, and like any true agnostic in trouble, I began to pray: *Dear Lord, make her journey painless . . .*

"Stand back!"

. . . give her peace . . .

"Again!"

. . . bring comfort to her family . . .

"Stand back!"

. . . and friends.

"She's gone."

Amen.

A Trash 'n' Treasures Tip

"You break it, you bought it." Don't you believe it. See Minnesota ruling, Ye Little Ol' Antique Shoppe vs. Kafer.

Chapter Nine
CLOCK ON THE WILD SIDE

The day after the death of my hospital roommate, my life began again.

My brain scan came back okay, and Dr. Englund came around for one last look, after which I was released. Even though I felt perfectly fine, and had been making my way to and from the restroom all by myself like a grown-up, a nurse's aide insisted on taking me out in a wheelchair — hospital policy, protection against lawsuits, no doubt. The aide, a heavyset young woman (who thankfully was not attired in the Teddy-Bear Brigade uniform), deposited me at the curb like luggage at an airport. Lawsuit threat or not, the aide disappeared back into the hospital with an automatic-door's *whoosh* while I waited alone for Peggy Sue to bring her car around.

The parking lot was busy with patients and visitors, and assorted others, including Jennifer, who had arrived for her stint in the flower shop and was getting out of her emerald-green SUV. She saw me and waved and summoned up a small smile. I half waved back and gave her a slightly bigger one, trying to meet her more than halfway. Like she'd said, this was a small town, and if we took a stab at civility, the notion of me going after her husband again would remain buried for both of us.

But I wasn't disappointed that Peggy Sue pulled her chocolate-brown Montana up to the curb in time for me to avoid another stilted exchange with Jen.

Peggy Sue was a chatterbox driving us to her house; she loves to take charge of a crisis, especially when it doesn't directly involve her.

She was saying, "We'll put Mom in the upstairs guest room, and you can have the daybed in the basement sewing room. It's small but not really cramped. It's just for sleeping, anyway."

I nodded.

She gave me her most patronizing smile (which was pretty damn patronizing). "Of course, I'll expect a little *help* out of you girls — you know, do your own laundry, cook a few meals now and then . . ."

I gave her a sideways look, and she corrected herself. "Well, *Mom* can cook . . . I realize that's not your strong suit."

"Remind me to be offended later."

She pretended to find that funny, then said cheerfully, "You better just stick with cleanup patrol."

"Aye-aye, Captain."

She chattered on, and I looked out the window, barely listening, only enough to recognize a cue where I was meant to leap back in; those wouldn't come often.

After a while, my sister took her eyes off the road for a moment. "You're kind of . . . quiet."

"Mm-hmm."

". . . Are you feeling all right?"

"I guess." I gave her an arched-eyebrow look. "You know, I did just get out of the hospital."

We turned off the bypass and onto a blacktop road that led to her upscale housing addition.

She asked, "Brandy, is it . . . is it that woman who passed away that's got you down? The one in your room?"

I nodded.

"These things happen," she said. "I'm sure God had a reason."

"For a woman dying of complications of a hysterectomy? And what reason would that be?"

Peggy Sue pulled up into her driveway. "Well . . . I don't claim to know. . . . But I'm *sure* there is one. The Lord works in mysterious ways."

I said, "Doesn't He, though?"

She shut the car off, sighed. "Brandy, we're going to be sharing living quarters until the new house is built . . . so I hope you're not going to make your stay unpleasant. . . ."

I gave her my sweetest and most insincere smile. "Not any more than usual."

"You *are* guests. . . ."

"I know. And I appreciate this, Peg. I really, really do. But let's just try not to impose on each other, any more than we have to."

She blinked, as if trying to translate my words from Esperanto. "What do you mean?"

"I mean, Mom and I will stay on only as long as we absolutely have to. And we'll do our share. But spare me the 'Christian' values. You're red state, I'm blue state, and never the twain shall meet."

Peggy Sue looked mildly horrified. "You and Mother *are* Christians — *aren't* you?"

"By our definitions, yes. Maybe not by yours. And that's somewhere I think we shouldn't go."

"Well . . ."

"I'll gladly sleep in the sewing room and be grateful for the privilege — really, truly. But Mom and I don't need to be preached at, in either the spiritual or secular sense. *Capeesh?*"

"What a terrible thing to say."

"It's Italian."

Peg's eyes and nostrils flared. "That's not what I meant!"

I held out my hand. Absolutely straight, I said, "Truce?"

Her hard look melted, and for a just second there, I thought maybe she really did love me.

"Truce," she said, and took my hand and squeezed it.

Uncle Bob, Ashley, Mom, and Sushi were waiting in the large sunny kitchen where a computer banner welcoming me home — well, welcoming me to *their* home — had been slung across the doorway. Nearby, on the round oak table in the casual dining area, was a white sheet cake decorated with one word: KA-BOOM! (Mother's touch, I'm sure.)

There were hugs and kisses and promises to get along, and I even got a little teary-eyed; maybe it was the extra medication. Then we served up the cake and Whitey's peppermint ice cream, my favorite. I even gave a little tiny spoonful to Sushi (but don't tell the vet).

When the dishes were done — by yours truly — Mother helped me get settled into my temporary digs downstairs. Tina, bless her generous heart, had earlier in the day dropped off a big box containing some of her summer clothes, shoes, and purses, which Mother and I unloaded, and began hanging on a portable clothes rack. A note pinned to a Trace Reese dress of hers I'd coveted last year claimed that the donation hadn't even made a dent in her closet.

What a pal!

I don't care what anybody says: it pays to have a clotheshorse for a friend.

If you're wondering what Mother was doing to take the place of her demolished attire, here's the wacky if not unexpected lowdown: she raided the community theater's wardrobe department. At the moment, Mother was dressed as the title role of *Madwoman of Chaillot* in an 1890s black lace blouse with mutton sleeves, a black alpaca skirt, a half dozen long-beaded necklaces, and a white feather boa. But instead of button-top shoes, she wore Birkenstocks.

The most chilling thing about the ensemble was how natural it looked on her . . .

My temporary quarters consisted of a brass daybed, a modern white dresser, and a full-length oval mirror on an oak stand. An expensive, state-of-the-art sewing machine against a wall meant I had no excuse for walking around with a split seam.

On the pale yellow walls were framed samplers Peggy Sue had created, her initials in the corners. A few were sayings, painfully cornball, like HOME SWEET HOME and A PENNY EARNED IS A PENNY SAVED (like she'd ever saved a penny!), but others were sentimental scenes of bygone times, like Christmas carolers, and Victorian children sliding down a snowy hill. I had no idea my sister was into that kind of thing, and it gave me a twinge of sadness that I hadn't.

Mother, finished with her fussing, joined me on the edge of the daybed.

I began, "There's no sense worrying Peggy Sue, so let's keep this conversation between us. . . ."

Mother, always up for a conspiracy, nodded, eyes dancing with childlike excitement . . . and deviltry.

I continued: "It's now become crystal clear that . . ." I found myself goggling at her madwoman getup. "What *else* was available in the wardrobe room?"

"That *fit* me? Lady Macbeth."

Define "fit."

"Oh," I said. "Well. Nothing contemporary?"

"Just *Everybody Loves Opal,* but I can't risk wearing costumes from an ongoing production. That way lies madness."

She always has a reason, yes she does; deeper you probe, the more likely you are to find one, and the less likely you are to like it.

Mother patted my hand. "Go, on, dear. . . . Your line was, 'It's become crystal clear that . . .'?"

"It's not a 'line,' Mother — it's real life!"

"I know, dear. Our house exploded. I was there."

I gave her a disgusted smirk. "Well, keep that in mind. Because what's clear is that I'm somebody's target."

"Target? For what?"

"For what else, Mother? Harm!" I leaned closer. "What if I really *was* meant to drive out to Carson's house that night, straight into a murder frame-up?"

I was immediately sorry I'd used the words "murder frame-up," because her eyes went wide at a term her Red-Hatted League had encountered many a time in the pages of Agatha Christien unreality. And I needed her to focus on the reality of the threat that she herself had pointed out, days ago, and that I was increasingly convinced of, myself.

She clasped my hand, too tight. "What has brought you around to my way of thinking, dear?"

The notion that I had come around to her way of thinking was unsettling.

"Oh, I don't know — maybe . . . our house blowing up?"

Mother's eyes narrowed behind the magnified glasses, as much as they could, anyway. "Good point."

"And what if it was *me* who was supposed to die last night? Not Linda Taylor."

Mother shook her head, waved that off. "Brandy, that poor woman died from complications of her operation. It was her time, that's all."

I lowered my voice. "What if it was supposed to be *my* time — what if it wasn't God or the Devil or the Guy with the Scythe who came around that hospital room, last night, looking for Linda Taylor . . . rather, Clint Carson's *murderer* looking for *Brandy Borne?*"

The eyes were huge and buggy now. "How is that *possible?*"

"It's ridiculously possible, Mother — and

I caused it."

"You?"

"I traded beds with her. Trying to be nice."

Mother was shaking her head. "But wouldn't the . . . the *murderer* have recognized his own victim?"

Now I shook my head. "The room was darkened, Mrs. Taylor sleeping, covers pulled up around her face. I was in the next bed, sleeping, not looking like me. It was something that had to be done quickly — would have been easy for the murderer to be interrupted, so haste was unavoidable."

Mother still wasn't getting it. "Why didn't *you* look like *you?*"

I gestured with open hands, in frustration and bitter amusement. "Tina had come in and given me a hospital room makeover, to improve my spirits — straightened my hair. . . . Don't you see?"

Mother's expression went from disbelief to realization in three seconds flat. "Oh my . . ."

"And after they took Mrs. Taylor out, they moved me . . . up to the next floor, in a room by myself, right across from the nurses' station . . . *and didn't put my name on the door.*" I shook my head. "Everyone was acting so *weird.*"

Mother said, "Well, they had just lost a

263

patient, after all."

Shaking my head firmly, I said, "No, it was more than that . . . it was lots of things, including the way the nurses were whispering. Once, in the night — I couldn't sleep — I came out of the room and they were like, 'What are you doing? Get back in there! Keep that door *shut!*' and all. Not mad, *concerned.* And not just concerned, but . . . spooked."

"Oh dear."

" 'Oh dear' is right, Mother. Those hospital types, nurses and doctors, they've seen it all — since when do *they* get spooked over a death in the night?"

"Seldom, I would say."

"I would, too. And I thought I heard Officer Lawson's voice out in the hall, but was too doped and sluggish to go have a look . . . besides thinking those nurses would jump on me again."

Mother was frowning in alarm. "The police came?"

"Well, I'm not positive about Lawson. But I am about Cassato."

"The chief himself?"

"That's right. No minor underling like Lawson this time, oh no. Chief Tony Cassato, Serenity PD numero uno, started asking me lots of questions, like about who I remembered came into the room that night and when."

"What did you tell him, Brandy?"

"About who came in?" My frown made my chin crinkle. "That's just it, Mother . . . I don't remember who all came in. That's the downside of that pain medication — and you can even hallucinate on the stuff, so my memories aren't reliable."

"When you spoke to Tony — Chief Cassato — did you learn anything? Get anything out of him?"

I shook my head. "Bubkes. Not that I didn't try — but you know Tony, half professional, half enigma. He was typically tight-lipped."

Mother's voice was soft and unnervingly sane. "And what did you garner from his reluctance to share information about your own dire situation?"

"His clamming up only confirmed my belief that my roommate's death was suspicious."

"He didn't confirm that, directly? Didn't tell you what it was that caused Mrs. Taylor's death?"

"No. Oh, I asked, and he said only, 'Autopsy will tell.' When it does, though, I bet *he* still won't. . . ."

Mother stood suddenly and began to pace

in front of me, like a lawyer in front of a jury box, during summation. But Mother wasn't summing up; she was still question-ing — me.

"Dear, whoever would want to harm *you?*"

I said, "Honestly, I can't think of anyone — a few people have grudges against me, but nothing that justifies murder. And I haven't been home long enough to make any new enemies."

"Then why you?"

"Maybe it isn't me, personally, so much as something I . . . *we. . .* have stirred up."

Mother nodded. "You could be right, dear." Then she asked, "Who did come to see you in the hospital? That you can re-member?"

I shook my head. "Coming up with a list of visitors is pointless, Mother."

"Why?"

"It's a hospital, not a prison — visiting hours or not, anybody can get on any eleva-tor in that place and come up to whatever floor he chooses. Anybody who walked by my door could see my name, and what bed station I had been assigned."

She planted herself suddenly and her eyes blossomed hugely behind the glasses. "Some of the Romeos were at the hospital!"

"Really?"

"Yes, yes — the day after you were admitted — Harold and Marvin. You were still unconscious, but they came in while I was with you and —"

I cut her off: "What significance could *that* have?"

"Well, both gentlemen had serious run-ins with the murder victim. Neither exactly shed a tear when Clint Carson went to that great flea market in the sky . . . or, more likely, rummage sale down below. What if one of them killed him?"

I was shaking my head again. "And, what? Tried to pin it on me, and when that didn't work, attempted to murder me? I could see one of them waging a vendetta against Carson, but involving me, in that convoluted fashion? And sacrificing *you,* who were also in the house when that gas was turned on? That doesn't make any sense."

Mother sighed, obviously disappointed that her old friends hadn't wanted to kill her. "You're right, of course, dear. Anyway, Harold and Marvin were probably principally at the hospital to lend support to Floyd Olson, who was in Short Stay for a colonostomy."

Little in town got past Mother.

She said, "Well, it becomes painfully apparent that you need protection, Brandy. Why don't we go see that nice young handsome policeman — Officer Lawson? Is he married, by the way?"

"Mother . . ."

"Tell him our concerns. Perhaps he can help."

"No. Absolutely not."

She frowned. "Why ever not?"

"Because I don't trust him."

And I told her about Lawson possibly being seen with Mia at Wild Cat Den.

Wearily, she plopped down next to me on the daybed. "How terrible. Seems you can't trust anyone these days. . . . Why didn't you *tell* me about your Wild Cat Den adventure before?"

I hadn't wanted to encourage her in the amateur sleuth area, but I said, "I wasn't sure I'd come up with anything pertinent. . . . Anyway, why didn't you tell me about my old friend Mia? Clue me in about this whole police-force drug scandal?"

Knowing Mother, she'd have followed every aspect of the case in the local media down to the smallest detail.

"Because you and Mia were friends, once," Mother replied, "and I didn't want you getting involved with her again. A good parent doesn't want a child running with a rough crowd, you know."

My eyes popped. "Mother! I think I'm old enough, and wise enough, to make that decision myself."

She raised an eyebrow, eloquent in its reminder that my life had recently fallen apart and I'd had to come running home to, yes, Mother.

We fell silent, lost in thought.

After a moment, I expressed mine. "And Mia was seen recently with Ginger. . . ."

Mother's brow knit. "Who?"

"Oh — that clerk at Carson's store . . . that's how I think of her — Ginger, not Mary Ann."

"Tanya, dear. Her real name is Tanya, or at least that's what she uses. Who knows if anyone in Clint Carson's life is what he or she professes to be!"

I let that pass, and got back on point: "Tanya could be the key to this whole mess. Can you think of anyone who'd know more about Carson and his business?"

And we both knew that the call that had begun all this, left on our answering machine, was left by either Tanya or someone claiming to *be* Tanya.

Mother perked up. "Shall we go talk to her?"

I laughed humorlessly. "Oh, sure. We'll go

do that right away — only, we don't know where she lives, or if she's even still around town. She could've blown this pop stand, particularly if she was involved with Carson's meth biz."

Mother was thinking again; not always a good sign. "I'm not so sure, dear. Remember, I ran into her at Carson's store, not so long ago."

"Sure, but that was right after . . . You're not saying the store is still *open,* are you?"

Mother explained patiently: "Not 'open,' per se. But some of the merchandise was on consignment, and therefore not part of Carson's estate — I understand Tanya has been contacting those people to come by and pick up their antiques."

I just looked at her. "How do you know these things?"

Mother seemed shocked. "Dear — I'm Vivian Borne! What goes on in Serenity that I *don't* know about isn't *worth* knowing."

Maybe Peggy Sue could sew that on one of her samplers. I looked at my wrist and realized my watch was one of the many casualties in the house explosion.

"Mother, what time is it?"

Mother checked her watch, which (like her) had survived the blast intact. "Two PM."

I stood. "Well — what are we waiting for? We're the Snoop Sisters, aren't we?"

"I prefer to think of us as the Borne to Win Detective Agency. . . . I'll just get my hat and parasol."

"Do you really need those?" I asked, wincing as I took in the items hanging on the end of the clothes rack — the wide-brim hat smaller than a tractor wheel (just), loaded with faded silk flowers of every variety and color, and covered with white netting. The parasol was pink and was, well . . . a parasol!

"Of *course,* dear," Mother said, grandly patient. "The hat *makes* the outfit, and, anyway, I heard it was going to rain."

I sighed. "Well, all right . . . but hanging around with you, I feel underdressed. . . ."

My eyesore of a car — my only insured possession, and unharmed in the blast (damn!) — was hidden away in the Hastings family's third garage. I told Peggy Sue that Mother and I were going out to run a few errands, which she was fine with as long as we weren't late for supper. So now my older sister had taken on the role of my mother and her own mother's mother. *Please God, make our stay here short. . . .*

The warm, sunny morning had surrendered to a cloudy, dark afternoon, cool wind

271

whipping in from the north. Big drops of rain had begun to fall, just the occasional warning pellet, but enough to prompt turning on the car's wipers, which sounded like fingernails dragged across a chalkboard. When we cruised slowly by Carson's store, I noted that the heavy wooden and very much tightly shut front door wore a CLOSED sign, visible behind its etched glass.

I swung my Taurus around the corner, then drove down a narrow alley behind the building, where a sky-blue Mercedes sat in an alcove adjacent to the back door of the shop.

Mother and I exchanged raised-eyebrow looks.

"Tanya must be doing well," said I.

"Very well, indeed," said she.

I parked, purposefully blocking the Mercedes; then we got out and went to the door. I knocked.

Nothing.

I knocked again, really, really loud.

Really, really nobody answered.

"Might be unlocked," Mother said.

"Isn't that breaking and entering?"

"It's entering," she said with an innocent little shrug, "but not breaking."

The door, indeed, was unlocked, almost as if Mother had willed it so.

The air within was oppressively dust-laden as Mother and I climbed a flight of wooden steps that led to the first floor. We arrived and promptly announced ourselves by sneezing three times each (mine: chipmunk; Mother's: moose in labor).

After this unintentional proclamation of our presence, I expected a glaring Tanya to greet us as we emerged onto the main floor, perhaps with a weapon in hand, to ward off intruders; but neither woman nor weapon appeared.

In fact, as we moved deeper within the first floor of the venerable building, Tanya was nowhere in sight.

The shop was still full of antiques, primarily furniture but also occasional display cases of collectibles; here and there outlines in the dust spoke of consignment items that had been carried off by their owners.

I walked over to the raised cash-register island and peered over the counter. A computer monitor had gone into screen-saver mode, indicating that Tanya had been away from it for at least a while. Resting by the feet of the office chair was a brown Gucci hobo bag. So the woman hadn't left the store. Briefly I had a flash of that tale of the woman declared missing because her purse had been left behind; suddenly it seemed less ridiculous. . . .

Walking around big old empty buildings has a certain built-in creep factor, but — despite a core skepticism of anything mystical — I had a real sensation that something was wrong here, that something (all right, I'll say it) sinister was in the dust-mote-floating air.

And a sense that we were not alone.

I turned to speak to Mother, but she had disappeared.

At least she'd taken her *purse* with her.

Fighting panic, knowing Mother was as capable as any small child of wandering off unattended, I nonetheless ran to the back where I had seen her last, my footsteps echoing off the hardwood floors like machine-gun fire.

"Mother! . . . *Mother!*"

Suddenly a door next to the stairs flew open, and Mother stood framed in the archway, adjusting her girdle.

"Well, the girl's not in here," she announced, adding, "By the way, I wouldn't use the toilet — it doesn't flush."

I waited for her to approach me; then I took her by both arms, firmly, and my eyes locked on her buggy ones. "Mother . . . please stay with me . . . *don't* go wandering around."

"Of course, dear. But you can't blame a girl for having to tinkle."

I let go of her. "Well, you didn't have to scare the piss out of me doing it!"

She gave me the reproving "language!" look.

I sighed and said, "Okay, now you've tinkled — any other urges or impulses, check with me, first, before acting on them."

"You're treating me like a child!"

"Right . . . now stay with me."

And admittedly there really was little difference in taking Mother out these days and Jake at age three — I'd have been better off with Sushi.

I sighed. Swallowed, not relishing the dust taste. Then I said, "Let's check upstairs."

Taking the lead, I navigated the narrow paths between antiques, some stacked on top of each other. We were nearly to the stairs when Mother shrieked.

I spun, hair on the back of my neck standing up straight. "What is *it,* Mother? What's *wrong?*"

Mother pointed to a particularly ugly bowl on a table. "That carnival glass — it's marked at seventy-five dollars! Anyone can *see* that it's chipped."

My eyes tightened to where I couldn't see much, and what I could see was red. "*Mother*

— can you *please* behave?"

Mother frowned, half cross, half hurt. "Have you been taking your medicine?"

"Have *you?*"

Mother, indignant, snapped, "Certainly," sounding just a little like Curly in *The Three Stooges.*

I let out yet another sigh, a very, very long one. Then I said, "Okay — okay. We're both properly medicated. So let's both just settle down. . . ."

We climbed the stairs, which were wide enough for us to do so side by side.

Near darkness awaited. The second-floor ceiling lights were off, and with the storm brewing outside, the row of windows facing the street offered little help for our vision. Those windows rustling with wind, however, did aid and abet our fear.

Up here, very little of the merchandise had been cleared out, a looming armoire looking like a large tombstone, and an ornate floor lamp a skeleton. A row of grandfather clocks stood like weird figures staring at us from the darkness, waiting to strike. Suddenly this was a graveyard of antiques, and I shivered.

"Tanya?" I called out.

Silence.

"Tanya!"

Mother, her eyes searching the vast, dim expanse of furniture, said, "Maybe she's in the basement."

"But we came *in* that way."

"We didn't look around, though . . . and there are lots of rooms down there."

She had a point.

"Let's do it," I said, fighting crankiness and not succeeding terribly well.

As Mother moved away from me, I asked, "Where are you going now?"

"The basement."

"The stairs are over there . . ."

Mother's condescending expression granted me dispensation for being young and foolish. "Why climb down two flights of stairs, when we can take the freight elevator?"

"Maybe . . . because we don't know how to use it?"

But Mother had already disappeared into the darkness, her voice emerging to say, "I do, dear. Nothing to it!"

Managing not to bump into anything, moving down an aisle of strange shapes like Snow White through the scary forest where the wicked witch sent her to die, I caught up to Mother at the elevator as she was about to enter.

"Mother! *Stop!*"

As she took a step into dead air, I grabbed her arm, and for one heart-stopping moment, I thought we were both going to tumble down the shaft!

But I also had hold of the retracted wooden gate, and with some difficulty pulled us back, where we collapsed on the floor in an undignified (but at least alive) pile.

I squawked at her: "You can see a *chip* in some *carnival* glass at *fifty feet* — but you couldn't see that *elevator* wasn't there?"

Mother, alarmed, said, "But . . . but the gate was open! The gate shouldn't be open if the elevator's not waiting. . . ."

I spotted a mag-light hanging on a nail, got up, and fetched it. Then I knelt on my still-shaking knees by the edge of the elevator shaft and beamed the flashlight upward.

"There it is," I said, "just above us — I think it's stuck in between floors."

Mother, still seated on the floor, huffed, "Whoever used that elevator last should have been more careful. It would have served them right if I'd fallen!"

Deciding not to dignify that with a response, I couldn't help directing the beam downward into the yawning mouth of our near-fate, to morbidly assess what would have been waiting for us.

For one thing, we would have had company. . . .

"And when I see that Tanya," Mother railed on, "I'm going to give her a stern talking —"

"I wouldn't bother, Mother." I gulped. "She . . . she's down there."

"Where?"

"Right where you said she was — the basement."

Mother crawled over and looked down the shaft where the flashlight's beam revealed the limp, twisted body of the store clerk.

"Oh dear," Mother gasped, and touched her bosom delicately. "She must have made the same mistake *I* almost did . . . fell down there by accident."

"Accidental, like Clint Carson's body waiting in the road for one of us to run over . . . accidental like our gas fireplace getting turned on in the summer and our house blowing up . . . accidental like my hospital roommate dying after I traded beds with her . . . *that* kind of accidental, Mother?"

Mother thought for a moment, then, absurdly, "You're suggesting she was pushed, aren't you, Brandy?"

"Yeah," I said dryly. "That's what I'm suggesting. And I'd suggest, now, we call the police."

"That," came a deep voice from the darkness, startling us, *"won't be necessary."*

Officer Brian Lawson emerged from the gloom and stood a few yards away; his gun was drawn — not quite pointing at us, but not quite *not* pointing at us.

Where he had come from, I couldn't say. I certainly hadn't heard him approach. Maybe he'd been hiding in the dark the whole time; if so, he knew how to minimize his breathing.

And yet I'd had that sensation that we weren't alone here.

Several things clashed in my mind, not completely formed thoughts, just snippets: *Wild Cat Den, Mia, meth, Carson, Lawson . . .*

Had my knight in blue armor had something to do with the death of Tanya?

Mother said, "Thank goodness you're here, Officer! That poor woman is lying at the bottom of the elevator shaft."

I got to my feet and helped Mother up. "Yes, it's a good thing you happened to be here," I said, putting no suspicion in my voice, but remembering that he'd happened to be patrolling in the area at the very time our house blew up.

Taking Mother's elbow, I gently guided her away from the open mouth of the shaft.

Lawson, his gun still aimed in our general

direction, wore a decidedly nasty expression — damn near a sneer. "You girls just can't stay out of trouble, can you? Had to continue sticking your noses in."

I huffed with forced indignation: "I don't know what you're talking about! We're here on business . . . to pick up some antiques we had here on consignment."

He was at the edge of the elevator now, body turned so that his torso faced us while he looked down, grimly. "Looks like somebody consigned Tanya to the bottom of this shaft."

I kept working at indignation, but it wasn't flying. "We just happened to find her, Officer — right now. You must've seen us!"

Lawson stepped a few feet away and talked into his shoulder — some of it was official numbers that I frankly can't remember, sort of *Adam-12* cop-speak; but he seemed to be calling the death in.

Then he swung back toward us. "You two're coming with me."

"Where?" Mother and I asked.

He didn't answer, but motioned again with the gun. "Get going."

Was Mother as afraid as I was?

If so, she hid it well, demanding, "Young man, are you arresting us? If so, on what charge?"

He ignored this and just said, *"Move."*

"Move *where?*" I asked.

"Downstairs," he said, and thankfully holstered the gun. "My car's in back."

I took Mother's hand. Were we going back to the station — for another round in the "Interview Room"? Or was Lawson a dirty cop, up to his badge in meth and other drugs and the murder of Clint Carson?

Either way, I didn't know what to do about getting Mother and me out of this situation. One could be answered with a call to Mr. Ekhardt; the other didn't present any solution at all, unless I wanted to tackle him or something, wrest that gun on his hip out of his holster. . . .

I was still frantically thinking it through when we were outside, where Lawson put us once again in the backseat of the police car, which was blocking mine, blocking Tanya's.

He stayed outside the vehicle talking into his shoulder again, but I couldn't hear what he was saying to whoever was on the other end of the radio. After a good minute or even two, Officer Lawson got behind the wheel, slammed the door, and we headed down the alley.

Mother and I were quiet on the short ride along Fifth Street to the Safety Building.

But when the car went on by, we both broke out in protest.

Fear spiked through me. "Where are you taking us?"

Mother shouted at the wire separating us from Lawson and the front seat, "I demand to see my lawyer!"

Banging on that wire with both hands, I yelled, "This is kidnapping! We haven't been charged! You won't get away with this!"

Mother's cries were overlapping mine: "If you don't pull over, young man, we're going to sue the city of Serenity for every cent in its coffers!"

Lawson said nothing.

Not a peep.

At the end of Fifth, we bumped over some train tracks, sped down a dirt road between a defunct tool factory and a condemned grain silo, and came to a dusty halt in front of an abandoned warehouse.

My heart was pounding.

Lawson got outside the vehicle.

"Mother," I whispered, "after we get out, I'm going to rush him — I'm going to grab his gun and toss it to you and then I'm going to claw his eyes out."

"Well . . . it's a little rash . . . but —"

"But nothing — if he gets us inside that warehouse, we're finished. He's the one behind all this — he's a dirty cop."

Mother looked out the window at him, frowning, as if looking for dirt smudges and finding none. She turned to me. "A small suggestion, dear? You kick him in the nuts, and I'll gouge his eyes out. Two are better than one."

"Okay. Okay, Mother. We'll go with *your* plan. . . ."

Lawson was about to open the door with his left hand, his gun out again, in his right.

Mother said hurriedly, "Brandy, there's something I should tell you . . . something about Peggy Sue. . . ."

"Another time, Mother." Lawson had his hand on the back door handle. "Get *ready*. . . ."

But my blue knight played it smart.

After opening the car door, he backed away as we climbed out, letting his gun do the talking.

"After you, ladies."

Mother and I clutched hands as we walked slowly, tremblingly toward the warehouse, Lawson bringing up the rear, keeping a safe distance.

"Inside," he ordered.

We could do nothing but obey.

The building we stepped into — once owned by a company that made office furniture — was now neglected and empty. Rusty, bleeding pipes ran the length of the high metal ceiling, the concrete walls peeling green paint.

"Mother," I said, "I'm sorry for every lousy, selfish thing I ever did or said, and for any trouble I've caused you."

"Brandy, dear, don't talk like that. Perhaps Officer Lawson will listen to reason."

"No, Mother, I don't think so. And it's my fault. I let us get in over our heads, this time. . . ."

"Through there," Lawson commanded, his gun pointing to another closed door, bearing a timeworn, barely decipherable title — FOREM N'S O FICE.

I turned the knob with a quavering, old woman's hand — and a woman about to die is about as old as a woman can be.

The door swung inward.

Mother gasped and I just stared, open-mouthed.

The office was a high-tech hideaway of flat-screen computers, security monitors, neon wall maps, and other gizmos worthy of the Bat Cave. This inner chamber was as modern as the building's exterior was not.

Though the room was good sized, only one other person was there: a dark-haired woman seated at one of the computers with her back to us.

Mia swiveled in her chair.

She rose, strode toward us, stood, hands on hips, brown eyes blazing, nostrils flared, lips a tight, thin line — I hadn't seen Mia this mad since camp, when I threw her Chatty Cathy doll down the outhouse toilet.

"What the hell do I have to do," she snapped, "to keep you two morons from blowing my cover?"

A Trash 'n' Treasures Tip

When buying antiques and collectibles via the Internet, use the same kind of caution and scrutiny you use when snagging a pair of Louboutins.

CHAPTER TEN

DO TELL MOTEL

We sat at a very low-tech card table in the high-tech chamber — indignant, irritated officers Brian Lawson and Mia Cordona, and chagrined would-be sleuths Brandy and Vivian Borne.

"You will understand," Lawson said tightly, "that there isn't much we can tell you . . . other than that you've stumbled into — and seriously *endangered* — a major ongoing investigation into drug trafficking in eastern Iowa."

"Oops," I said.

Mother said, "Involving Clint Carson, you mean?"

"I mean," Lawson said, "you've stumbled into and endangered an ongoing investigation into drug trafficking in eastern Iowa."

"Oh," Mother said.

"We are doing you a favor," Lawson continued, "by talking to you ourselves — you can see by the size and sophistication of this operation that a couple of cops from the Serenity PD aren't the *only* law enforcement professionals involved."

"You mean," Mother said, "Chief Cassato and the state police and even the DEA are in on it?"

"I mean," Lawson said, "that a couple of cops from the Serenity PD aren't the only law enforcement professionals involved."

Mia's big eyes were boring into me like dark lasers. Her words were crisp, uncompromising: "I didn't purposely sully my reputation as an officer of the law so you two chuckle-heads could ruin all the months and months of groundwork I've put in."

"This is about Juan, isn't it?" I asked, sheepishly. "About finding the people responsible for your little brother's death . . . ?"

She exchanged glances with Lawson, who nodded his permission to Mia.

"Yes," Mia said softly. Then the hard edge returned: "But Juan is only *part* of it. He represents scores of other kids, and adults, too, who throw everything away when they spiral into meth addiction. This is a serious business you're playing with."

My embarrassment gave way and irritation surged forward. "Do you think we don't *know* that? We lost our home, and almost our lives! Somebody tried to frame me for Clint Carson's murder, and I'm supposed to sit back and take that lying down?"

Mother said, "I don't think you can sit and lie down simultaneously, dear."

"Shut up, Mother. Brian — Officer Lawson — what do you have to say to *that?*"

His expression was hard and unapologetic. "Someone may have set you up for the Carson killing, but thanks to your mother here, that didn't come off. I don't blame you for that — no one can, or even would. But you two, both of you, have blundered around asking questions and causing trouble and damn near blowing this undercover operation, when you should have sat back, or lain down or whatever the hell, and let us do our jobs."

"I . . . I am sorry," I said, my irritation back to chagrin.

Mother chimed in, "Me too," then added lamely, "But we were just trying to help."

Lawson closed his eyes momentarily, then opened them and said, "Your kind of help, Mrs. Borne, we can do without."

Mother's chin went up. "I don't think it's necessary to be rude."

"Perhaps not," Lawson said. "Let's hope it's also not necessary to charge you with obstruction of justice."

And with that, Mother and I both swore to keep Mia's undercover identity a secret, and not (heart crossed) (fingers, too) do any further meddling. . . .

I asked for a moment alone with Mia, and Lawson sighed, flashed an annoyed look at Mia, who rolled her eyes and sighed back at him . . . but they both allowed it.

My brown-eyed blue knight escorted my mother toward the door and left Mia and me at the card table.

"That's why you told me to stay away from Todd, isn't it?" I asked. "He's a suspect or something, maybe somebody dangerous — it's not because he was your boyfriend. You were concerned about my safety."

Expressionless, she nodded.

"Would you consider telling me one thing? Is there a possibility Clint Carson was having an affair with a respectable local woman?"

Mia frowned. "Why do you ask?"

"It's an impression I got, that's all . . . from my snooping."

"Be more specific."

"I can't. I'd just like to know if there's any truth in it."

Mia considered the question. Then she gave me a curt nod.

"Who?" I asked.

"We don't know. But we have reason to believe he did have such a relationship, yes. It factored into his ability to take advantage of prominent local elderly people — the way he did with your mother, virtually stealing her precious antiques."

"I see. Thank you."

She said nothing.

"Mia, I value our friendship," I said. "Or anyway, the friendship we used to have . . . and I hope maybe someday we can pick back up where we left off."

She looked at me coldly. "Is there anything else?"

"I . . . I guess not."

I got up and moved away from the table.

Halfway to Lawson and Mother and the door, Mia's voice rang out in the cement-walled chamber: "Brandy!"

I turn and froze — after all, she was a cop.

She walked up slowly, her face as unreadable as a carved wooden mask, and, suddenly, she took me in her arms and squeezed me in a warm embrace.

I thought I saw a tear trailing down a dark cheek as she whirled away, putting her back to me as fast as she could.

A smug Lawson escorted a chagrined us into the backseat of the squad car again, then headed toward downtown. He said nothing as Mother and I sat behind the wire barrier, our seat belts buckled, our hands folded in our laps, two scolded children.

As Lawson turned into the alley behind Carson's antique store, an ambulance was pulling away, no siren — if the "patient" within was Tanya, as I expected was the case, no siren was necessary. A dark green Buick pulled out after, and I recognized the driver as our county coroner.

Two other police cars, lights flashing, blocked the immediate area around the rear door of the building, crime-scene tape draped ominously around the periphery.

Depositing us near our parked car, Lawson opened the door and gave me a blandly contemptuous look as we emerged — and having passed through fear and embarrassment, I was now approaching boiling mad.

I asked, "Could we have a word, Officer Lawson?"

"I told you that —"

"This isn't about the case. Not really."

He let out a bunch of air and nodded. Mother stood out of earshot, giving us a respectful privacy (except I think she was trying to read our lips) as we spoke.

I began: "Was it really necessary to scare us like that? You could have told us right away that we'd intruded into an undercover operation, and needed to brief us elsewhere — how were we to know you weren't the killer?"

"Me?" He blinked in surprise and indignation. "Are you kidding? How was I to know you two weren't the perps? That you didn't push that Tanya character down that elevator shaft yourselves?"

"You were watching us — you saw us discover the body!"

His eyes got tight. "I'll tell you what I was watching. The alley. We've had this building under surveillance for days now, and've logged the names of everybody who's gone in and out of that back way, picking up their consignment goods. And I saw Tanya help them out with their stuff, in every instance — right up to where you and your mother went in there."

Frowning, I said, "And . . . and you came in after us?"

"That's right."

I tried to parse that. "So we're . . . suspects?"

He shook his head. "No. You're right — I saw you discover that body. I know you didn't do it."

"Then who *did* do it?"

Now he was the one who seemed embarrassed. "Must've been somebody Tanya let in the front way. . . . We're a small force. We couldn't afford two cars and two officers to properly watch that place."

I gave him a "poor you" look. "Oh, that must be *frustrating* — so you took the frustration out on *us,* scaring the bejesus out of us."

His hands went to his hips, heel of one on his holstered gun; his brown eyes were very attractive, even when they were filled with anger. "I *saved* your silly asses, getting you out of there, fast as I could — how could I be sure the killer wasn't still in that building, somewhere in the dark? I did you a favor!"

"Well, next time you 'save' me, Officer Lawson — don't be such a jerk while you're doing it!"

We glared at each other.

Mother strode up, and she'd heard that last part, because it had been shouted — I couldn't fault her for eavesdropping (in this instance).

Arms folded grandly over her bosom, she looked down her nose at the officer and said, "My daughter is right — we're both deserving of better treatment, and more respect — after all, I'm seventy years old."

Seventy-four.

His frustrated face moved from me to

Mother and back again. "All right, all right ... maybe I was a little heavy-handed about it, but neither of you seems to grasp the seriousness of this. . . . Three people are now dead as a consequence of this situation, and —"

"Three?" I said. Now my eyes tightened. "Then that means my hospital roommate *was* murdered — and I was the intended victim."

"Yes," he said, "and yes, some sicko injected cleaning fluid into Mrs. Taylor's IV."

Mother's mouth dropped open like a trapdoor. "Oh . . . oh my. . . ."

I, of course, was not surprised.

Lawson's face softened; he touched my sleeve, tentatively. "Please — accept my apology, cut me a little slack, and will you *please* let us do our job? Stay out of mischief. Keep out of harm's way. Go home."

Which we did.

The latter, anyway.

Before long Mother and I were sitting at the kitchen table at Peg's, coffee cups in hand. As Mother poured me another round, she said cheerfully, "Well, look at it this way, Brandy — at least Mia isn't a drug dealer!"

"I just hope nothing we've done has put her into any danger."

Mother frowned at me thoughtfully. "Why did you want to talk to her without *me* around?"

I couldn't tell her that I was hoping to find out whether her daughter — my sister, and under whose roof we were residing at the moment — had been having an affair with Clint Carson. Of course I ruled Peg out as a murder suspect — she would hardly have tried to murder us! But what Ashley had told me about the woman at that motel, who'd argued with Carson and gone off in a vehicle like Peggy Sue's, well . . . that might put my sister in the middle of this mess.

And if that were the case, Peggy Sue could be in as much danger as the rest of us.

If only I felt comfortable enough with my sister to ask her!

But I shared none of these thoughts with Mother.

And when she asked again, "Why didn't you want me to hear what you two girls were talking about?"

"It wasn't that," I lied. "I just thought, since we were old friends, that Mia might open up a little, one on one."

"But she didn't?"

"No."

"She gave you a hug."

"That's all she gave me, Mother."

Mother studied me, and I wondered for a moment if she suspected I wasn't being wholly forthcoming. But she didn't ask anything else, merely excusing herself to go take a nap — she had *Opal* rehearsal tonight.

I was staring into about half a cup of coffee when Peggy Sue wandered into the kitchen.

"Can I fix you something to eat?" she asked me. "We're not having anything here tonight, I'm afraid — Bob and I have a dinner dance at the country club."

"I can take care of myself, thanks. Sis . . . would you sit down for a minute? And talk?"

This seemed to surprise her, understandably.

"Let me get myself some coffee first," she said, and did.

Then she was seated across from me, sipping her cup, waiting for me to take the lead.

"Sis . . . I don't mean to be out of line, but — is everything cool with you and Bob?"

Her smile had a frown in it. "What brought that on?"

"Please don't ask. Just . . . this isn't easy for me. Please be honest with me. I really don't mean to pry."

Her blue eyes flashed. "Well, what else

would you call it? Bob and I are fine. I love him, he loves me, and I think he loves me no less even though I've invited my strange family members to live with us indefinitely, which makes him quite a guy, wouldn't you say?"

I wasn't sure how much sarcasm was loaded in there; I never am with Peg.

"Did you know Clint Carson?"

She laughed. "What, am I a suspect now? Aren't you taking this Nancy Drew thing just a little too far?"

If I never heard the words "Nancy Drew" again, it would be too soon. . . .

I shrugged. "I just wondered if you knew him. I mean, antiques aren't your thing, really."

"No. I like new things. But I saw him that day at the Red Hat luncheon, of course."

"Had you ever gone into his shop?"

"Brandy! What is that *about?*"

"Why is that such a terrible question? He was murdered, and somebody tried to frame your own sister for it! And said sister has now been the subject of *two* attempted murders growing out of —"

"Well, I want to strangle you right now. Does that count?"

I sighed. Pushed the coffee cup aside. "Fine. Never mind."

I got up and was halfway out when Peggy Sue said, "I knew him a little. He . . . he hit on me when I was in the shop."

Swiveling to her, I said, "Really?"

She touched her shellacked hair. "Don't sound so surprised. A few men on the planet might still find your ancient sister attractive."

"I didn't mean —"

"I would buy collectible trinkets in there, from time to time, for Mother. And now and then for you. Remember that autographed David Cassidy LP I sent you for your birthday last year?"

"Yes . . . I forgot about that."

Her smile was frosty. "I'm glad it meant so much to you. Well, I bought it at Carson's shop. And that, Brandy, is the extent of it. After he got a little too . . . familiar . . . I never went in there again."

"Thanks, Sis."

"Why? Why are you asking?"

"Nothing. Just a loose end, a thread."

Her expression took on seemingly genuine concern. "Well, careful. You know what happens to sweaters when you start pulling on loose threads."

"Nothing good."

"Nothing good," she affirmed, and returned her attention to her cup of coffee.

Later that evening, Peggy Sue and Bob drove Mother to her play practice on their way to the Serenity Country Club. Ashley was, typically, out with friends.

I played with Sushi for a while, then wandered around the house, taking an inventory of furniture that would never gain value as antiques, no matter how many hundreds of years passed. As dusk set in, the restlessness became unbearable, and I went out to my car, leaving Sushi penned up and with water (Peggy Sue didn't want her to have the run of the house, and I couldn't blame her, even though Soosh already had the Hastings layout down pat).

After driving around the streets for a while, I wound up in Weed Park — I think I mentioned that the land had been donated to the city by a family named Weed. And as long as there was still a Weed rooted in Serenity, the city didn't dare change the park's name to something more inviting.

The park had once been home to a small but wonderful zoo. There was an elephant named Candy, and an assortment of ill-mannered monkeys, including a tattered old gorilla that looked like a person wearing a cheap costume in an Abbott and Costello movie. The orangutans were especially nasty; you couldn't stand too close because they could spit a country mile, and make the most obscene gestures. I'm sure the endless parade of teasing kids made them that way.

Most memorable at the zoo, however, was the vile-smelling log cabin snake house, home to a variety of slithering reptiles, which were truly frightening, not to say gross — watching the python eat his mouse dinner was enough to put you off your own meals for a week — and the rattlesnakes would strike at your hand on the glass, which was scarier than a Freddy movie.

As a kid, I felt sorry for the caged creatures . . . and apparently I wasn't the only one.

One sultry summer night someone released all the animals, snakes included, and major panic issued. The seemingly docile elephant, in a mad dash for freedom, overturned parked cars, knocked down phone lines, and trampled anything else in its path. The monkeys, taking no interest in making a break for the state line, ran roughshod over the downtown, smashing windows, scattering trash, swinging from the lampposts, terrorizing the riverside apartment dwellers.

Word spread like wildfire that the town was under siege. I happened to be at Mia's for a sleepover, and when we heard about the snakes getting loose, Mia grabbed baby Juan's toy rattle, and we sneaked out of the house.

Now, I can't say whose idea it was — back then Mia and I seemed to think with one collective, mischievous mind — but we ran through the neighborhood, crouching in bushes beneath bedroom windows, and shaking the toy loudly. We could hear the people behind the glass, rustling around in fear, sometimes screaming for their lives.

Eventually, through the long night, most of the animals were captured with the help of the National Guard . . . but for one holdout.

The gorilla climbed on top of one of our taller buildings — three whole stories, I believe — where he swaggered around and occasionally clung to a TV antenna like a low-rent King Kong. A photo made it onto the A.P. wire, and he was instantly, if briefly, famous all over the world. But by noon the next day, the gorilla was tired and hungry and came down with the bribe of a few ripe bananas.

One thing was clear to the town after the Great Zoo Escape: those animals were angry at us. After that, the zoo was dismantled, leveled, and turned into flower gardens . . .

. . . with one exception: the snake house.

Mother went before the city planning commission to plead for its life; I was in the seventh grade, and was along for the ride — this was one preservation cause I could sink my little fangs into. Mother produced old letters that proved the log cabin had been used as a secret way station for slaves heading north, and therefore had historic value. As for me, I regaled the council with such wonderfully poignant memories as the time Tubby Calloway got locked in there all night on a dare, and the tarantula got loose, and by morning his brown hair had turned white. (The white hair part wasn't true, but it really sold the story.) (The Underground Slave Railroad yarn somehow seemed to carry a little more weight with the council.)

As I drove slowly past the former snake house, the cabin looked forlorn and forgotten in the shadows of a park streetlamp.

How could I have been so wrong about Mia?

Now some things that had made my brain hurt previously were suddenly making sense: Mia's warning to stay away from Todd at the club, as we'd discussed; but also the sad, almost apologetic look she'd given me when I left the Octagon House; and her meeting with a cop who might have been (*was,* I now knew) Brian Lawson out at

Wild Cat Den.

What a dope I had been, blundering in the world of dope.

On the other hand, Mia might really have gone down the wrong road; *anybody* can — drugs are a potent force, and once hooked, a person can change from good to bad.

As I caroused around Weed Park, my thoughts gathered into possibilities, and suddenly my aimless driving took on a purpose.

I steered my pee-colored Taurus out a back road, which connected to the river road.

Dusk had given way to darkness when I pulled into the Haven Motor Hotel, the cluster of small cabins tucked back a discreet distance from the road.

I parked next to the main, much larger cabin, which was also the residence of the owner, and went into the front office, an old-fashioned bell on it jangling as I did.

I doubt that anything much had changed here in fifty years. I stepped up to a chest-high pinewood counter behind which hung an old wooden board with rusty hooks for real keys. A thin young man in his early twenties looked up from a *Maxim* magazine. He wore a short-sleeve white shirt with a red bow tie that was apparently his night clerk uniform; a badge identified him as Ron.

Not a bad-looking kid, but life had somehow put him behind this desk in a short, short haircut (Army Reserve?) and nature had provided a heavy five o'clock shadow, crooked teeth, and enough pimples to make his probable sex life revolve around a magazine with Pamela Anderson on the cover . . . a bitter irony, considering the constant thought of illicit sex taking place behind every closed door of the facility he was tending. Ouch.

"Sorry," he said, "we're full up." He seemed a little shy, and he obviously thought I was pretty cute. No Pam Anderson, but cute enough.

Piece of cake.

Giving out my prettiest smile, I said, "I don't need a cabin . . . just need a little help."

"Oh . . . sure." He closed the magazine. "I have a car jack, if that's —"

"No! No, no, thanks, that's generous. . . . I'm a reporter with the *Sentinel.*"

A mild look of alarm took over his pleasant, tortured features. "Oh . . . well, I'm sorry, but we respect the privacy of —"

"This isn't a current client — it's actually a deceased one. Maybe you've already talked to the police about him."

That really alarmed him. "Who do you mean?"

"Clint Carson. The antique dealer who was killed not long ago? Not far from here?"

Relieved that this pertained to a past client, he said, "Yeah, sure. I knew that guy. He came out here once in a while."

I leaned an elbow on the counter; was that Old Spice? Probably. "Was he here with the same woman every time?"

That question he didn't like much. "Ahhh . . . I don't know. . . . He'd come out here by himself, and check in. . . . I didn't really see who he was, uh, hooking up with. . . ."

"Not even a glimpse?"

"Well . . ."

I fluttered my eyelashes; yes, I did, so sue me. "Do you think it was different women . . . or just one? The same one?"

"Lady . . ."

Bad sign. I'd gone from a potential Pam Anderson replacement to a "lady."

But I kept trying: "For example, did she have red hair? Or was she a brunette, maybe?"

I was losing him.

And then the well-worn curtain separating the back living quarters from the office jerked open, metal rings clanging.

This was a relative of Ron's, and I didn't have to be Nancy Goddamn Drew to figure that out: he was a twenty-years-older, no longer skinny and badly acne-scarred version of Ron, probably his dad, also wearing the white shirt and red bow tie . . . a real professional. *Rob,* his name tag said.

"What does the little lady want, Son?"

Now I was a *little* lady. Was that a demotion, or a promotion?

"Just some . . . you know, information, Pop."

Ron's pop, Rob, frowned at me. "Lady, we specialize in *not* giving out information . . . and we're all booked up tonight."

I mumbled a "sorry," and threw in a "thanks" for good measure, and beat a hasty retreat.

Frustrated, I lingered outside in the glow of the Haven's yard light to collect my thoughts, and my eyes drifted to my car.

That was funny.

I looked from my Taurus to the light and back again.

Under the lamp's reddish bulb, my yellow car looked almost orange.

And then I knew.

Knew it all, knew damn everything.

But most of all, I knew the real color of the SUV the mystery woman drove, Clint

Carson's companion that night at the Haven when Ashley had been there, too, the woman with whom he'd shacked up and argued and, just maybe, provided with a motive for his own murder.

A Trash 'n' Treasures Tip

Estate "tag sales" are generally overpriced, so don't go until the last hour of the last day. Greedy relatives will be forced to take your offer, or face up to hauling the leftovers to the Dumpster.

CHAPTER ELEVEN
VASE THE MUSIC

The next week was the longest of my life, or at least the longest since I'd broken up with my husband. My elation over figuring out what had really been going on was soon dashed on the rocks of Officer Lawson's reaction, which was nothing compared to Chief Cassato's.

"After everything that's happened," the chief had said, with that handsome ugly face set in its sternest mode, "you *still* went out sticking your nose in?"

"It was something I had to do." We were seated in the chief's office, Officer Lawson and me — Mother wasn't along. "It was personal, and I won't comment further on that."

I wasn't about to bring Peggy Sue into this.

Cassato said, "I don't say there's not merit in what you've told me —"

"Merit! I've just solved your murders for you!"

I heard Lawson sigh beside me, but Cassato remained an imperturbable blank slate. The chief sat behind his desk, hunkered forward, hands folded.

"Let's suppose you have solved 'em," he said. " 'Solve' in the sense that you've pointed us toward the person who very likely did commit these crimes."

Perhaps too smugly, I said, "Let's."

His head shake was weary. "I can tell you right now that nothing we've turned up so far supports your theory."

"But —"

He held up a traffic cop palm. "Put the defensiveness aside, Brandy — I think you're right."

I blinked. "You do?"

"I do. So does Officer Lawson here, and the detectives on the case, both my men and the BCI group from Des Moines. But here's the problem — we could be weeks, perhaps even months away from having the forensics evidence we need to back your theory up."

I was shaking my head. "I don't care *how* long it takes you, just so —"

Another "stop" palm.

This time Lawson spoke. "Ms. Borne, we're concerned — for your safety, *and* your mother's. We have an individual, here . . . a killer who's taken three lives and made several attempts on yours . . . who is clearly out of control."

Cassato said, "We are frankly concerned about what this perpetrator might do between now and when we have our legal ducks in a row."

Lawson again: "You're going to have to play things very careful. We don't want to tip our hand to the killer, and set off another murder or attempted murder or God knows what. This is *not* a stable individual."

I sat forward. "How can I help?"

Cassato frowned. "Don't you think you've done quite enough for us already?"

I had searched for sarcasm in there, but wasn't good enough a detective to find it.

And now, a long week later — filled with sleepless nights and nightmares when I did sleep and stomach-churning concern for myself and my mother and my sister — I found myself stumbling out into the sunshine along Main Street's Pearl City Plaza with its pricey antique shops (Carson's closed, however), cute boutiques, and restaurants.

Noon at the Grist Mill restaurant was hopping as usual. I entered via the front, through the antique and collectibles portion

311

of the store, and stood in the arched brick doorway taking in the lunching patrons in the intimate eatery, hoping for a familiar face.

As it was, I saw nothing *but* familiar faces. . . .

At one of the larger of the many oak tables, with distinctive vases of silk flowers at every one today, a group of wine-drinking ladies of the Red-Hatted League chatted like magpies, some half crocked, a few fully loaded. At another, the Romeos hunched over cups of strong coffee and were having a serious discussion that I guessed to be political in nature, until the words "Cubs" and "this season" floated my way above the din.

Joe Lange was making a rare public appearance, dining with his middle-aged mother at a table for two. The pleasantly plump woman looked happy — pleased her son was back on his meds — he seemed uncharacteristically mellow, if typically uncomfortable in civilian clothes.

As for me, I was not at my best, and had definitely not walked right off the cover of *Lucky* magazine: I was wearing a pink blouse with coffee stains, a patchwork skirt with part of the hem hanging, and blue rubber flip-flops . . . and my grooming was not top-drawer, either, my hair straggly and with hardly any makeup on — I hadn't even bothered touching up my dark sleep circles.

No one paid me any heed, except for Peggy Sue, seated alongside her viperous friend, Robin — who looked at me with obvious alarm, as if I'd just crawled out of a crashed automobile (which, the way I looked today, was an insult to accident victims everywhere). Perfect in her latest Calvin Klein's, Robin followed Peggy Sue's gaze with a smirk. My state of dress and grooming confirmed every nasty opinion and suspicion she'd ever held about me.

I wandered between the various tables, looking for a place to land, wondering if it was too busy here to even find a seat, when a hand reached out and touched my sleeve.

"Brandy!"

"Oh . . . hi, Jennifer."

Jennifer looked strikingly lovely in a yellow Juicy Couture mini worn over slim jeans. Her lush auburn hair was perfectly coiffed, and that doll-like porcelain complexion was to die for.

"Are you all right?" she asked, head cocked.

"Not . . . not really," I admitted.

Her green eyes showed concern. "You . . . frankly, Brandy, you look *terrible.* Not yourself at all."

"Lately I don't *feel* like myself, either." I gestured limply to the empty chair at her table for two. "Are you meeting someone?"

"Yes," she said with a little smile. "As a matter of fact, I am — a mutual friend."

I frowned. "Tina?"

"That's right."

The disappointment must have shown on my face. "I haven't heard from her in . . . in ages."

"Really?" Jennifer's cell trilled a few bars of the *Love Story* film theme. "Excuse me, Brandy, would you? . . . Hello? . . . No, sweetie, that's all right, *really!* . . . No, I can wait . . . 'Kay. See ya."

I was about to move on when Jennifer said, "Speak of the devil."

"Tina?"

"Yes, she's going to be late, very late, actually. Why don't you sit down? Were you going to eat?"

"No, I just wanted something cool to drink."

"Then you *must* join me. . . . Why don't you sit down here, until she comes?"

"Are you sure?"

"Absolutely."

"Thanks." I took the chair opposite her

and she beamed at me across the silk flowers.

A waitress appeared and I ordered a lemonade. Jennifer already had an iced-tea.

I said, "I . . . I didn't know you and Tina were friendly. Missed that, somehow."

She smiled again, but now it seemed less friendly, something catlike . . . and catty . . . in there. "We became kind of friendly when you were in Chicago, and this past week or so, we've gotten together a few times. You know, I'm not lucky, like you."

"How's that?"

"I don't have a sister in town. Fun having Tina around — we went shopping in the Cities yesterday, then caught a movie. Let the husbands fend for themselves, I say."

"Yes. Right. Tina can be a lot of fun."

"I guess you'd know that better than anyone."

I sighed heavily. "Not so much lately. Haven't seen her in weeks . . . it's almost like . . . like she's trying to avoid me."

"Oh, I'm sure that's not the case."

I offered up a humorless smirk. "I don't think I've been much fun lately. Gotten myself all caught up in all kinds of paranoid stupidity. My, uh . . ." I lowered my voice. ". . . my doctor increased my medication."

"What are you on, dear?"

"Just Prozac, but it . . . it can make you kind of, you know, sluggish."

"That's what I hear. Might I make a suggestion? If I'm not being overly familiar . . ."

"Please."

Jennifer leaned in closer, eyes and smile hovering above the fake flowers, and that smile every bit as fake. "Maybe Tina's just, well, a little weary of hearing about your problems. . . . Friends need to exchange their troubles, of course, but sometimes, if one of them goes on and on and on and on . . . well, it can be a bit of a drag, don't you think?"

I sat back, and I'm sure my hurt feelings showed. "She . . . Tina *said* as much?"

Jennifer took a sip of her iced tea, shrugged. "In so many words."

I muttered, "I *thought* she was my best friend . . . and friends should support friends. . . . I mean, you need a sounding board sometimes, and . . ." I swallowed, then leaned forward, low self-esteem oozing out of my every pore. "What . . . oh, Jen, what *else* did Tina say?"

Jennifer raised her chin, looked down her well-formed nose at me with cold eyes. "Do you *really* want to know?"

"Yes . . . yes, of course."

A short, harsh laugh. "Well, all right . . . if

you insist." She took a breath, expelled it. "For starters, Tina told me that you stole money from her — several times — because you were so broke. You'd get into her purse behind her back. Everyone knows you came home from Chicago unemployed."

My eyes popped. "But I *didn't* steal from her! I would never —"

"And she said that you *lie* all the time."

"She . . . she did? I suppose I exaggerate sometimes. But, Jen, everybody does that . . . sometimes . . . right?"

"Whatever you say, dear." She shrugged again. "These aren't my opinions, understand — you wanted to know what Tina had been saying. Should I stop?"

"No! No, please . . . go on, you have to go on."

With relish, she did: "Well, she says she never wants to go clubbing with you again."

"Why not? We always have a wicked good time!"

"That's just it — you're a little too 'wicked,' Brandy — you have the morals of an alley cat. According to Tina, anyway." Jennifer's upper lip curled into an eloquent half sneer. "Of course, I already knew that."

I drew a deep breath. Let it out. "You've never really forgiven me . . . have you, Jennifer?"

She leaned forward, spoke through a clenched-teeth smile; no one watching us would have noticed anything untoward. "You thought you could come back here to live and start over and everything would be fine . . . like nothing had ever happened. Never mind what you might stir up."

"I had no intention of —"

Her eyes were as tight as a clenched fist. "Did you have any intention of starting back up with Brad?"

"I haven't even *seen* your husband since I got back to Serenity!"

"Maybe you just hadn't got around to it yet."

My lemonade came, but I didn't bother sipping it. My eyes were tearing up. "I'd never do that. That was one night, two years ago . . . one stupid night, one stupid mistake, and I hope you've forgiven him for it. I don't suppose you'll *ever* forgive *me.* . . ."

Her eyes were wild now. Somehow she kept her voice soft, but it was like a controlled scream when she said: "You have no idea, do you, of the trouble and misery you've caused me? That you ruined my marriage, and ruined *me.* . . ."

"If a one-night stand ruined your marriage, I'm not taking the blame — there must have been something wrong with that marriage already."

Her nostrils flared, her eyes, too. "You won't take the blame? But, Brandy . . . *all* the blame is yours. All the lives destroyed. . . ."

"*What* lives?"

Her expression turned inward suddenly; for all her apparent self-control, there was a wooziness in her voice as she muttered, "People dead . . . your fault those people are dead."

"*My* fault? *What* people?"

She was weaving as she sat there, just a little. "If you . . . if you hadn't had an affair with Brad, I wouldn't have . . ."

"Wouldn't have *what,* Jennifer?"

Still weaving, ever so slightly, Jennifer regarded me with wide eyes, her expression blank but for a tiny upturning of the corners of her mouth, which suggested bitter amusement.

Finally she said, "You *should* know. You really should know what you've done. *I* have to live with it. You should have to live with it, too."

"Live with what, Jen? Tell me. I deserve that much."

A crackle of laughter. "You deserve so much more . . . well, why not? I think I *do* want you to know what misery you've sown. And, anyway, it's not like anyone would *believe* you, if you told. Everybody in this town — *especially* the police — think you and that mother of yours belong in a loony bin."

My eyes were locked upon hers, but my emotions were barely under control, my lower lip quivering, and a tear sliding down my cheek.

"Just *look* at you," she said, with a contemptuous sneer. "You're *pathetic.* Beautiful Brandy Borne — an absolute loser. A pitiful Prozac-popping would-be home wrecker." A derisive horselike snort erupted from her. "What Brad ever saw in you I'll never know . . . he must have been *drunk* at that reunion." She gave her head and that auburn hair a toss. "I, on the other hand, am the wronged wife, respected in the community, with all the right friends . . . even *your* friends, now that you don't have any." A manic gleam came to her green eyes. "Yes. I think I *want* you to know . . . I want you to know and not be able to do a goddamn fucking thing about it!"

I wiped a tear away with a knuckle. I snuffled snot, and said, "You . . . you killed Clint Carson and tried to blame me for it."

She smirked. "You think?" She paused,

glanced around. No one was paying us the slightest attention, the chatter and occasional laughter covering up our conversation; but at our table her ominous whispering was all too audible.

I said, "That was *you* who left the message on our answer machine — not Tanya."

Leaning forward, upper lip curled back over tiny perfect teeth, Jennifer said, "I was there with him at his farmhouse, when I made that call — of course, he was already dead. You weren't my first priority, Brandy, don't compliment yourself — I just found it a fitting irony for you to take the blame, since my getting involved with Clint was, after all, your fault."

"*My* fault . . . ?"

"Obviously! I would have never tried to even the books with Brad, by having an affair with Clint, if you hadn't made that necessary. . . . I was a faithful, loyal wife before you came along and ruined everything."

"How can you —"

"And another irony I relished? Was drugging the drug dealer. I drugged that bastard, then 'drug' him outside and down the lane, positioning him for you to run over." She heaved a self-pitying sigh. "That should have worked — I didn't factor in your crazy mother. . . ."

I asked, "You'd been having an affair with Carson, how long?"

Her eyebrows knit. "Longer than I intended — just to get even with Brad, at first. He was a good-looking man, and he made a kind of play for me in his shop, and I thought . . . maybe if I have my own little fling, I'll be able to put my anger at Brad behind me. And it was fun, while it lasted — he wasn't tender, Clint, but he got the job done nicely." She'd been smiling at that thought, but now frowned. "Then Clint wanted me to keep supplying him with information . . . particularly from my candy striper position at the hospital, that helped him get him leads on loads of antiques. I'm well connected, after all. I knew what patients were sick or dying or dead."

So that's how Carson replenished his stock. . . .

"When I tried to break it off, that creep threatened to expose me." Her mouth tightened as if tasting something unpleasant. "He told me I'd have to keep him satisfied, both with 'leads' on antiques, and . . . with whatever he was in the mood for. . . . Well, I couldn't have that. He had to go." Her brow furrowed. "So do you understand,

Brandy? Don't you? How it was *all* your fault?"

"And then when I started poking around, Mother and I, you —"

"No. That wasn't it, at first. I had to make sure that that answering machine tape was never found — my voice might still have been on there. So I sneaked in to take it, and then . . . well, I just had an inspired idea. On the spot. You and your mother were causing trouble, so . . . why not tie it all in a nice bow?"

"How did you get into our house?"

She smiled. "Doesn't your mother *ever* lock the front door?"

Sometimes.

I asked, "And Mrs. Taylor?"

"Who?"

"The woman in my hospital room? I suppose the drain cleaner was meant for me."

Her eyes flashed, and I'd clearly struck a nerve. "Again, your fault, your fault, your *fault!*"

Her voice had risen now, and I glanced around to see if anyone had noticed; no one seemed to have.

Her upper lip tightened over her teeth. "Who but Brandy Borne would switch hospital beds with a roommate? Who ever heard of *that?* You did it to be selfish, right?

What, to be closer to the toilet? You are such a selfish, selfish, *selfish* bitch. . . ."

I chose not to argue that point, and pressed on. "Why kill Tanya? She seemed harmless enough. . . ."

"Harmless? *She* was a bitch, *too* — a *blackmailing* bitch!" Jennifer was trembling now, a tiny twitch at the left corner of her mouth making her seem to smile involuntarily every few seconds. "Clint, that stupid selfish bastard, he must have told her about our affair — he was seeing her, too, and he must have bragged or, or God knows what. I *tried* not to kill her — I even gave her ten thousand dollars from my personal savings; but, no, she wanted more, or she'd tell Brad." Jennifer shook her head and the well-controlled auburn locks landed in a wild tangle. "Did she really think a married woman could come up with fifty thousand dollars without her *husband* knowing? She was like you — selfish. Greedy . . . I lured her up to the second floor, and sent her back down to the basement."

I swallowed. "Isn't it getting a little too easy, Jen? Killing people?"

She laughed harshly. "That's right — blame *me!* Cause and effect, Brandy, cause and effect — your fault, your fault, *your fault!* If you hadn't slept with my husband, *none of this would have happened!*"

"I apologized for that, Jennifer, and I meant it."

"Words. What good are words?"

For the first time since I'd sat down at this table, I smiled. "Your words this afternoon? They'll do a lot of good."

Her sneer this time was as wild as her tangled hair. "You repeat anything that I've said here? I'll deny it."

"I figured as much. But the police are already looking at you — starting with a woman answering your description arguing with Carson at the Haven Motel, a woman with a green SUV, even if it did look brown under red light."

She sat back and regained her poise, though the mussed-up hair took the edge off. "I'll say you're a liar, a poor mentally disturbed woman who is still lusting after my husband. . . . No one will believe you."

"I figured as much," I repeated. "That's why I'm wearing a wire."

For a moment, Jennifer had the stunned expression of a clubbed baby seal. Then she laughed, trying a little too hard. "I'm *sure!* Brandy Borne — undercover airhead!"

So I unbuttoned my shirt, exposing the tiny microphone taped to my bra.

"There's a mike in the flowers, too," I

said, nodding toward the vase.

With a savage cry, she sprang to her feet, lurched across the table, upsetting the vase and the flowers and the drinks, long fingernails clawing at my blouse.

I slapped her face.

She pulled my hair.

I kicked her in the shins.

She jabbed a salad fork in my side.

It wasn't very dignified, even as catfights go, and a kind of small-stakes payoff for a murderess who'd taken three lives and blown up a house. But we were both adlibbing, and — off-script — you can only accomplish so much.

Joe Lange reached us first — which was a good thing because Jennifer, in her psychotic fury, was besting me. With some difficulty, Joe pulled us apart, then got her in a headlock, and frankly he seemed to me to be enjoying himself just a little too much.

A plainclothes Brian Lawson, who had rushed in when the fight broke out, slapped handcuffs on Jennifer.

Mother, on the heels of Lawson, was ecstatic. "Oh, that was just *wonderful,* Brandy!" she trilled. "Your acting was *superb.* . . . You were so utterly, believably *pathetic.*"

Peggy Sue, attending to my superficial side

wound by applying pressure with a napkin, said wryly, "A little too believable, if you ask me."

I looked at her and at Mother. "Well, it wasn't a stretch. Anyway, I wasn't really acting."

Mother waved her hands as if they were pom-poms (or is that pons?) and pshawed. "Nonsense, dear! It's in the DNA — the scene called for tears, and you summoned them up from sense memory. You had a *part* to play — to goad that woman into baring her horrid soul — and you performed it to perfection."

Tina, who had also been offstage (so to speak), where she had made the phone call to Jennifer, appeared to give me a gentle hug and asked, "Are you all right, honey?"

I gave my best friend a mock-hurt look. "You said I stole *money* from you?"

She responded sheepishly. "Hey, I was supposed to gain Jennifer's confidence, wasn't I? And she never seemed to have *any* trouble believing *anything* bad I had to say about you!"

Jennifer, having been read her rights by a uniformed officer who'd materialized, glared at us as she was walked out of the restaurant. Even going out the door, her hard, hating eyes shot their green laser beams at me.

I shuddered — being hated that much was unsettling . . . particularly by a sociopathic killer.

Mother clapped her hands loudly. "Everyone! Everyone, please! May I have your attention?"

The room settled and all eyes went to Mother.

"I don't believe individual notes will be necessary," she said grandly. "But I do want to thank all of you for being a part of this production . . . which was, by any measure, a complete success. And I look forward to seeing all of you at the cast party this afternoon, held at my daughter Peggy Sue Hastings's home. . . ."

Sis goggled at her. "The what party? . . . Excuse me! Wait a minute . . . *What* party?"

". . . So I hope you can *all* come, and we'll wait together for the reviews."

The reviews?

Had Mother finally lost *all* her marbles? Then I noticed a camera-toting, notebook-scribbling reporter from the *Serenity Gazette*. And on the periphery, a video cam was on the shoulder of a local TV cameraman, a good-looking female reporter at his side, her notebook at the ready, too.

Mother had arranged coverage for her directorial debut in the reality TV arena.

Officer Lawson was at my side, and touched my arm. "Are you sure you're all right? We should have that looked at."

I pulled the shirt up. "No, it's fine . . . see? Stopped bleeding. Must've been a dull fork."

He smiled at me — all the irritation gone. A nice, warm, maybe-something-more-than-a-friend kind of smile. After all, this time I'd been sleuthing and snooping with police permission.

I asked him, "You got it all on tape?"

"Every word." Then: "Thank you."

"Any time."

He frowned. "No, Brandy . . . *not* any time. Promise me."

"Well, *I* can promise you," I said. "For my part — but with Mother? You never know."

He glanced over at her, surrounded by friends and press and general admiration, and from his defeated expression, I knew he knew exactly what I meant.

A TRASH 'N' TREASURES TIP

If you see an item that makes your heart skip a beat, and the price is right, *grab it;* it may not be there ten minutes, or even ten seconds, later. At a flea market, Mother spotted an autographed photo of Errol

Flynn, turned around to get my attention, and another lady stole it out from under her.

Chapter Twelve

BAD HEIRLOOM DAY

Sometimes, at night, when sleep won't come, I find myself going to a bad place where I think about everything that snowballed from my one night of irresponsibility. In this place, much of what Jennifer said to me, and accused me of, makes perfect sense.

And, sometimes, at night, when sleep won't come, I wonder if Jennifer's husband, Brad, finds himself in that same bad place, going through those same sad thought processes.

Thankfully, my medication doesn't let me wallow there for long. And the odds are excellent that Brad and I will never compare notes on this subject.

About a week after the improvised one-act "play" at the Grist Mill Restaurant, a letter addressed to Vivian and Brandy Borne, in care of my sister, arrived . . . from the Serenity Safety Building, Police Department.

Mother — not waiting for me — opened it, then came running downstairs to my sewing-room hideaway, where I was playing with Sushi on the daybed, one hand under the protection of the blanket, pretending to be a striking snake, while Soosh didn't pretend at all as she attacked it with her sharp teeth.

"Brandy!" Mother's face was flush with excitement, her eyes behind the glasses comically huge. "Chief Cassato has been kind enough to send us information about our antiques." She had to pause to catch her breath. "They'll *all* be going up for auction tomorrow morning!"

I jumped off the bed, peered over her shoulder at the letter, and read the important part aloud: " 'Be at Klein's Auction House at six AM sharp. Good luck, Tony.' "

I looked at Mother. "Where's that?"

"About an hour's drive from here."

"Well, what are we waiting for? We've got to rent a trailer!"

"Can we afford anything?"

Mother had come clean with the insurance company about the contents of the house, so the two hundred grand for contents had been knocked down to about twenty thousand.

"We have to refurnish, don't we?" I asked.

"We have some insurance money to play with . . . Certainly we can get *some* of our memories back!"

"Yes!" she said, and began to hop up and down. "Yes! *Yes!*"

I resisted hopping up and down myself, but just barely, and off we went to rent our trailer.

That night Mother and I sat up late at the kitchen table trying to devise a game plan. We had lots to think about: *How many of our prized possessions would be auctioned? What dollar limit should be bid on each? Who should do the bidding — me or Mother? Would our emotions run amok? Would we overdo our bids on a few pieces and lose out on many other, more precious ones?*

Peggy Sue and Bob weren't going with us; Bob was leaving for a weekend business conference, and Peggy Sue said she had a social obligation she just *couldn't* get out of (while this was true, I knew Peggy Sue could not face an antique auction with Mother and me) (could you?).

But the Hastingses didn't hesitate to give us their opinions.

Bob: *Keep within your budget, and don't expect to get every single piece.*

Peggy Sue: *Mother, the actress, should*

weep and moan whenever one of our items comes up for bid to get the sympathy of the crowd (great advice coming from somebody who wasn't going to have to witness that!).

In the end Mother and I arrived at the same conclusion: we were willing to spend all of that twenty thousand in insurance money to get back everything we could, however much, however little. . . .

It seemed like my head had barely hit the pillow when one of the two alarm clocks I'd set trilled on my nightstand. The other, across the room on the sewing machine table (a strategic placement that would force me to get up to shut it off), sang out shortly thereafter.

Four AM and all was well.

So far.

Mother was already up, and dressed.

Don't ask.

All right, all right — as Lady Macbeth. I only hoped she could be as devious and cunning as her wardrobe; I was certainly willing to help wash any blood off her hands. I wore a sky-blue Grist Mill Restaurant T-shirt (they'd earned the publicity) and jeans and Rebox, wanting to look vaguely well off to an auctioneer but not threatening to other buyers.

After stopping for coffee and messy donuts, we headed north along the scenic river road, the pink sunrise magnificent, shimmering with promise on the Mighty Miss. Mother seemed lost in her thoughts, perhaps beating herself up a little for losing this stuff in the first place, but probably also girding her loins to make up for that lapse; I was concentrating on keeping my protesting car and the attached fishtailing trailer on the road, peeved that I couldn't go any faster than fifty-five.

At a quarter to six, however, we pulled into the gravel lot of the auction house, a large, tan-metal, no-frills affair set off between cornfields.

Except for a van parked along the side of the building, we were the first ones there. That was good — Mother and I exchanged greedy-little-kid looks. Then the Borne girls got out, stretched, and headed to the front door, which we, unhappily, found locked.

We glanced at each other, puzzled.

Was this the right day? The right time? Maybe PM instead of AM?

Mother was digging the chief's letter out of her purse when the gunmetal-gray door cracked open and an old man poked his head out.

"Are you girls the Bornes?"

The Borne girls nodded.

"Then come on in. Come on in!"

We followed the toothless gent inside — and it must in fairness be noted that this man who considered us "girls" looked like Gabby Hayes on the Western Channel — where he handed us a booklet listing the items that would be auctioned today. Then he ushered us over to a disturbingly large area of folding chairs, placing us in the first row, directly in front of a podium, and disappeared.

We were still the only ones there.

Mother whispered, "The auction must not start until seven."

I grabbed her arm. "Mother! *Look!*"

Among the vast assortment of items up for bid around the perimeter of the floor, I spotted our furniture, grouped together. We sprang out of our chairs and ran like the idiots we were, arms waving.

Standing in front of our roped-off antiques — labeled as Lot Number One — Mother clasped her hands.

"I . . . I believe everything's here," she exclaimed.

I consulted the booklet. Lot Number One was on the auction block first.

Showing the entry to Mother, I asked, "Does this mean our things will all be auctioned *together?*"

Mother nodded, frowning. "It appears so, dear."

"Then . . . then . . . we'll being going home with everything, or . . . or —"

"Nothing."

My heart sank into my stomach. So much trouble, so much excitement, and now . . . so much pressure. Glumly, we returned to our seats to wait.

But not for long.

At six-fifteen, a woman wearing a plaid shirt, tan slacks, western boots, and wielding a gavel, stepped to the podium.

I looked behind me.

Our butts remained the only ones in these chairs. Mother and I stared at each other with raised eyebrows.

The lady auctioneer dispensed with the microphone since we were six feet away, and announced, "Now auctioning Lot Number One." She then read the contents of our former living room, dining room, and china cabinet, concluding with, "Do I have an opening bid?"

I was so flabbergasted, I couldn't find my voice.

Mother, however, had hers and shouted, "Twenty thousand dollars!"

I stomped on her foot as if I'd spotted a particularly nasty-looking spider. Not acting at all, Mother screamed.

I recovered from my muteness. "Mother didn't mean that! What she meant was *one dollar!*"

Mother, aghast, cried, "Brandy! Our things are worth much more than that! Why, the Chippendale chairs alone are —"

I clamped a hand over her mouth. "One dollar!" I repeated to the auctioneer.

Mother bit my hand. And, not acting at all, I screamed.

But what I screamed was: *"One dollar!"*

The lady auctioneer came to my rescue by breaking protocol and slamming down the gavel.

"Going, going, gone — sold for one dollar! Pay the man at the front desk."

And, with a tiny smile, she exited the podium.

Mother and I sat in stunned silence.

Then Mother asked, "What just happened there? Other than you stomping on my foot, and me biting your hand — that Polident is a wonder, by the way."

"I . . . I . . . *think* we just bought everything back — for one dollar."

And then we threw our arms joyfully around each other and began to shout and babble in joy.

At the front desk, Officer Brian Lawson

was lingering nearby, in plainclothes — wearing a yellow Polo shirt and black jeans and an elfin smile.

"Did *you* arrange this?" I asked, as Mother stepped up and paid Gabby Hayes one dollar.

"I'd like to take credit," Brian said, "and maybe get on your good side. But our resident hard guy, Chief Cassato, bless his soft heart, arranged this private presale . . . just for you."

"I have to thank him!"

"No. Never mention it. He said for me to tell you, consider it payment in full . . . for undercover work."

I grinned. "Kind of a bonus!"

He arched an eyebrow. "Consider it a pension plan for your mother, Brandy — you two're leaving the detective business, remember?"

"Sure. Sure thing, Brian."

And we hired a couple of enterprising teenage farm boys — who hung around for just such a purpose — to help Brian load everything into the trailer, although it all didn't fit.

Smaller things, like lamps and chairs, went into the trunk and backseat of the car, some parts protruding out the windows. And the dining room table — wrapped in a moving blanket, sweetly provided by Mr. Hayes — had been turned upside down and roped onto the roof.

Brian waved as we finally took off, looking like the Beverly Hillbillies with all their worldly possessions stuffed in one vehicle, slowly creeping away, big grins on our faces, all the way.

Mother and I didn't even mind the car horns and occasional middle finger we received holding up traffic on the river road.

Sure was good to be home.

A Trash 'n' Treasures Tip

If you're a fidgeter, always insist on a number card to hold up at an auction. Mother once scratched her nose and became the proud owner of a Civil War chamber pot.

ABOUT THE AUTHORS

Barbara Allan is the joint pseudonym for husband-and-wife mystery writers Max Allan and Barbara Collins.

Max Allan Collins, a five-time Mystery Writers of America "Edgar" nominee in both fiction and nonfiction categories, has been hailed as "the Renaissance man of mystery fiction." He has earned an unprecedented fourteen Private Eye Writers of America "Shamus" nominations for his historical thrillers, winning twice for his Nathan Heller novels, *True Detective* (1983) and *Stolen Away* (1991).

His other credits include film criticism, short fiction, songwriting, trading-card sets, and movie/TV tie-in novels, including *Air Force One, In the Line of Fire,* and the *New York Times*–best-selling *Saving Private Ryan.*

His graphic novel *Road to Perdition* is the basis of the Academy Award–winning

DreamWorks feature film starring Tom Hanks, Paul Newman, and Jude Law, directed by Sam Mendes. Collins's many comics credits include the *Dick Tracy* syndicated strip; his own *Ms. Tree; Batman;* and *CSI: Crime Scene Investigation,* based on the hit TV series, for which he has also written four video games and a *USA Today*–best-selling series of novels.

An acclaimed and award-winning independent filmmaker in his native Midwest, Collins wrote and directed *Mommy,* premiering on Lifetime in 1996, as well as a 1997 sequel, *Mommy's Day.* The screenwriter of *The Expert,* a 1995 HBO World Premiere, he wrote and directed the innovative made-for-DVD *Real Time: Siege at Lucas Street Market* (2000). His latest indie feature, *Shades of Noir* (2004), is an anthology of his short films, including his award-winning documentary, *Mike Hammer's Mickey Spillane.* A DVD boxed set of his films, *The Black Box,* is currently in release.

Barbara Collins is one of the most respected short story writers in the mystery field, with appearances in over a dozen top anthologies, including *Murder Most Delicious, Women on the Edge,* and the best-selling *Cat Crimes* series. She was the coeditor (and a contributor) to the best-selling anthology *Lethal Ladies,* and her stories were selected for inclusion in the first three volumes of *The Year's 25 Finest Crime and Mystery Stories.*

Two acclaimed hardcover collections of her work have been published — *Too Many Tomcats* and (with her husband) *Murder — His and Hers.* The wife-and-husband team's first novel together, the baby boomer thriller *Regeneration,* was a bestseller; their second collaborative novel, *Bombshell* — in which Marilyn Monroe saves the world from World War III — was published to excellent reviews.

Barbara has been the production manager and/or line producer on *Mommy, Mommy's Day,* and *Real Time: Siege at Lucas Street Market,* and other independent film projects emanating from the production company she and her husband jointly run.

"Barbara Allan" live(s) in Muscatine, Iowa, their hometown; son Nathan recently graduated with honors in Japanese and computer science from the University of Iowa in nearby Iowa City.

The employees of Thorndike Press hope you have enjoyed this Large Print book. All our Thorndike and Wheeler Large Print titles are designed for easy reading, and all our books are made to last. Other Thorndike Press Large Print books are available at your library, through selected bookstores, or directly from us.

For information about titles, please call:
    (800) 223-1244

or visit our Web site at:
    www.gale.com/thorndike
    www.gale.com/wheeler

To share your comments, please write:
    Publisher
    Thorndike Press
    295 Kennedy Memorial Drive
    Waterville, ME 04901

Anderson County Library
300 North McDuffie Street
Anderson, South Carolina 29621
(864) 260-4500

Belton, Honea Path, Iva,
Lander Regional, Pendleton,
Piedmont, Powdersville,
Westside, Bookmobile